Another Family Reunion Novel—Wisdom of the Ancestors Series
–Book 24–

PROTECTIVE INSTINCTS

An Alex-Mont Kids Saga, Episode 5

ANN JEFFRIES

Published and Distributed By
New View Literature
820 67th Avenue N, #7603
Myrtle Beach, South Carolina 29572
info@newviewliterature.com
www.newviewliterature.com

Jessica Tilles, Editor
TWA Solutions, Cover and Interior design

ISBN: 978-1-941 603-12-3 paperback
ISBN: 978-1-941603-41-3 eBook

Library of Congress Control Number: 2022917623

First printing November 2022

This is a work of fiction. Names, characters, businesses, places, events, and incidents are either the products of the author's imagination or used in a fictitious manner. Any resemblance to actual persons, living or dead, or actual events is purely coincidental.

For inquiries, contact the publisher.

Acknowledgments

I bow in humble gratitude to:

The Creator
My Ancestors
Jessica Tilles, TWA Solutions
The Carolina Forest Authors' Club
Kelley Hazen, Storyteller Productions
The Carolina Forest Library, Horry County, SC
Faithful Family, Friends, and Fans

The struggle for literary perfection continues and will never cease.

I remain faithfully yours,

Ann Jeffries

Ann Jeffries Titles
Family Reunion—Wisdom of the Ancestors Series
In Print and eBook formats

Southern Exposures
Another Point of View
Northern Exposures
Uncommon Choices
An Unguarded Moment
Moments to Remember
The Better Part of Valor
Walking On Uneven Ground
Ask Me No Questions. . . I'll Tell You No Lies
Touch Me in the Morning
All Goodbyes Aren't Gone
A Different Frame of Mind
Judicial Indiscretion
Crystal Clear Persuasion
Sweet Justice
Bittersweet Memories
All in the Family
An Ulterior Motive
A Forever Kind of Love
Walking on the Wilde Side
All That Glitters Ain't Gold
Regrets
City Chic, Country Cool, Continental Class

In audiobook format:

Southern Exposures, Narrator Kelley Hazen
Another Point of View, Narrator Glen Pavlovich
Northern Exposures, Narrator CJ McAlister
Uncommon Choices, Narrator Kelley Hazen
An Unguarded Moment, Narrator Richard Dennis Johnson
Moments to Remember, Narrator Richard Dennis Johnson
The Better Part of Valor, Narrator Richard Dennis Johnson
Walking on Uneven Ground, Narrator Richard Dennis Johnson
Ask Me No Questions...I'll Tell You No Lies, Narrator Pam Dougherty
Touch Me in the Morning, Narrator Ginger Walton
All Goodbyes Aren't Gone, Narrator Julian Thomas
A Different Frame of Mind, Narrator C. J. McAllister
Judicial Indiscretion, Narrator Kelley Hazen
Crystal Clear Persuasion, Narrator C. J. McAllister
Sweet Justice, Narrator C. J. McAllister
Bittersweet Memories, Narrator Richard Dennis Johnson
All in the Family, Narrator Kelley Hazen
An Ulterior Motive, Narrator Kelley Hazen
A Forever Kind of Love, Narrator Kelley Hazen
Walking on the Wilde Side, Narrator Kelley Hazen
All That Glitters Ain't Gold, Narrator Kelley Hazen
Regrets, Narrator Kelley Hazen
City Chic, Country Cool, Continental Class, Narrator Kelley Hazen

I'm setting you free now,
releasing you through my protective instincts,
because I love you too much to watch you suffer
and you only suffer because I let you in.

–Saffie

Chapter 1

"Hey, Doc? Wait up!"

Professor Dena Montgomery heard the young man loudly hailing her as she turned off her mobile phone and hurried down the steps from her office in MIT's McNair Building. Her students' appointments kept her long over the allotted time for her office hours. She would have escaped free and clear if she had left one minute earlier. Instead, all Dena wanted to do this evening was go home, make a batch of vegetable soup, curl up in front of her fireplace, and read her cousin's latest novel in her Fireside Chat series. If she didn't hurry, the grocery store would close, and she needed to pick up a substantial number of items before going home to make the soup. Still, her students were important and she would never deny them whatever time they needed with her.

Sighing and slowing her quick pace, she allowed her student, a gangly, freckled-faced, redheaded young man, to catch up before continuing down the staircase. "How's it goin', Chad?"

He shrugged, adjusted his heavy, eye-searing fluorescent green backpack on his left shoulder, and jogged down the steps with her. "So far, so good, Doc."

"Great. Did you have a good holiday?"

"Yeah, but you know, Doc, I tried to catch you during your office hours for the past couple of weeks to chat about that, but your schedule fills up so fast. You see, my parents and I had to go to Aruba for the holidays. So, you see, it was like this. My sister, Carol, announced that she's pregnant. So, suddenly, she wants this destination wedding rather than doing the June-wedding thing at home in The Hamptons the way she originally planned. So, we had to hustle and do a lot of work to pull off the wedding in a new place. That took the time I needed to complete my research. So, I may need an extension on my thesis."

Dena shook her head in sympathy. "You know, I hate when that happens. First, my parents insisted that we—me and my nearly forty siblings—go to the Pocono Mountains to ski for two weeks instead of one week over the holiday break. Then all of a sudden, my mom gave birth to a baby during dinner on Christmas Day, and then my sister-in-law, KiLe, went and did the same thing. Well…" She dismissively shrugged as they continued down the broad staircase past other slower-moving students and professors. "…my mom and sister-in-law both had boys, so now somebody in my family has to go and have girls to balance the numbers again. We may have to wait a while, though, because only my brother, Brian, and my sister, Linda, are married at this point, and they both have two boys.

"Did I mention in class that my sister, Eve, is getting married on Juneteenth? I sincerely hope she and her fiancé don't decide to elope before June. That's just the kind of thing they would do and that would screw up everything we've planned." She frowned as they rounded another level on the stairs. "Still, no matter when they marry, I don't think Eve and her fiancé, Simon, plan to start a family right away because she's only in her mid-twenties. However, my sister, Samantha, who is even younger than Eve by six months, will probably accept an engagement ring from her guy friend, Quentin, this coming Valentine's Day. Smart money says that she will, but who knows when it comes to weddings? You just had that experience with your sister's wedding, right?"

They stopped walking just as they reached the heavy doors of the main exit. Dena looked up at the blank expression on the young man's face. "Oh, I apologize, Chad. What were you saying?"

"Doc, I just wanted to know whether you'd give me an extension on submitting my thesis?"

"Oh, Chad, I thought we were just sharing our holiday experiences. Sure, don't worry yourself about it. You can take all the time you need to complete your research. If you miss the deadline this year, I plan to be here next year, too. You can turn in your thesis then." She shook his hand. "Thank you, Chad. That will take a load off of me this year. I wish more of my students were as considerate as you. Now I will only receive maybe a hundred to two hundred projects to review by the spring break deadline. Have a good weekend." Dena guilelessly smiled and walked out of the door into the skin-burning cold on Vassar Street, leaving Chad with a decision to make.

Fifteen minutes later, Dena's quick-booted steps echoed on the bodega's tile floor. She carried a red hard plastic basket that, so far, only held fresh fruit and vegetables. Dena could remember the calculus of the Pythagorean theorem as if it were her address but couldn't, for her life, remember what was on her grocery list. She chastised herself for forgetting to take a picture of the list on her refrigerator door this morning before leaving for class. At least this time, she remembered to make a list, but details of other math theories clouded her mind.

She would use those theories to stump three of her younger brothers: Spencer, Darren, and Andrew. They were the most challenging of her thirty-plus siblings, as they, like her, were mathletes. They won several math competitions and were now gleefully gunning for her title. Dena, a mathematical Olympiad, won competitions on the world stage and was giving her brothers a run for their effort. Although her IQ was genius level, her family dubbed her the Absent-Minded Professor because she often forgot basic things…like picking up groceries or eating three meals a day. Dena sighed as she marched up and down each aisle, scanning left and right to jog her memory. Unfortunately, nothing came to her mind, and she knew the list was very long. Hell, she hadn't been shopping for groceries or anything else in a month of Sundays.

Frustrated, she looked at the fresh produce in her basket, shook her head, and headed for the checkout counter. For now, this would have to do.

It was Friday night, dark and cold outside. Mounds of snow and ice were piled up on the ground, and more snow was in the forecast. That was typical for New England in the dead of winter. Resigned to stopping for a takeout order for dinner again tonight, she'd simply have to go for an early run in the morning and then take her grocery list to stock up before the Nor'easter hits. Dena made a mental note to photograph the list as soon as she got home so she wouldn't forget it in the morning…again.

Dena dumped her fresh produce on the counter and stacked the basket on top of the others. There were carrots, onions, green peppers, and celery to make vegetable soup. She had a taste for a pineapple upside-down cake with fresh pineapple, maraschino cherries, and brown sugar. So, she also had navel oranges, lemons, limes, green apples, pears, seedless grapes, and a large cocoanut to make a fresh-fruit Waldorf salad to go with the soup.

Mr. Armegos folded his muscular arms over his chest in his Mr. Clean pose, shook his hairless head in amusement, and waited.

Dena dug into one after another of the deep inside pockets of her floor-length leather duster for cash. It took a few moments, but she finally found the right pocket and pulled out a few bills. She cheekily grinned up at him as she put the mangled bills, assorted change, a large paper clip, and a ball of lent on the counter. "See, I didn't forget this time."

He shook his head and sighed. "Chica, you cannot survive on only fruit and vegetables for long." He reached behind himself and placed a giant cup of hot New England clam chowder on the counter and a small loaf of freshly baked brown bread beside it. "Here, you take home this soup that I made fresh today. The bread, my Alice, she make, is still warm from the oven." Then he weighed the fruit and vegetables and rang up her order.

Dena pounced on the soup, pried open the lid, and breathed deeply before taking a quick sip. The heat singed her tongue, but she closed her impressive diamond-black eyes and sighed in delight. "Thanks, Mr. A. I missed lunch today."

A man accustomed to his favorite customer's forgetfulness, he sighed. "What will it take to fatten you up? You are too skinny. The wind will just whip you away. I tell my son, Paolo, he should marry you just to fatten you up. He say no because you'd probably forget you're married." He bagged her order and sighed dramatically again.

Dena grinned and shrugged. "Paolo is a very smart man. You should listen to him." She accepted her change and then dumped it in a large, clear plastic donation jar. Then, with a cheeky grin and a tip of her Stetson,

Dena scooped up her paper bag by the handles and waved as she backed out of the door.

The icy wind off the Charles River immediately took her breath away. Pulling up the collar of her wool sweater to cover part of her face, she then pulled her black Stetson down more securely on her head and used the chin strap so the wind wouldn't rip it away. Digging in her pockets, Dena hoped she had at least one pair of gloves in her coat. Her hands would be icicles if she didn't find them before walking one more block toward her home.

As she crossed an alley, Dena heard the distinct sound of a child's pitiful cry in terror. Quickly, she turned into the alley, which was wide enough for a car to drive through. She forgot about the search for a pair of gloves. From a distance, Dena could hear two voices arguing and a child's continued pathetically miserable cries. She picked up speed, unmindful of the rutted ice where car or truck tires had made crisscrossing tracks. When Dena was closer, she saw two small, poorly dressed young children bound by ropes around their frail bodies and necks. Her anger bloomed red as she yelled just as shots rang out. One man fell to the ground while the shooter put his gun in his waistband and started to drag the bound children to his van.

Dena's second shout momentarily stopped him. Then, before he could draw his gun, she was on him in a flash. With a quick fist to his jaw and another to his left eye, he was fleetingly stunned. A big man, but not one with quick reactions, he attempted to backhand her. She ducked under his swing and came up with a karate chop to his Adam's apple that gagged him and a knee to his groin. Reaching under his bent torso, she grabbed the gun and smashed him in the jaw with it before tossing it away. Then Dena kicked his legs out from under him and got him on the ground when one child screamed.

Taking her focus away from the choking man, curled up like a boiled jumbo shrimp, she turned to see another man attempting to drag the children into the van. Dena levered up with a one-two kick to the man's jaw, heard the distinct sound of teeth cracking, and saw blood spurt from his mouth. He screamed like an animal, let go of the rope holding the children, and charged toward her. Unfortunately, the man was a wiry sort with skills. He got a hold of her sweater and yanked to choke her, but her skills were better than his. She head-butted him, stomped on his instep with her booted heel, and slammed him against the van with a sharp elbow to his solar plexus. When he turned away from her to block her next assault, she kicked him in his rear, and he fell to his knees with his upper torso inside the van.

Then she turned back in a fighter's stance in time to see the first man crawling into the van. The second man, holding his bloody mouth, scrambled into the van's open side panel door, his feet dragging on the icy ground just as it sped away.

Dena held her defensive pose for humming seconds while scanning her surroundings to ensure there were no other threats. Then she moved to check the fallen man's pulse. Finding none, Dena gathered the children, removed the ropes, and huddled with them under her coat in the dead man's truck with the heater on blast. Fortunately, she found her cell phone quickly, turned it on, and dialed 9-1-1. When Dena ended the call, she noted there were many calls from her students. So as not to be disturbed during this emergency, she turned off her phone again. She would make time to return her students' calls or hand them over to her teaching assistants in the morning.

Chapter 2

Cambridge, Massachusetts, Police Lieutenant Darrius Pappas lifted his topcoat from the rack in the corner of his small drab gray office. Stretching as he stuck one arm and then the other into the sleeves, he yawned and could feel his fatigue. He had worked a double and several hours over the end of his shift, catching up on the paperwork that went along with managing detectives and other police officers. Cambridge streets in his district were not hotbeds of crime, but rowdy college students still generated a lot of ink and paper.

Checking his watch, he figured there was enough time to pick up a bottle of wine before he was due at Gail Henley's place. She was making something Italian for dinner, so he'd get a couple of bottles of red and a supply of condoms for the evening. Pulling a skull cap and heavy scarf from the rack, he checked his pockets to ensure his heavy-weather gloves were still there.

It was on wintry days like this that Darrius wished he were back in his homeland of Greece. Still, he liked America and thought he might try living in a warmer part of the country. Most police departments were about the same, and he didn't worry that he wouldn't find another position in law enforcement elsewhere. He thought Southern California around San Diego might be the right place to look when time permits. He had gone there for a police association conference and liked the area. They had temperate weather, the beaches were beautiful, and the women were plentiful. *Yes, that may be a place to consider in a few years,* he thought. He would plan to take his vacation there, scout the housing situation, and check the Internet for positions in or around the city.

Darrius was about to turn out his office light when Detective Bob Brewer stuck his head in the open door.

"Hey, Lieu, I'm glad I caught you. There is something I think you ought to see." He grinned.

Darrius sighed and eyed the younger detective. "Let's pretend that you didn't catch me. Go find Lieutenant Coleman and show her what you want me to see. She's got the night shift."

Brewer shook his head. "Can't do it, Lieu. This call came in during your shift."

Darrius sighed again. "I'm already thinking how soon I can demote you to dog catcher, Brewer."

"Well, that's one step up from Harbor Patrol. You promised to demote me there last week because you know I can't swim, but the transfer papers must have gotten lost somewhere on that mountain of paper in your inbox."

Darrius shook his head remorsefully. "I thought you were still out at a crime scene."

"I was, but I had to bring in my wits."

"Where's your partner?"

"Stony is still at the crime scene doing the door-to-door interviews with a couple of uniforms. He's about wrapped it up and should be in the house shortly with video from local security systems."

Darrius shook his head and sighed again, but relented and followed Brewer down the hall to a dark observation room. Once inside, he looked through the one-way large glass window at a female with a waist-length fat braid, dressed in all-black from the top of her black Stetson to her authentic Tecovas Western ostrich leather boots. A thick black sweater with a cowl neck molded snuggly around her ample breasts and tucked into the trim black jeans. A black leather belt with a large, round, intricately designed silver buckle rode low on her curvy waist.

Darrius nodded toward the female. "What's with the Halloween get-up? This is frekkin' January."

"Beats the hell out of me, Lieu. Her ID says her name is Dena Montgomery. She's a professor on staff at MIT."

Darrius skeptically looked at Brewer and frowned. "Can't be. She's just a kid. Double-check her credentials and see whether you can find a picture of the person she claims to be on MIT's website."

"Yes, sir." Brewer left the observation room and quick-stepped up the hallway.

Darrius, now more engaged, took off his coat, cap, and gloves, placed them on a table, and continued to observe.

When the door opened again, Darrius's captain, Russ Noland, stepped in, followed by Alana Fulton, a Police Special Victims Unit, social service supervisor. Darrius nodded to both, but only got an icy glare from Alana. Clearly, she was still smarting over his decision to end their intimate six-week relationship. He ignored her pique and turned his attention back to the scene in the interrogation room.

Captain Noland motioned to the youngsters. "Who are the kids?"

Alana shook her head and consulted her notepad. "We don't know that yet. The Police Dispatch records indicate that a woman identified as a Ms. Dena Montgomery called in a 9-1-1 murder and attempted child abduction. First officers on scene said they found this woman huddled with those kids in a van with the motor running. She claimed that she didn't know the dead man or the children.

"The van was next to a dead male. He was shot at close range, once in the head and the heart. The medical examiner will have to confirm the time of death. Registration on the vehicle comes back to the dead man. One of my agents was dispatched to collect the children, but they sent up a racket and clung to this woman like glue. My agent called me because she didn't want to inflict further emotional trauma on the children."

Captain Noland nodded. "Your people caught the case, Pappas?"

"Yes, sir. Brewer and Stonewall. I haven't been fully briefed yet. I sent Brewer to confirm specific details, and Stonewall is still at the scene. I should be able to brief you in the morning."

"You pulled a double again, didn't you?"

"I did, but this is my squad's case, so I'll work it with them."

"Aren't you off duty tomorrow?"

"I am, yes, but I'll come in for this. I want to ensure that those kids are protected."

"Don't overload yourself. Lately, you've been pulling a lot of extra duty, particularly during the past holidays. You also skipped your vacation time, Pappas."

"I'll probably take some time in a few weeks, sir."

"Good. We need you on top of your game. I'm heading out now. I'll see you in the morning."

"Yes, sir."

Captain Noland looked hopefully toward the woman. "Alana, do you need a ride?"

"No, thank you, Captain. I still have to determine who these children are. If Pappas leaves after this, I'll catch a ride with him."

Noland nodded and sighed. "Good night, then." He closed the door and left.

Silence fell like an avalanche between Darrius and Alana.

Alana sighed. "We should talk tonight, Darrius. It's important."

Darrius shook his head. "I don't believe there is anything left to say, Alana. You and Russ are the ones who need to clear up whatever is going on between you. I'll give you a lift to your home if you need it, but otherwise, I'm out of it."

Alana rolled her eyes. "What? So you can see Gail Henley, the woman you met at Stigger's birthday party? You have a date with her tonight, don't you?"

"Yes, as a matter of fact, I do. I've never lied to you, Alana, and I won't lie to you now. I'm interested in her, and we plan to spend time away from the city together in a few weeks. At least she's not involved with anyone else, especially not my boss. So, stick a fork in it, Alana. Whatever we had is done."

When she started to argue, Darrius turned away. Then, less concerned about Alana's pique, Darrius activated the sound to listen as the female and two tender-aged children continued to talk.

Dena smiled at the boy. "I have brothers and sisters your ages."

He shook his curly haired head. "Brothers, sisters? I don't know this."

"No? Well, how old is your sister?"

He frowned. "Sister?"

"Yes, is this pretty girl your sister?"

The boy frowned and shrugged. "She girl."

"Ah, and you're boy?"

Nodding enthusiastically, he pointed a thumb at his small chest. "Boy."

"Okay, Boy, we will work with that for now. Do you have a father and mother?"

The boy's frown deepened, as if the words were also foreign to him. Dena was getting the drift. These children had no social interaction whatsoever. The boy was barely verbal, and the girl hadn't spoken. She only watched what transpired between Dena and the boy. When Dena heard the girl's stomach growl, she remembered she hadn't eaten dinner either. When she stood, the children tensed and rose, too.

Dena smiled at them. "I'm hungry. How about you?"

When they mutely continued to stare up at her, she rubbed her abdomen in a wide circular motion and then pantomimed eating. The boy nodded and pointed to his abdomen, too.

Dena smiled and pointed. "Do you see those paper cups and plates by the coffee maker? Would you go get two of each?" She held up two fingers.

The boy seemed to understand, but he locked hands with the girl. They moved together as a unit. When they returned to the table with the items, Dena reached inside her grocery bag, retrieved the large soup container, and divided it into two cups. The small loaf of brown bread she tore into three equal slices. The children didn't hesitate to drink it and devour the bread, so Dena poured the remaining soup into the cups and only ate her share of the bread. Again, the children gulped it all up. She realized they must be starving. So, Dena took the pineapple out of the bag, retrieved her Swiss Army knife, and sliced off the top and bottom of the fruit. She was about to cut the pineapple in half lengthwise when a tall man rushed into the room with his weapon drawn and pointed at her, followed by an attractive woman with blond hair and the two detectives she had spoken with earlier.

The tall man shouted at her. "Drop your weapon!"

Dena eyed him up and down and frowned at him, but didn't stop what she was doing. When the commotion started, the children clung to her legs. Then, like a Ginsu Master, she sliced the pineapple and handed a piece to each child to soothe their fears.

"Put your weapon away. You're frightening these children."

Dena wiped off her knife, closed it, and put it back in one of her many inside pockets.

Bob Brewer put his hand over his lieutenant's weapon, pressing his hand down toward the ground. "It's all right, Lieutenant."

Lieutenant Pappas frowned at Detective Brewer but holstered his weapon.

"Doctor Montgomery, this is my lieutenant, Darrius Pappas, and Alana Fulton, from our Special Victims Unit." Brewer handed a file to Pappas as he made the introductions. "Doctor Montgomery is an assistant department head at MIT."

As he read the file, Lieutenant Pappas briefly lifted his gaze to her. "Doctor Montgomery, the next time a police officer instructs you to drop your weapon, I strongly suggest you do so immediately."

"If the safety on your weapon wasn't engaged, perhaps I would have. However, I hope that the next time you will not engage in bullying with young children in the room. Would you like a piece of pineapple?"

The two detectives snickered behind the lieutenant's back. Pappas silenced them with a look and continued to read the file. According to data gathered by his detective, Dena Montgomery was MIT's assistant dean of science, professor of astrophysics, a principal investigator at the MIT Kavli Institute for Astrophysics and Space Research, a math Olympiad and a rodeo star in her youth. A picture of her from MIT's website and her bio were also in the file.

Alana extended her hand. "Doctor Montgomery, you seem to have developed a rapport with these children. So, I hope that you'll help me with them. First, I need to have them examined. Then I'll try to find warmer clothes for them and space in one of our facilities until their parents can be located."

"I agree that they need to be examined, but I don't believe you will find parents for these children. In the truck, while we waited for the police to arrive, I tried communicating with them in several languages.

They didn't respond to me. They were more responsive when I spoke to them in English. Their speech patterns indicate that they've been living in isolation. The boy is likely Cuban, but the girl, I'm not sure. If I had to guess, I'd say she's from the Louisiana Bayou area. Given how they are dressed, they have been brought from a warmer climate to this area.

"They are witnesses to a crime. The man who was about to sell the children to the traffickers was murdered right in front of them. Given the number of restraints and chains I saw welded into the van's walls, other children were at one time in the vehicle. They were likely sold off along the route here. So, your social services facilities will not be safe with them anywhere in the system. You will have to keep them and me off the radar."

The police officers stood silent and stared.

Lieutenant Pappas signaled to the others and headed out of the room. "Give us a moment, Doctor Montgomery."

Dena shrugged, sat, and shared most of the remaining fruit in the grocery bag.

"What have you got, Stoney?"

"You won't believe this, Lieu." He pulled a jump drive from his evidence bag and inserted it into a computer terminal. "I downloaded this from several security cameras in the area." They watched as two men argued. Then one pulled out a gun and shot the other. Finally, a figure clad in black with a coat flapping like wings flew up the alleyway and attacked the shooter. The rest of the video unfolded just as Dena had informed the on-scene officers. "Doctor Montgomery went all Jessica Campbell Jones Cage on the UNSUBs. Talk about a super shero? Man! She kicked ass!" He enthused until Darrius eyed him. Then he became less animated and continued. "Still, we wouldn't have found the gun if Doctor Montgomery hadn't told us where to look."

Darrius had to admit that Doctor Montgomery looked like some type of avenging angel and fought like a tigress. He dug his left hand in his pocket, raked his right hand through his pelt of dark hair, and paced. From what he could read, she was not only a professor-in-residence at MIT but also some type of hand-to-hand combat master.

Alana watched him pace and recognized the affectations as Darrius's thought mode.

Darrius stopped pacing and faced the other three people in the room. "She's right, damn it. This looks like a major case to me. Does anyone disagree?"

Brewer shook his head. "No, Lieu, but she's also right that we can't put this case in the system. The fewer people who know about it, the better to protect the witnesses. If this is interstate or international human trafficking, then it's an FBI or CIA case. We can only investigate the murder aspect of this situation."

Darrius looked at Stony. "Do we have a ballistics report on the gun yet?"

"The lab is working on it. We've got clear prints for two of the perps, but I didn't find a match in CODIS. However, thanks to Doctor Montgomery's righteous beatdown of the perps, we've also got blood samples to work with and the tip of one of the perp's tongue."

Alana shook her head. "If this is international, the prints may not be in our statewide or even national system. So, if you're trying to keep a lid on it, we can't even go through Interpol."

Darrius agreed and sighed. "For tonight, we have to put them in a safe house. I'll talk with Captain Noland in the morning and then contact the local FBI Field Office. Let's get those children examined, in warmer clothes, and into a safe house to get some rest. By the way, Stoney, if you or Brewer allow a perp to enter the precinct without being frisked, you'll both be skinny dipping off a lifeboat in the harbor until April Fool's Day."

Stony shook his head. "Beggin' your pardon, sir, but Doctor Montgomery wasn't a perp. She was a wit. Still, I'd take on the job, but my wife would divorce me for patting down a woman who has an hourglass figure like Doctor Montgomery."

Bob Brewer held up his hand. "I'm not married and can't swim, but I'd wear a Speedo and happily take the plunge on the coldest day of the year. Beggin' your pardon, Alana, but the Doc looks like a cover girl, and she's stacked."

Just after Darrius, Alana, and the two detectives returned to the room where Dena sat with the children, the door opened again. Everyone except

Dena froze when the Police Commissioner entered with FBI Agent Jenna Baker and Washington, DC, police lieutenant, Eve Montgomery.

"Uh oh," Dena breathed the words, rolled her expressive eyes, and got to her feet.

"Sir." Darrius frowned, but extended his hand to the commissioner. *This case is getting more curious by the second*, Darrius thought.

The commissioner shook hands and regarded the rest of the people in the room. "If you'll let us have the room, I'd appreciate it. You stay, Lieutenant Pappas."

The two detectives and Alana didn't have to be told they wouldn't be included in whatever conversation was about to occur. So, they quickly left the interrogation room.

Once the door closed, the commissioner extended his hand to Dena. "I regret that we had to meet under these circumstances, Doctor Montgomery. Please tell your father that I said hello. We were undergrads at Boston College together and lived in the same dormitory. I was in the school band and played the tuba. I'm still one of his avid fans." He handed a business card to her.

Darrius frowned. *Her father?*

Dena pocketed the card and then shook the commissioner's hand. "I'll do that, sir. He'll be pleased that you remembered him."

The commissioner regarded Lieutenant Pappas. "You are, from this moment going forward, assigned to a special task force. You will work under the FBI's direction. Is that understood, Lieutenant?"

Pappas nodded. "Yes, sir," and then watched as the commissioner left the room. Yet, Darrius was even more confused than before. Turning, he regarded the three women in the room, particularly Dena Montgomery. *Her father? Who is this kid?*

Jenna Baker turned to Darrius and nodded, as if reading his thoughts. "Lieutenant, the less you know about us for the moment, the better. For all concerned in your police department, we were never here. Nevertheless, what you do need to know is that the FBI is taking over this case with your police commissioner's full knowledge and approval. As he has instructed, you will be temporarily assigned as liaison between your police department and the FBI on the murder case part of these crimes. I'm assured that you are fully capable of conducting the murder investigation on your own.

"Shortly, you will be taken from the building with Doctor Montgomery and the children to an airfield, where you will be flown to an undisclosed location. You will leave all forms of communication, your keys to your car, and your condo here in your office under lock and key until the conclusion of this assignment. New equipment will be provided as well as your personal effects. You will tell no one of this assignment now or going forward. Questions?"

"Many, but I presume that this is an urgent matter. The questions can wait."

Jenna smiled. "Good man. Then let's head 'em up and move 'em out. We're burning moonlight."

Chapter 3

Within the hour, Jenna Baker waved goodbye at a small, remote airfield. Eve Montgomery fired up the Cessna Citation's jet engines, took the aircraft down the runway, and smoothly lifted off into the night sky. Once they were safely away, Jenna climbed into the back seat of one of three black SUVs, and the trio of blacked-out windowed vehicles pulled away.

Dena sat quietly in the aircraft's snug fuselage with the children asleep, wrapped in warm blankets with their heads on her lap while Darrius looked on.

"You don't seem surprised at this turn of events, Doctor Montgomery."

Dena shrugged and yawned. "Not entirely, no." She sighed. "You'll learn this soon enough. The woman piloting the aircraft is my sister, Geneviève Montgomery. We call her Eve. She's a police lieutenant like you. However, she's also a part of a joint FBI and CIA task force representing the DC Police Department's Major Crimes Division. She's a bit territorial when it comes to our family members who might be in danger. Still, I have yet to figure out how she knew—." She broke off and frantically reached inside the collar of her sweater.

Darrius thought it was strange how Doctor Montgomery felt around inside her clothes. He didn't want to think about her hands on her body, touching herself. Nevertheless, the observation had his blood uncharacteristically warming. When she pulled a broken gold chain from inside her clothes, he wondered what the significance was when she sighed, seemingly in relief or concern. Then she pulled her mobile phone from a pocket in her multi-pocketed duster and frantically thumbed a text message.

"Did your necklace get broken in the altercation with the perps?"

"Yes, it did." Dena knew better than to comment further about the significance of the chain. To most people, it was just a pretty piece of jewelry that intricately spelled out the word **FAMILY**. However, it was much, much more. Now Dena knew how and why her sister found her so quickly. When broken, the chain emitted an emergency communication that sent a crisis distress signal to the closest cell towers in the vicinity. From the towers, signals were sent to one of the many security satellites in geostationary orbit around the globe. Within seconds, the signal triggered a Code: Red alert at CompuCorrect, a Silicon Valley tech firm. Cameras and scanners on a grid of geostationary satellites went into action to identify the signal's location and record any activity within a ten-mile radius, starting an hour before the signal was received. The satellite was so powerful that it could read the year on a dime on the ground.

By now, her entire family was on red alert and focused on what had transpired. If she had thought to check her phone, she could have saved her family a great deal of anxiety. Given the position of the stars that she could see above the Nor'easter's cloud cover, they were heading for the Pennsylvania Mountains to her family's retreat. Fortunately, her family wouldn't be there since they had left for Maryland before New Year's Eve after spending two weeks there during the Christmas holidays.

As she suspected, they had only been in the air for about an hour when Eve started her descent through the turbulent atmosphere. With the amount of snow falling, it looked as if they had flown right into the Nor'easter and landed just in the nick of time. Eve taxied the aircraft into a hangar, where the giant doors rolled up into the ceiling. As soon as they cleared the doors, Eve cut the engine off, and the doors rolled down.

Eve came back into the aircraft's cabin. "We're going to have to hurry. Visibility is limited, but I don't want to spend the rest of the night in the hangar. These children are not properly dressed, and they look exhausted. They and both of you need a warm, comfortable bed. So, I'll fire up the Sikorsky. Can you two carry the children?"

Dena gingerly hoisted the sleeping girl onto her shoulder. Eve tucked a blanket around the girl and did the same as Darrius lifted the sleepy boy. They eased down the short steps of the jet and waited while Eve battled the blowing snow to the big helicopter outside the hangar. Once Eve had the blades whirling and the cabin warm enough, she motioned for Darrius and Dena to come out and climb aboard. They were underway in moments, but the going was treacherous, with visibility near nonexistent and turbulent winds whipping around the mountainous terrain. Still, following a beacon, within fifteen minutes, they hovered over a round space surrounded by powerful landing lights.

Once safely on the ground and the blades stopped turning, Eve activated a yellow covering that extended and sealed around the helicopter's left door. It was made of slick canvas cloth woven through accordion rings large enough to walk through. When Eve opened the door, they walked down the short steps through the tube that blocked the brunt of the icy wind and snow. Eve closed and locked the helicopter door and followed her sister and the detective into the house at garage level. When they were inside, Eve activated gears that retracted the tube just as the ones at airports did and folded away.

Darrius followed Dena through rows of tall, decorated Christmas trees with the root balls attached and in wide tin tubs. Once in the hallway, Eve led the way to a set of elevators. Still carrying the children, one elevator took them up three stories to the first bedroom level. They put the children in bed, and Eve activated the video monitor to hear and see them as they slept. Then they returned to the lobby level, where they were met by a tall, slim, sturdy-looking middle-aged woman wearing tennis shoes, thick socks, jeans, and a heavy sweater. Her hair was liberally streaked with gray and braided.

"Good morning." She hugged Dena and then Eve before she extended her hand to the tall man who looked to be of Greek extraction. *A young Apollo Greek god,* she thought. *He is an unusually handsome one, too. He dressed well as if he knew the style suited him.* "Althea Hardyston. I'm the grandaunt-in-law to these two babes." She noted he had a nice, firm grip and looked into her eyes.

"Lieutenant Darrius Pappas, Cambridge, Massachusetts Police Department."

She released his hand. "Welcome, Lieutenant Pappas. You can call me Aunt Althea. Everyone does. Grand aunt-in-law is too much of a mouthful and we don't stand on ceremony here. Calling me Miss Hardyston only makes me feel like an old spinster aunt. Please make yourself to home." She turned to the two women as he moved away and spoke more quietly. "Your uncle Seth called me at three o'clock this morning to relay your messages and to say you were crazy enough to take that bird up in this type of weather. He told me to notify our security team and that you should be here within two hours because you were on your way." She shook her head and sighed. "I'm surprised to see you made it through the mountains in one piece."

Eve grinned at Althea. "I flew above the mountain range and only dropped down when I could hover over the landing pad."

Althea just rolled her eyes. She loved her sister's daredevil grandchildren to distraction. The whole lot of them never backed down from a challenge. God rest her soul; her sister would be so proud of them. Althea sighed. "Still, it's going on five in the morning. I've already started breakfast. It should be ready in about thirty minutes. I imagine you want to freshen up and talk before or while you eat. When you're finished, show Lieutenant Pappas to Suite 101. A change of clothes is already there with the equipment he will need."

Eve smiled. "Thanks, Aunt Althea. You're right. We need a briefing first, but we'll be in for breakfast on time."

Dena handed her grocery bag to her grandaunt. "I bought these fresh last evening from a bodega in Cambridge. I hope you can use them."

Althea peeked inside the bag and shook her head. "Forgot your grocery list again, didn't you?"

Dena rolled her eyes and sighed. "I almost remembered, Aunt Althea."

Althea smirked, sighed, and left, taking the bag with her and closing the door behind her.

Eve activated the gas fireplace while Dena and Darrius settled in the small salon off the front lobby entrance. Then Eve and Dena opened their phone apps to monitor the children.

Darrius looked up and around the well-appointed space that resembled a cozy men's club before regarding the two women. "Where are we?"

Dena sighed and stretched out on a long, burgundy wine-colored leather sofa. "We're at my family's home in Monroe County, Pennsylvania. It's an old hotel that was once a ski resort."

"Are your parents here and asleep?" He was surprised they didn't hear the helicopter and wake up.

"No, they left after Christmas. My father grew up here. He is the youngest male in his family of thirteen siblings. Many of his close and extended family members still live and own farms in these mountains. Actually, the Montgomery family is so large that they should call Monroe County Montgomery County. In addition to farming, the family also works in the construction industry. So they renovated this hotel before we moved in and made this land and buildings a working farm. Our brother, Brian, is the general manager." She yawned and covered her face with her Stetson.

He frowned. "Your family is so large that you need a three-level hotel to house you and a farm to feed you?"

Eve snorted a laugh, leaned forward in the tufted, wine-colored leather chair that matched the sofa, and placed her elbows on her knees with her fingers laced together. "You have no idea, but what is pertinent here is that it's a safer place than anything your police department could offer, given the nature of what I believe my sister unwittingly uncovered. In addition to my police duties as a lieutenant in Washington, DC, Police Department's Major Crimes Division, I am also the liaison with the FBI, CIA, and Interpol."

Darrius cocked his head toward Doctor Montgomery. "Yes, your sister told me that much." He knew Washington had over thirty-four hundred police officers and six hundred civilians in its department. One of the places he considered an exciting place to relocate was the nation's capital. So he had done extensive research on the area. The weather in the mid-Atlantic was more temperate, and access to beaches along the southern coastline was cleaner and more plentiful. In addition, the DC Police Department served more than seven hundred thousand residents. So, Eve Montgomery's role as a lieutenant likely held more responsibilities than his and, therefore, it would be more challenging than what he was doing now. Nevertheless, he liked the idea of working harder and more innovatively, particularly if it involved working with challenging law enforcement entities like the FBI, CIA, or Interpol.

Eve tilted her head in a nod. "Good. What you need to know is that the joint task force has been investigating white slavery among the Baltic states of Estonia, Latvia, and Lithuania. Estonia is a significant source country, trafficking women to Norway, the United Kingdom, and Finland for forced prostitution. Unfortunately, some Baltic countries don't have or don't enforce criminal laws against white slavery. However, the United Nations does ban the practice. That's why Interpol is a part of the task force.

"Estonian men are used within the country to work in hard-labor projects like rock quarries. Other men have been forced into committing criminal acts like kidnappings, murders, and thefts. Even more victims are shipped to Ukraine for forced labor in the construction industry. Healthy men are required to impregnate young girls on baby farms and for ethnic cleansing. Some babies have been sold to the highest bidders internationally. What happens to the babies after that is anyone's guess. We have a keen interest in the Baltics at this point for other reasons, considering what is going on in Ukraine. We're in an all-hands-on-deck mode with Switzerland and Finland requesting admission to NATO.

"We know Russian oligarchs are behind the human trafficking crimes in the United States. We also suspected that white babies and children were kidnapped from the Baltics and trafficked for high-cost adoptions and pedophiles. We didn't know that South and North American criminal cartels also sell children to the highest bidder. We believe that's what my sister inadvertently uncovered. So, we're having the vehicles' recent locations tracked through their GPS systems to determine where they have been over the last year. We want to rescue as many children as possible and try to reunite them with their parents. What concerns us is that, in many cases, the parents may be illegals who are hiding from the authorities. They are not likely to complain that their children have been kidnapped. In some cases, they have their own means of tracking down child abductors, which often leads to bloodshed."

When her phone signaled, Eve held up her hand. "Hold one. I have to take this." Then, she rose and stepped out of the room. As she left, he could hear her saying, "Go for Eve."

Darrius sat back in the comfortable chair and crossed his right leg over his left knee. He was weary, but he now understood the sheer magnitude of the problem and the impact this situation could have on Dena Montgomery and the two young witnesses. Yet, he was brought in and expected to solve the murder case. To do that, Doctor Montgomery and the children were his responsibility and in his custody as his witnesses. He also had to become their bodyguard to ensure their safety.

Darrius observed Dena Montgomery's lean body stretched out on one of the sofas with her face covered by her Stetson. He could hear her lightly snoring. He had never known anyone like her. She looked like a kid, wore Western-inspired clothing and boots as if they were a fashion-forward statement, and was a high-fashion model. She could fight like a Karate master, yet she was as warm and caring toward the children as the nuns had been to him in the orphanage where he grew up in Greece. He was more than a little curious about her, but Eve Montgomery interrupted his thoughts when she reentered the salon.

"Hey, kid, did you forget that Drew was coming to visit you?"

Dena lifted the Stetson from her face and frowned at her sister. "He isn't scheduled to be in town…" she trailed off, fluidly stood, and retrieved her phone from one of the many pockets in her coat. "Oh, hell." She sighed after checking her calendar. "Is he at my place?"

"He was. He coded into your place twice. I presume that he's still there."

Dena paced as she dialed his number. "Drew?" His handsome face filled the screen.

Drew Hamilton sighed, yawned, and rubbed his eyes. Then he looked at Dena's face and smiled. "You forgot I was coming, didn't you?"

Dena rolled her eyes to the ceiling. "I didn't forget…exactly. I just failed to remember what weekend it was."

Drew laughed. "Okay, are you all right?"

"I am, but I'm not sure when I'll be back."

"That's okay. I was just worried when you didn't come in. I fell asleep waiting for you. I tried to call you several times, but each time my call went to voice mail."

Dena shook her head in frustration as she paced. "I apologize, Drew. I turned off my phone after my last student conference today. Then something came up. I had a bunch of messages, but I didn't thoroughly check them."

He shrugged. "You missed a great dinner and some exciting news."

"Drew, I didn't have any groceries."

He laughed. "I know. I saw the grocery list on your refrigerator. I came into town early because of the expected storm. My flight landed at three. So when I got to your place and saw the list, I went back out and picked up your groceries. I figured that you forgot the list this morning."

Dena sighed. "You know me too well. So what's the exciting news?"

"Will has agreed to consider opening another **INDULGENCES** facility here in Cambridge or elsewhere in the Boston area. He wants me to scout out locations and do the preliminary research."

Dena smiled. "Really? That is great news. How long can you stay in town?"

He shrugged. "I've never done anything like this before, so it may take a while. First, I need to find a commercial real estate agent to show me around."

"Wait. I know someone in real estate in Boston." She frowned and thumbed through her phone. "She's a friend of my mother's. They went to school at Spelman College together in Georgia. She helped me find housing for visiting lecturers." Dena flipped through her addresses, but Eve handed her cell phone to Dena. It had the name and contact information on display. "Thanks, Eve. Drew, I'm sending the data to you via text from Eve's phone. The agent's name is June Austin-Andrews. She and her daughter, Alexandra Andrews, own and operate The Austin Real Estate Agency in Boston." Dena handed Eve's phone back to her.

"Got it! Thanks, Dena, and thank Eve for me, too."

"You're welcome, Drew. Look, stay at my place while you're there working—*Mi casa e su casa.* My car and my bike are in the garage. You know where my parking spots are located. The keys are hanging on the peg in the front closet next to the security keypad. If you use either one, check the gas. I don't recall the last time I filled up."

Drew laughed. "Thanks. So, if I don't see you while I'm here, are we still on for Seychelles for spring break?"

Dena closed her eyes. "Yes. As far as I know now, we're still on. I'll give you a heads up if anything changes."

"Good deal. I'm looking forward to getting out of the cold for a winter break. Take care of my pal."

"Will do. You do the same." Sighing, she disconnected the call and then looked into her sister's eyes. "Am I going to make the Seychelles trip?"

"If I have anything to do with it, yes, you will."

"Good. I don't want to disappoint Drew again."

Eve put her arm around her sister for a quick squeeze. "You won't. We'll be sunning in Seychelles for spring break."

"Good. Now, let's eat. Talk later. I'm starving."

Darrius quietly sat listening and watching the interaction between the sisters. He noticed that although they were both about the same height, they didn't resemble one another in any other dimension. Dena Montgomery had a warm brown complexion, diamond-black irises, and thick black hair she wore in a single, long fat braid that ended at her hips. They were both stacked, seemingly physically fit, with a subtle musculature. However, Dena was thinner than Eve, who had a *café au lait* complexion, silky shoulder-length hair, and whiskey-colored brown irises. He frowned. Yet, love and warmth radiated between the women. When they spoke with one another, they looked directly into each other's eyes. Curious, he would continue to listen and observe, making his own judgment about these two. He was also curious about Drew, who had unfettered access to Doctor Montgomery's condo. According to data in the records, she lives in a condo with a panoramic view of the Charles River. That was a pricey neighborhood for a kid her age, even if she was a professor at MIT. *Curiouser and curiouser,* he considered.

Eve looked back over her shoulder at Lieutenant Pappas. "Finished with your mental gymnastics, are you?"

Surprised at her accuracy, he simply shrugged. "Not quite yet, but I'll let you know when I am."

Eve grinned as they left the salon and headed to the back of the mansion to the industrial kitchen. They grabbed plates and filled them with breakfast foods from a lavish steam-filled buffet before sitting in what appeared to Darrius to be an employees' dining area. However, it had a panoramic view of the swirling snow and gusty winds. Once they sat, Althea joined them and poured coffee all around before sitting down to eat.

CHAPTER 4

A while later, midway through their meal, Eve and Dena noticed movement in the room where the children were resting. They both were mid-standing when Dena motioned to her sister to stay seated. "I'll get them. They may be uncomfortable with too many people around. I want them to bathe so that I can check them for injuries. Aunt Althea, did you—?"

"I did, yes. There were plenty of warm clothes and shoes to fit them in your brothers' and sisters' rooms. I left everything in the bedroom on the dresser."

Dena left while Eve, Darrius, and Althea continued to eat.

Althea eyed Darrius while she sipped her coffee. "So, Lieutenant Pappas, may I call you Darrius?"

He shrugged and wiped his mouth with his napkin. "Sure."

"You're from the Greek Isles?"

Surprised, Darrius looked up into her eyes and frowned. "Yes, Koufonisia."

"Where is that exactly?"

"Geographically?"

"Yes."

"It's located on the south-southeast side of Naxos and on the west-northwest of Amorgos. It's a part of the archipelago, the Lesser East Cyclades."

"Really? I've visited Greece a number of times, but I've never been to Koufonisia. Do you have family there?"

"No, none that I'm aware of."

"What brought you to the United States?"

"I came to America to attend college. I earned a full-ride scholarship for competitive swimming and diving. I planned to try out for the Olympics."

"You competed?"

"I didn't make the cut for the official team. I was on the support team."

"That's too bad."

Darrius shrugged. "Not so bad. After I graduated, I became an American citizen. I was offered an opportunity to train younger people with the potential to become Olympic swimmers and divers."

"That's a leap to becoming a police officer."

"Not so much. The police department hired me to train officers who worked on police boats. I worked two jobs for a while, but the pay was better with the police department. So, I decided to join the force. I took the test, moved from harbor patrol as positions opened up, and now I have a squad of detectives."

"Do you plan to stay with the police department?"

"Yes, I want more significant challenges. I'll take the captain's exam when it's offered next fall."

"You're ambitious."

He shrugged. "I feel that what I do is necessary to serve the common good. So, if that's considered 'ambitious,' then you're probably right."

"Anyone special in your life?"

Darrius frowned. "I have people I consider friends and others I consider acquaintances… Look, am I being vetted for something I'm unaware of?"

Eve shook her head and grinned. "No, not by the FBI, CIA, or Interpol. Aunt Althea is just naturally curious about people in general. Your background and credentials were already established before you were approached at your police department. I could probably tell you things about yourself that you've forgotten. Like, for example, your third date with a Ms. Gail Henley, an account executive with a shoe manufacturer you met recently at a birthday party held at a club for a friend of yours, your former police academy training officer, Jack Stiggers. Stiggers' baby sister, Melony, is Gail's best friend from college. Gail is sorely disappointed that you had an emergency and had to leave town. However, she did appreciate the fact that you sent flowers and a bottle of outstanding red wine to her. When the gifts were delivered, she opened the door wearing something straight out of Victoria's Secret and very, uh…comfortable. She's, obviously, looking forward to your return."

Darrius cursed liberally under his breath. He had forgotten entirely about his date with Gail. Then he smirked. There was no doubt that if Eve Montgomery and her FBI pal, Jenna Baker, could learn that much about him in a short time, they knew more than they stated. They were smart, too. No doubt, Gail called his cell phone or office looking for him. So, someone had been dispatched to check her out. The gifts were a nice touch. Gail would appreciate such things. Victoria's Secret, huh? It seemed that he missed out on more than an Italian dinner. He'd have to remember to get a supply of condoms before he saw Gail again. Absence makes the heart grow fonder and all that jazz. He cleared his mind of the image of Gail wearing something from the Victoria's Secret Collection. "Uh, thanks. However, I'd prefer to know more about the plan for protecting my witnesses?"

Eve nodded, pleased by how the lieutenant handled a sticky situation, and then rose from the table when her phone signaled an incoming call. "Hold one. I may be able to answer that question shortly." She put the phone to her ear and left the room. "Yes, go for Eve."

Darrius watched her go and then turned back to the very observant Althea Hardyston. "So, I've told you what you wanted to know about me. How about telling me something about the Montgomery sisters?"

Althea raised an eyebrow. "What do you want to know?"

"For starters, who are they?"

Althea frowned. "You live and work in Cambridge near Boston, and you've never heard of the Montgomery family?"

He shrugged, confused. "No, I haven't."

"You've never heard of Chuck Montgomery? He graduated from Boston College and was a first-round draft choice who played in the NBA in Boston. He has three Olympic gold medals, multiple championship rings, and he's in the Basketball Hall of Fame. He often comes back to Cambridge for events on campus and his name is included on the sports arena's endowments boards."

"Vaguely, I remember the name because the police department has to support campus police for crowd control when celebrities come to the area, but I don't follow basketball that closely."

"Then you've never heard of the gold medalist, Vivian Alexander, either?"

"No. I'm drawing a blank."

Althea shook her head. "You must have been living underwater for the last twenty years."

"Yes, likely, I was. I would have been thirteen years old twenty years ago and swimming daily to learn how to be a champion."

"Charles and Vivian Alexander Montgomery are parents to Eve and Dena Montgomery, along with thirty-plus siblings. We call Charles Chuck. He's my deceased sister's twelfth child of thirteen and one of my nephews. He and his siblings all grew up here in Monroe County. I've told you about Chuck. However, as I've said, his wife, Vivian, is a basketball gold medal winner. Her brother, Kenneth Alexander, is the former two-term California governor. He also owns CompuCorrect Global, a Silicon Valley tech firm, one of the top ten in the country. His wife is US Senator JeNelle Towson Alexander. Vivian's second brother, Benjamin Alexander, is a five-star general and US Air Force jet fighter pilot. We tease him and call him Benny and the Jets. He has flown the last five space flight missions to SPACEHOME, so he is also an astronaut. His wife is US Navy Admiral Stacy Greene. They are both deployed as military attachés to the American Embassy in Tokyo, Japan.

"Vivian's younger brother is Gregory Alexander, a basketball icon that the press and news media call Alexander the Great. Before he retired from professional sports, he and his friends opened what has become one of the most prestigious financial firms on Wall Street. He is married to the actress and supermodel, Angelique, who has become a Le Cordon Bleu certified chef and restauranteur. Then there is Aretha Alexander, who is working on her post-doctorate at Cambridge in England. So, the families, Alexander and Montgomery, are legion and legend."

Darrius just stared, dumbfounded.

Dena entered the room with the children and helped them serve their plates from the buffet. She had overheard a part of the conversation. "Actually, Aunt Althea, that number is closer to forty at last count if you include the Phillips' kids and the others who were rescued, but I haven't seen my family since New Year's day a few weeks ago. As you know, the number of my siblings is always fluid." She brought the children to the table to sit on booster seats and eat while Althea served fresh-squeezed orange juice and hot cocoa to them.

"You see, Lieutenant Pappas, my parents had a baby born during Christmas dinner, and so did my brother, Brian, and his wife, KiLe. My dad, my brother, Vincent, and my grandmother, Sylvia Benson Alexander, delivered the babies. So, the Alexander-Montgomery family had a very merry holiday last year."

Darrius frowned at Althea. "I thought you said that Chuck Montgomery was a basketball star."

Dena picked up the story. "He is, and he still plays a couple of times a week for fun and exercise with a team of medical personnel. The team is called The Body Snatchers. In addition, my mother still plays with a group of female law students, lawyers, and judges. Their team is known as Final Justice. So, after he retired from professional sports, my dad became an emergency room doctor. He now has a small private practice and owns and operates Physicians' Hospital in rural Maryland. He also takes primary care of the little people in our family and the rest of us. He's more or less a stay-at-home dad these days. So, we sometimes call him Mr. Mom. However, he considers himself a cowboy and gentleman rancher."

Dena continued while she ate. "My brother, Vincent, is an emergency room pediatrician and pediatric surgeon. My grandmother, Sylvia Benson Alexander, is a registered nurse and the Director of Nursing at Summer County Hospital in Goodwill, South Carolina."

"Unless your parents hold some type of world record for the birth of biological offspring, I presume that many of you are adopted."

"You presume correctly. However, as I said, my parents just added to the family two weeks ago."

"You mentioned that your mother plays basketball with females in the legal profession. Does she work in the court system doing something outside of your home?"

Dena laughed. "Uh, yes. My mother is one of the US Supreme Court Jurists."

Again, Darrius just stared.

Eve returned to the room and slipped her phone into her back pocket. "That was Jenna Baker. The van matching your description, Dena, was found in a remote area on fire with two bodies inside. She hopes to match the blood from the crime scene to the bodies in the van. Jenna is also using the GPS systems in both vehicles to trace their routes over the previous twelve to twenty-four months."

Dena frowned, looking between Eve and Darrius. "What does this do to your case if the blood samples match the bodies in the van?"

Eve sighed and eyed the children before she spoke. "We're S-O-L."

Darrius looked Dena in the eyes. "We will have to hope that the GPS tracking turns up actionable results. First, of course, we have the body of one of the perps. Then, I can begin my investigation by determining who he is and how he came to have possession of my witnesses. Otherwise, we're also up the proverbial creek without a paddle."

Chapter 5

With the children fed, bathed, hair scrubbed, dressed warmly, and curious about their surroundings, Dena took them on a playroom tour and provided crayons and coloring books. Then Dena explained to Althea what she believed to be the children's level of exposure. Althea nodded her understanding and sat with the children in one of the playroom's cubicles at a table, naming the items they colored or drew. The boy repeated the words and seemed to understand what Althea was teaching him. However, the little girl said nothing and continued to watch everyone around her.

Althea had no children of her own, but she was like a fawning grandmother, praising every little hieroglyphic the children drew or colored. Althea's attention and encouragement finally drew a smile from the little girl. Their apparent comfort with Althea allowed Dena, Eve, and Darrius an opportunity to slip away and go to their rooms for some necessary downtime.

Eve and Dena led the way to one of the interior staircases. As they walked up the wide, spiraling, marble steps, Darius couldn't help but look up the four stories to a high skylight over the wide circular staircase and down three levels. At the second-floor landing, Eve held open the heavy door for Darrius and pointed. "To your left."

Once through the heavy fire-rated doors, they entered a long, wide, carpeted hallway. Suite 101 was the first door they came to on the right. Eve waved, but kept walking further down the hallway. Dena opened the door to the suite and led the way inside, flipping on the lights as she went. "This is your suite of rooms. You should find toiletries in the bedroom bath and clothes and shoes to fit you in the closet. The electronics you need are here." She pointed to the new boxes stacked on a desk with a cellphone, iPad, and laptop computer.

WOW! Darius thought when he stepped inside the ultra-modern suite. First, he inspected the boxes of electronics. They were high-end equipment that he would never have been able to purchase on the open market, even with a police officer's discount. Then he looked up and around at his environment. To his right was a sofa in a sitting area complete with a desk, coffee table, and wall-mounted flat-screen above a wide, squat water-vapor firebox. A wall to his left partially bisected the room where a king-sized bed could be seen with a dresser against the opposite wall, a small round table, two chairs, and another wall-mounted flat-screen above the dresser. Wide barn doors provided closures for the bedroom space and a sumptuous four-piece bathroom and closet with clothes inside. A small kitchenette spanned the wall by the entrance to the suite. Bridging both ends of the suite were wall-to-wall, ceiling-to-floor glass bi-fold doors. Charming exterior lighting provided an unencumbered terrace view, with attractively arranged furniture with potted plants and trees. *The view must be phenomenal from here*, thought Darrius.

After checking the clothes in the closet and drawers, Darrius stood looking into the murky dawning light of the vastness of the mountain range. It seemed to go on unspoiled forever. "This is incredible." His voice was a reverent whisper.

Dena looked around. "The view is pretty spectacular when the wind isn't blowing snow all over the landscape. This slow-moving storm is predicted to clear out in about twenty-four to thirty-six hours on its way to New England. So, sometime while we're here, you should be able to see the sunrise on the snow-capped mountains to the east and the sunset to the west in the early evening. It's difficult to see in the daylight, but at night you can sometimes see the lights from the homes of our family members who live here in the mountains year-round."

Darrius turned from the view and looked at Dena. "I'm curious about how you knew what size I wear and where you were able to find clothes and shoes for me in a frekkin' winter storm."

Dena shrugged. " It wasn't me, but I'm sure my sister figured it out and sent a message ahead of our arrival. You'll probably learn this later, but our granduncle is the sheriff of Monroe County. His name is Seth Montgomery. He's kept abreast of when any of us plan to be here at Point of View. That's the name of this farm. As was mentioned before, my brother, Brian, manages the farm here and hired a K-9 security officer, Claudia Shaffer, to protect the property. She's a military veteran who worked with service dogs in Afghanistan. I think she has eight dogs and a security staff of six here in Pennsylvania. That's why Eve felt we could come here for a while until she had time to work out a plan to keep us safe.

"I believe Eve will show you more of the security setup later today. For now, is there anything else you need?"

Darrius shook his head, constantly surprised by how unique Doctor Dena Montgomery and this entire situation appeared to be. "No, for now, I just need some sleep."

"Good. My room is right across the hall." Dena turned toward the door to leave.

"Uh, Doctor Montgomery?"

Dena turned back to look at him. *He certainly isn't hard on the eyes,* she thought. "Yes, Lieutenant?"

"Thank you for your hospitality."

She gave him a warm smile. "You're welcome." She opened the door and was gone.

Darrius watched her cross the hall and open her door before closing his door. Then, shaking his head in wonder, he began disrobing on the way to the bedroom. By the time his head hit the pillow, he was out like a light. Yet, the visions of Doctor Dena Montgomery were ever-present in his dreams.

Chapter 6

"Yeah, I love you, too, boyo. You be safe," Eve said into her phone as she watched Dena exit the bathroom, fresh from her shower and wrapped in a towel. Her hair was loose and still damp. However, Dena's hair was thick, and it always took more time to get it completely dry. Even when they were children and did each other's hair, hers was the last to be finished. Yet, Dena wouldn't cut it and always wore it from the crown of her head in one long fat braid down the middle of her back. Standing before a mirror, she bent at the waist, blow-drying and brushing her hair until it crackled with electricity. Then she brushed it into the shape of a bowl around her head and covered it in a silk scarf.

Overhearing Eve, Dena plucked the phone from her sister's hand. "I love you too, brother-in-law-to-be, but if you don't get that list of names you've chosen as your groomsmen to me before the end of this month, you can't marry my sister on Juneteenth this year."

"Oh no, kid." Simon Wilde laughed. "Do you know how hard it was for me to convince your sister to marry me?"

"Yes, I do, and I was on Team Wilde, but I may be persuaded to change my mind. I need that list because I have to pair your groomsmen with Eve's bridesmaids."

"You'll have it as soon as I get back to town."

"Where are you or should I ask?"

Simon laughed again, his grin sexy and his blue eyes vibrant with mirth. "Yeah, no, don't ask."

"Okay, you be safe no matter where you are. "

"You be safe, too. Eve showed me what you did to save two tender-age children. Apparently, your training paid off and we need to step you up to the next level. I love you, too, kid, but try not to take on two UNSUBs at a time, particularly if they are armed with a gun. We'll need cardiac care if you do anything like that again."

She grinned. "As Mom always says, 'I'll consider it.' Here's Eve, the blabbermouth." Dena handed the phone to her sister and crawled into bed beside Eve.

"I'll talk with you later. Take care of my man."

"Will do. You take care of my woman."

"Will do. Bye for now." Eve disconnected the call and sighed.

Dena reached for her sister's hand for a light squeeze. "He's a former Navy SEAL. He'll be okay, Eve."

"For Simon and his SEAL Team pals, there is no such thing as a *former* SEAL. They are just dormant unless or until called on to protect and defend. He's now a world news correspondent and television reporter who is known around the globe. Unfortunately, he's also not exactly welcome in certain countries, and some countries would like to get their hands on him to string him up by his gonads."

Dena grinned at her sister. "Not a problem. Simon has other plans for his gonads and has no intention of letting anyone else use them except you." Her grin turned to a serious expression. "Just based on what he and his brothers and sisters-in-arms have taught me about self-defense, I believe that Simon is very good at what he does, Eve. So, remember that when you start to worry."

Eve smiled at her sister. What Dena and millions of other fans didn't know was that Simon Wilde was not only an award-winning journalist, but also a covert agent for The Nursery, a super-secret enforcement organization created by the G7. Eve never knew what his mission was or exactly where Simon had been sent. She may not learn where he had been even after his mission was over and he was safely home again. Still, he had five crew members posing as cameramen, drivers, and guides with him. All like him were somewhat dormant US Navy SEALs. They were from Simon's old command when he was a captain, running and gunning on active duty. A female sniper handled his overwatch. She was unobtrusive and wore a burka to obscure her identity. No one paid attention to her, but she carried more deadly weaponry on her person under her clothes than most geared-up warriors.

When Simon did his stand-up interviews in some war-torn country, he held his microphone in his left hand to display the engagement ring she gave him when he asked her to marry him. That was his signal to her that all was well. He was one of those rare ambidextrous people, but that was his little affectation, especially for her. Still, Eve was former military, too, so she knew how dangerous his missions could be. For now, she had other tasks of her own to complete. So, she tuned out her concerns about the love of her life and turned to Dena. "I'm very proud of you and what you did to save the children. However, you scared the living shit out of me. Still, I believe that Simon is right. You're ready for the next level in your training."

Dena tilted her head and looked at her sister, her face devoid of mirth. "Yes, I'm ready. This is the first time I've had to use deadly force in any situation, except when guys came on a little too strongly, but I didn't even think about it. I never lost my focus. I was in a zone and my muscle memory knew exactly what to do."

"That's precisely right. When we got the signal that your chain broke and we couldn't immediately get a call through to you, I was afraid that something had happened to you. I know you prefer walking to work and home rather than riding your bike or driving your car. If you had taken either of those modes of transportation, you wouldn't have encountered the UNSUBs or the children. So, your preference for walking saved two young lives. Then I saw the video of you attacking those UNSUBs. I was so proud and so scared simultaneously."

"That's when you called a Code Red, got on the horn, and called Jenna Baker at the FBI?"

"I did, yes. Jenna has a greater reach and more clout outside Washington, DC, than I do. New England was my old stomping ground when I was flying choppers in the Coast Guard, but a current FBI bureau chief tops a former Coast Guard captain any day of the week. I was so confident of Jenna's skills and abilities that I told Slade Richardson and Richardson Security to stand down. When Jenna asked me to wait for her, I was on my way to the airport to fly up to find you. She had already checked the police reports and found information about the shooting. We were in the air when Jenna got more details. By the time I landed the jet, she had as much information as we needed to find you. Then she scrubbed what limited information was already on the wire. Nothing is there now about what you found in that alley or anything about you and the children. What she left available on the police blotter and for the public news report was the murder. There is nothing about when, where, or how the incident occurred. Now it reads like two men argued and one man ended up shot twice. Police are investigating, yada, yada, yada."

"I didn't realize my necklace was broken until you scooped me up and we were on the way here. If I had known, I would have called in to let everyone know I was all right."

"It's okay, but I have to get a new necklace for you immediately and then new mobile equipment in your hands so your phone can be activated even if you've turned it off. The alert has been reduced to a holding yellow, but you know that Dad and Mom won't settle until you show your face."

Dena sighed. "I know. We'll have to go home at some point. I don't want to bring this problem to our doorstep, but I feel responsible for the children. I believe that they've been abused, Eve. From what I could see when I helped them bathe, they have recent signs of bruising. I didn't do an exam, but they both have what I believe is a surgical implant under the skin at the base of their spine."

Eve frowned. "You think it's some kind of tracking device?"

"It's that or something that administers pain when they don't do as they are told. Eve, these children don't know how to use basic toiletry items like toothbrushes, washcloths, and soap. They cannot speak in sentences or understand simple words. They have no sense of their own identity. Yet, I believe they've been together for a while because they depend on each other."

"You would know about such things. On the other hand, I don't have experience with little people other than our siblings. They don't have any problem verbalizing because we've always been encouraged to be expressive and to question. Dad and Mom taught us to debate without being disagreeable. So, if these children don't have the motor skill of a newborn, you're the best person to teach them."

"I think our youngest brothers and sisters will be a huge help because they are about the same ages. These two children see me as a protector. They saw me fight the men who were abusing them, so they know that I can be aggressive to the point of violence. I believe they have keen insights because they allowed me to leave them with Aunt Althea. Because I trust her, they trust her. That's the first step in the love, respect, and trust triangle we all learned growing up. I also believe they will respond positively to the little people in our family easier and faster than our adolescent, teen, or young adult siblings. Of course, that may take a little longer until they know them better."

Eve shrugged. "You're probably right. Since we don't know what type of device they may have implanted, I don't want to stay here for more than two or three days before heading home. I want Vincent to take a look at what it is and remove it if possible. So, we'll move out after the storm clears."

"That's good, but I don't want to leave Aunt Althea unprotected if it is a tracking device. I know that you suspect the bodies found burned to a crisp in the van are likely the two men I fought to save the children. Still, they didn't commit suicide because I gave them a righteous beat down. Someone murdered them, Eve. That someone or whatever criminal organization that person represents won't take kindly to losing their products, namely these two children. Or I've considered that these children could also be used as drug mules. The UNSUBs may have gotten enough information to try to track me down. That may lead them here."

"Already handled. I've alerted Uncle Seth, Claudia, and Uncle Kenneth. Aunt Althea knows about our concerns. She'll be careful. Also, Jenna Baker is still in Cambridge. She's scrubbing all indications of your existence and covering up the lieutenant's departure from the area. Jenna's good and she's thorough."

"That's good, Eve. I know that this house is like a fortress. So, with that many eyes on this place, Aunt Althea should be all right."

"I'll keep checking, so don't worry so much."

Dena looked into Eve's eyes and sighed. "You're the security expert, but I still think Aunt Althea should come to visit her nephew, namely our father, and her grandnephews and nieces, better known as The Family. She could stay in Maryland with us for a few days or a week to be on the safe side. At least, Aunt Althea should stay until we determine what kind of device the children have implanted in them."

Eve sighed, but agreed to allay her sister's concerns. "Okay, kid. You've got good instincts and have been in this situation since the beginning. So, you get some rest, and I'll see whether I can convince Aunt Althea to come with us."

Dina smiled at her sister, hugged her, and then tucked under the heavy quilts and covers.

Eve shook her head, rolled off the bed, turned out the light, and went to her room to get some rest, too. The next few days would be busy, and she would need to be on high alert.

Chapter 7

When Darrius woke, he did so slowly. It took time to orient himself to where he was and why. Staying in the warm bed a while longer gave him time to mull over the previous days' events. First, he'd had plans, and apparently, so did Gail Henley, for him to wake up in her bed. Instead, here he was, waking in a different, unfamiliar bed several days later... except that he was alone. Still, it was a very comfortable bed which caused his dreams each night to be filled with images not of Gail, but of the kid, Dena Montgomery.

Next, he had to remind himself that Dena and the two young children were his witnesses to a murder. He was a detective and a reasonably good murder cop. However, there hadn't been a lot of homicides in Cambridge that didn't solve themselves in a matter of hours. The Police Department had only three hundred twenty employees, of which two hundred eighty were police officers. The rest were civilian support staff. Cambridge, the home of Harvard University, Harvard Law School, The Massachusetts Institute of Technology, Radcliffe College, Lesley University, and his alma mater, Cambridge College, wasn't a particularly large place. Instead, it was essentially a suburb of Boston with around one hundred thousand residents. However, even with a small police department presence, the crime rate was less than one percent. Yes, there were property crimes, such as motor vehicle theft, arson, larceny, and burglary. Still, the chance of becoming a victim of any of these crimes in Cambridge was negligible. Darrius and the rest of the Cambridge Police Department were duly proud of these factors. Even though the murder wasn't officially on the books and the FBI had taken over the case, he didn't want this particular homicide to smear his department's sterling record.

Now that he was adequately rested and his head was clear, he'd get into solving the murder case. So far, everything he learned came from FBI agent Jenna Baker and DC police detective Eve Montgomery, Dena's sister. So, he would start from the beginning by interviewing Dena Montgomery again.

When Darrius found his way to the hotel's first level, he saw two unfamiliar people, a Caucasian man in a wheelchair and a cinnamon-colored woman, sitting in the kitchen, sharing coffee with Eve Montgomery and Althea Hardyston.

Eve noticed Darrius's hesitation when he entered the kitchen. "Please, come and join us, Lieutenant. I'd like to introduce you to Claudia Shaffer, head of the K-9 Security Force for the Alex-Mont family properties." Claudia stood and extended a hand as Eve continued. "Claudia is a former Army Ranger."

"It's a pleasure to meet you, Lieutenant." Claudia shook his hand and then sat again.

Darrius inclined his head. "You, too. Thank you for your service."

"You're welcome."

"Next," Eve continued, "we have another Montgomery. However, this time he's a cousin of mine and Dena's, one of many. Anderson Montgomery, who we call Andy."

"Among other unflattering names you call me from time to time," he joked as he rose to a standing position in a mechanical contraption like a Transformer toy made for adult-sized people. Moments before, it was a wheelchair. Andy grinned as he shook Darrius's hand.

Darrius frowned, amused. "Impressive."

Althea placed a mug of coffee on the table in front of Darrius when he sat. He acknowledged her gesture with a quick thanks.

Eve narrowed her eyes at her cousin. "Yes, we call him unflattering things with good reason. Do not play cards or any board games with Andy. He always wins. We think he cheats, but we just haven't figured out how… yet. Even when we go bowling, play basketball, or go skiing with him, he wins."

However, Andy just grinned at Eve, his handsome face angelic. He negligibly shrugged. "It's mind over matter."

"Bull hockey!" Eve exclaimed, making everyone laugh. "Andy is the Montgomery family's resident genius. He invents *things*, all kinds of *things*, including the *contraption* he's whipping around in now."

Claudia agreed. "Also, the combination tractor, plow, and snowblower he used to get us here through this blizzard. It looks like something out of a *Star Wars* movie. My boys got a big kick out of it."

Eve laughed. "See, that's what I mean. Andy just invents *stuff* for the hell of it."

Claudia laughed. "I can attest to that." She pulled up her pants legs. "Which one is the prosthesis?"

Darrius regarded Claudia's lower legs and really could not discern a difference. He shrugged. "Beats me."

Andy just continued to grin, his face mischievously angelic.

Eve nodded. "See what I mean?"

Darrius shrugged, but he noticed that Ms. Shaffer was an intriguing woman who didn't wear a wedding band. He also noticed how Anderson Montgomery looked at her. It didn't take his skill as a detective to deduce that there was a story involving the two new arrivals. Ms. Shaffer had a military bearing, but wasn't unattractive or masculine. She wore no makeup or other enhancements. Her hair was in a tight ball on the top of her head, leaving her face unframed. However, her face was luminous, with expressive eyes, a narrow nose, and a wide mouth. From what he could see of her body, she was tall and fit in a heavy sweater, jean jacket, and pants. Darrius spotted her weapon in a shoulder holster under her left arm. If he didn't miss in his observations, Ms. Shaffer likely had other weapons secured on her body. She struck him as someone who knew how to use guns and wasn't afraid to do so.

On the other hand, Anderson Montgomery was clearly more than one might think on the surface. It appeared that he was paralyzed from the waist down, but Darrius noticed that he had large, upper-body, well-defined muscles, pronounced six-pack abs, and strong hands. Still, despite the diamond that winked from his left earlobe, the rimless eyeglasses, wavy, midnight-black, shoulder-length hair, and startling deep blue eyes, Anderson Montgomery was much more than an inventor. Given what Eve said about the sports Anderson participated in, the man was physically fit and no pushover. On the contrary, he radiated strength and intelligence, much as his two cousins, Eve and Dena, did.

Darrius looked around the kitchen area and then at Eve. "Are your sister and the children still sleeping? The children might enjoy seeing this."

Eve shook her head. "Uh, no, they already saw it and met Claudia and Andy. Dina took Claudia's two sons and the two charges to go swimming."

Darrius frowned and looked out the window at the heavy snow and brisk wind.

Eve noticed and smirked. "Uh, they're two levels down in the house. If you want to check on her, take one of the lobby elevators down to G2. It's the closest location to the indoor pool. Once you've assured yourself they are well, Claudia and I will show you the security measures we use here on the farm after breakfast."

Darrius finished his cup of coffee. "If you'll excuse me, I think I'll check on them, and then I'll return."

"Take your time, Lieutenant. We'll be here for a while. Unfortunately, this weather system is moving even slower than originally thought. Claudia brought her sons with her so they wouldn't get cabin fever cooped up at home."

He rose and placed his empty cup in the sink. Althea walked with him and pointed him toward the bank of elevators in a part of the hotel he hadn't explored before.

When Althea returned to her seat at the table, she dramatically sighed. "Eye candy. I'd be a cougar in training if I were only twenty or thirty years younger."

Everyone laughed as she playfully fanned herself.

When Darrius stepped off the elevator, he heard the squeals of youthful laughter. Before entering the pool area, he stood and watched four youngsters trying to capture a big blue globe ball that Dena kept pushing away from them in a kiddy pool. The water came to about waist high on the children, but most of Dena's fine figure was above the waterline. His witnesses seemed to be having the time of their lives with two young boys who looked so much alike that they could have been twins. However, it was clear that one was older, maybe six or seven, while the other boy was maybe four or five.

They must be the sons of Claudia Shaffer, the K-9 Security Chief, Darrius surmised. They had the look of her, but their complexions were much lighter. That fact confused him. Was Anderson Montgomery the father of Ms. Shaffer's sons? If so, how? He was in a wheelchair and seemed paralyzed below the waist. Of course, his injury could have come after the boys were conceived. Darrius shook his head. He didn't need to know whether his theory about a relationship between Anderson Montgomery and Claudia Shaffer was accurate. It didn't have a bearing on his murder case.

However, at the moment, the vision of Dena Montgomery's voluptuous, yet shapely slender figure in a one-piece black swimsuit was attempting to take root in his brain. He was accustomed to dating women with some…heft? However, Dena Montgomery's body was as close to sculptured perfection as he had ever seen.

People of Greek heritage always celebrated the human form as a masterpiece. In his spare time, he created statuary in clay or blown glass to pay homage to the arts his hands could form. Darrius could imagine capturing her form in a sculpture. Today, she had that thick braid coiled in a crown on top of her head, freeing her slender neck. Her musculature was subtle but clearly evident in her arms, mid-section, and legs. He had seen her in action. Dena Montgomery may be Barbie-doll slender, but she was powerful and no lightweight. As he continued to study her, she looked up in his direction as if sensing him. Their gazes held for humming moments before she summoned him inside with a tilt of her head. When he opened the glass door, the humidity engulfed him.

"Good morning." Somehow, Dena had felt eyes on her and had looked up to see Lieutenant Pappas observing her, the children, or both. It was a strange sensation to be observed as if she were a curiosity. It was clear to her that he hadn't quite figured her out…yet. However, Dena admitted to herself that it gave her a little thrill to have a man a bit off-center where she was concerned. Her mother often said that the fact her father couldn't line her up to fit in any box kept their marriage interesting. Her father agreed with her mother and claimed that it was one of the reasons he loved her to distraction. Yet, they still discovered exciting things about each other that kept them seeking to learn more about one another. Dena felt that her parents, Chuck and Vivian Alexander Montgomery, never seemed to run out of conversation.

Dena also felt that if she were to consider having someone permanently in her life, her parents' marriage prototype was the type of relationship she would relish. For now, she and Drew Hamilton were pals and could talk about anything and everything. However, their closeness came from sharing that they had both been molested as children. In her adolescence, her biological mother's pimp had consistently raped her while her mother, a high-priced and in-demand escort, was out of the house. He claimed that he was getting her ready to service his exclusive clientele. However, one night, her mother returned home early from one of her dates to find her pimp sodomizing her. All Dena remembered were the loud voices, a terrible fight, and gunshots. Numb from constant abuse, she was taken to a hospital emergency room, where Doctor Derrick Jackson examined her. The pimp and her biological mother were taken to the morgue. With no other known relatives to claim her, she became a ward of the District of Columbia government. Dena was placed in an orphanage until Derrick and Vivian Alexander Jackson adopted her at age six. Five years after Derrick Jackson's death, she was a flower girl in Chuck Montgomery and Vivian's wedding and was again adopted by them.

Drew Hamilton's life in New York City's Harlem neighborhood was similar, except that a priest molested him. He and his two older brothers attended an all-boys Catholic school all their lives. He was an altar boy, and with other tender-aged boys, they were told this was what they had to submit to doing to ensure the Devil would not take their families to hell. So, for years, the youngsters submitted until one of Drew's brothers,

Will, came to get him early and caught the priest molesting him. Even at eleven years old, Will, a baseball star, beat the priest to within an inch of his life with his bat. The police were never called, the priest was transferred to a monastery, and the matter was swept under the rug. His parents accepted a monthly stipend and free tuition for all three Hamilton boys.

Dena and Drew became close when her sister, Linda, a prima ballerina known internationally as The Black Swan, married Drew's brother, Will "The Hammer" Hamilton, an American baseball icon. Linda now owned a renowned dance studio, the New York School of Dance, for youngsters and teens with the potential to be superstars. After Will left professional sports, he owned and operated the prosperous private sports, fitness, and health club, **INDULGENCES**, in New York City. Will and Linda had two boys now under five years old. Given their horrible experiences at a young age, Dena and Drew were very protective of their nephews.

Dena never let her guard down when it came to her siblings or any youngsters while in the company of others. She didn't sense anything sinister about Lieutenant Pappas, but she watched him as intently as he seemed to watch her. "Were you looking for us or just exploring?"

"I, uh, asked where the children and you were, and your sister directed me here. In light of our information so far, I want to interview you again about what you may have heard once you entered the alley before the shooting started. I don't think interviewing the children will be productive, and I don't want to stress them out. They seem to trust you and feel more comfortable around others because of you."

"I don't think I heard distinctly what the men were arguing about because I was focused on the child's wail. Nevertheless, I'll try to recall what I heard and we can talk later, if that's all right with you. The children and I have only been down here for a short time. Could we do the interview after breakfast? I'm attempting to determine the level of socialization the children experienced before they are subjected to the hoard, which constitutes my family."

Darrius shrugged. "After breakfast, Claudia Shafer and your sister plan to give a security briefing to me. We can talk after that."

Rather than ogle Dena, the Ph.D. professor-in-residence at MIT, her alma mater, Darrius stuck his hands in his pockets and looked around the six-lane pool area. He had never been shy or out of sorts around women. Yet with her, he felt like he was on a slippery slope and could not seem to get his footing. She looked into his eyes when she spoke with him and her diamond-black irises seemed to stare right into his soul. So, he looked away at the water vapors evaporating from the bubbling spas, which spilled into the swimming pool. Chaise lounges were positioned before twelve-foot-high curved glass windows. The windows allowed a panoramic view of the mountain range through the curtain of fat, white snowflakes.

Dena noticed Darrius scoping out the area and frowning at a structure against two walls. For some reason, he seemed nervous to her. She had to keep her eyes on the children, but she didn't dismiss his presence. Instead, she decided to converse with him and figure out why he seemed on edge around her. "The structure you're looking at is a paneled decay-resistant cedar sauna. It can hold eight adults or twice as many children at one time. The walls and benches were kiln-dried, constructed, and installed by one of Andy's three brothers, Liam Montgomery, at the Montgomery Mills not far from here. Feel free to use it and the pool."

Darrius turned to look at her, but she was again playing with the children. Still, he noticed how observant she and her sister appeared to be. He felt as if they could almost read his thoughts. Their sense of awareness was uncanny and seemed more heightened than most people. In addition, the way Dena reported her experience during the initial interview at the murder scene was textbook perfect. He couldn't have designed a better witness if asked to do so. These factors caused him to be very curious about these Montgomery sisters.

"Uh, Doctor Montgomery, if you don't mind, I'd like to take a few laps in the pool. I presume there is swimwear somewhere in my suite or elsewhere in the hotel?"

"Sure. A closet on the other side of the sauna contains clean or new swim shorts that should fit you. Help yourself."

In the closet, Darrius found a multitude of swimwear, Speedos, trunks, shorts, and briefs, in his size. He preferred the briefs but chose the longer shorts with a matching cover-up. He tended to be at half-mast around Dena Montgomery. Grabbing a couple of rug-sized towels, he carried them to a chaise lounge just in case extra coverage was needed.

Dena did a double-take when Lieutenant Pappas came onto the pool deck, wearing black thigh-length shorts and a matching sleeveless T-shirt. Before, she hadn't given much thought to Lieutenant Pappas as a man. If she thought of him at all, it was to evaluate whether he would be the right person to help her sister solve the murders and protect the children. Now, she paid more attention to his physical characteristics.

Dena knew, as she continued to study him, people of Greek heritage derived their physicality from genetics, diet, and geography. Like Lieutenant Pappas, they typically have olive-colored skin due to heritage, the Mediterranean climate, and a diet rich in olive oil, fish, and other sources of skin-rejuvenating omega-3 and omega-6 fatty acids. As a result, the physical characteristics of the Greek people distinguish them from other Europeans.

Lieutenant Pappas was a sterling example of the best physical attributes of his heritage. He was tall with broad, muscular shoulders and arms, a well-defined chest, and six-pack abs leading to a narrow waist. His torso was typical of a swimmer's build, with long, muscular thighs and legs.

It isn't as if I haven't seen fine physiques before, Dena cautioned herself. In fact, among her brothers, uncles, and male cousins, there wasn't a roly-poly ounce of extra fat to be found. Even her dad's nearly seven-foot-tall physique looked like he was still in his youth. However, there was something different about the lieutenant's impact on her senses. So, when he executed a perfect dive into the pool's deep end, Dena turned back to the children. Still, she was hard-pressed to ignore him cutting through the water with precision and speed.

Chapter 8

Later that morning, as the adults began settling at a round table in a breakfast room, the children sat at an age-appropriate table of their own. Dena watched as her two wards attempted to communicate with the Shaffer boys. The little girl still watched more than tried to mimic what the boys said or did. However, during their time in the kiddie pool, she was as aggressive as the boys in chasing the globe ball. To Dena's way of thinking, this was a good sign. Because there were many fun things to do in the house, Dena intended to expose the children to as many things to stimulate their brains to be curious as possible.

Another good sign was that the children were not as uncomfortable around other people as they had been initially. Yes, they were very observant, but they were not clinging to her legs as often as before. Andy's motorized wheelchair fascinated the boy and the girl. Claudia's boys were very helpful in determining how well the children could interact and socialize.

Dena helped them select food from the buffet, then sat for a while to help them use utensils to feed themselves. They tended to pick up the food with their hands and stuff it in their mouths, but it didn't take long for them to become familiar with a spoon and fork. They were bright despite their inability to communicate using words.

Darrius noted that the boy and girl looked clean and their hair neatly combed. Before, they looked like street urchins with matted hair, dirty faces, and filthy clothes which reeked to high heaven. Now, dressed in warm, colorful clothes and appropriate shoes and socks, the two children couldn't look more unlike they did when they were in his police station.

However, they still looked a little gaunt and skeletal. Nevertheless, he felt that with time and attention, the children would thrive under Doctor Montgomery's ministration. She saw to their every need and made her time with them a teachable moment. If he didn't know that she was a professor who taught complicated math theories to adult students, he'd believe that she taught kindergarten or in an elementary school. She was so tuned into the children that one would think that they were her own.

Meanwhile, back in Cambridge, Massachusetts, two people, a man and a woman, hurried into The Padlock, a crowded restaurant and bar, out of the strong winds created by the Nor'easter. The local LEOs, law enforcement officers, from the Cambridge Police Department, frequented the place. The new arrivals wore uniforms that identified them as police officers from Brookline, Massachusetts, another small community outside Boston. Still, nothing could have been further from the truth of their identity.

First, they scanned the room and identified their targets, several police detectives from Darrius Pappas's squad. Then, positioning themselves in close proximity to the table where their targets sat, they ordered their food and struck up a casual conversation with Detectives Bob Brewer and Clay Stonewall, Lieutenant Shirley Coleman, and SVU Supervisor Alana Fulton.

"So, do any of you know a Lieutenant Pappas?" one of the imposters conversationally asked.

"Sure," Stoney answered while covertly cellphones were clicked to their record function. Then, two phones were used to clone the imposters' phones. "He's my lieutenant."

"Oh really? That's good to know. You see, we came here to talk with him about a case and found out that he's out of town."

Lieutenant Coleman shrugged while she continued to eat. "Yeah, you should have called before coming here through this storm. What case is it? I know most of his workload, and I'm covering for him with two other lieutenants in the department."

"Well, uh," he hesitated, "we were instructed to speak only with him about it. You understand, we have to follow orders. When will he be back in the office?"

Stonewall shrugged. "I'm not sure, but he has a lot of unused leave. He rarely takes time off. He was called away on personal business, but Pappas didn't tell anyone why he had to leave, where he was going, or when he would be back."

Alana chimed in and frowned. "He left several days ago and we assume he is back in Greece by now. That's where he was born and grew up, right, Clay?"

Detective Stonewall nodded. "Yeah, that's right. Pappas doesn't have family here in the states." He held up his cup to signal the waitress to refill his coffee. It was also a signal that these two were asking questions about Lieutenant Pappas.

The waitress, one of the FBI's operatives, had just finished refilling the coffee mug for FBI Agent Jenna Baker, who sat in a secure and discreet location in the restaurant, listening via cellphone to the conversation. Her special-ops team had tracked these two imposters for some time. The Cambridge police were playing their roles exceptionally well. No one would suspect that they were trained to give false leads to anyone who approached them looking for Lieutenant Pappas.

Stoney grinned. "Me and the Mrs. will be glad to be out of this icebox. This time tomorrow, we'll be sunning ourselves at my sister's place in Panama."

"It won't beat the Caymans." Alana laughed. "My flight leaves early tomorrow morning."

Shirley smiled. "I'll be right behind you. My sister and I are doing the Florida Keys for a few weeks."

Bob Brewer frowned. "I *would* end up drawing the short straw on vacation time, but when all of you get back, I'll be on my way to Mardi Gras in Argentina. *Yeah, Mon!* I can see it all now. All of those beautiful women will be dancing in the streets! Mid-February is the *worst* time to be in New England."

From across the restaurant, Jenna nodded, pleased as the conversation continued. Bob Brewer had agreed to be the one left behind. All the protective services were going to focus on him. If the FBI's strategy worked, the imposters would contact Brewer again rather than the others who had established that they would be out of town. They would not be going to the locations they spoke about. Instead, they would be in protective custody and moved to undisclosed locations shortly after leaving the restaurant.

Because of the UNSUBs' persistence *vis-à-vis* these two children, Jenna now believed they were being sought for more than sex. They had something or knew something vital to this kidnapping case, something that Jenna had yet to discover. She would have to bring Eve Montgomery and Darrius Pappas up to date. This situation was becoming more complex and convoluted than initially thought.

CHAPTER 9

After speaking with FBI Agent Baker, the next morning, as soon as the weather cleared, Eve took the jet down the Monroe County Municipal Airport runway before dawn and smoothly lifted into the air. It was a relatively short flight to the private airport in the rural Maryland countryside outside Washington, DC, where she landed. After deplaning, they again boarded a large Sikorsky helicopter for the short run to the Alexander-Montgomery farm.

Upon arrival, Chuck and Vivian Alexander Montgomery waited just inside the ballroom of their home for the sight of their daughters and the children Eve informed them to expect. When the blades above the helicopter slowed to a stop, dawn was breaking. Chuck and Vivian came out onto the covered veranda, holding hands and forming a welcome-home line.

Everyone was aware that the two children were apprehensive about meeting new people. So, Eve and Dena's multicultural siblings, of which there were nearly forty, waited in the breakfast room to share a meal with the new arrivals. They were accustomed to welcoming new people, particularly children, into their home.

However, it only took one look at Chuck's and Vivian's faces in the growing morning light for Eve and Dena to realize something was terribly wrong. They hurried their steps toward their parents, with Darrius and Althea bringing up the rear with the children in hand.

Eve questioned quietly, searching their faces. "What is it? What's wrong?"

Chuck shook his head and ran a comforting hand over his daughters' shoulders. "We'll talk about it after…" Tears flooded his eyes, but he brushed them away and held on to his composure. He and Vivian stooped on their haunches to welcome the children. His nearly seven-foot height was usually intimidating to most people and his wife was tall, too. "Hello, my name is Chuck." He pantomimed his words with hand gestures.

"My name is Vivian, and we are happy to meet you two." She followed her husband's lead and held out a hand to each of them.

Dena and Eve helped the children reach out and shake hands with Chuck and Vivian. When the children reacted correctly to the introduction, Dena forced a smile. "This is my father and mother."

Surprising everyone, the little girl hugged Vivian around her neck. Vivian buried her face in the child's embrace. She looked up and waited until the boy approached her for a hug. Then Chuck's arms went around his wife and the children. When they released one another, there were warm smiles all around.

Dena, pleased with the warmth exhibited between her parents and the children, stood alongside Eve to make introductions to the lieutenant. "Dad, Mom, this is Lieutenant Darrius Pappas with the Cambridge Police Department. Lieutenant, these are Eve's and my parents, Charles and Vivian Alexander Montgomery."

Darrius was awed by the nearly seven-foot man with porcelain-colored skin who wore authentic-looking, Western-inspired clothes and boots, as did his daughter, Dena. He wore his shoulder-length brown hair in a queue at the nape of his neck, and a diamond winked from his left earlobe. Chuck's wife, whose warm brown complexion made her look to be the same age as her daughters, wore jeans, tennis shoes, and a hand-knitted, oversized red sweater. Her hair was a cap of dark curls plastered to her well-shaped head. "It's a pleasure to meet you both. Thank you for letting us intrude."

Vivian shook her head. "There is no intrusion. Our daughters have explained the situation and we're happy to help. Please come in and make yourself and the children comfortable. We're about to have breakfast."

Darrius watched as Chuck and Vivian warmly embraced Althea Hardyston. Then they held the children's hands and slowly walked to accommodate their short strides through an ante-room outside the ballroom. The multiple entrance doors were open and Darrius observed workers setting up round tables that easily sat twelve and chairs around the ballroom's perimeter.

Beyond the anteroom, they entered the central mansion and then into a great room. Darrius held his shock at the sheer size of the place to a minimum. He looked up three stories in the great room to see a massive skylight. Modern chandeliers hung down, casting beautiful filtered light on the walls, and large fans silently turned slowly, moving the palm fronds placed strategically throughout the space on each level. A polished wood frame and wrought-iron railing circumnavigated the balcony on each level, where flower boxes hung and overflowed with healthy-looking greenery and fall foliage perfuming the air. A hint of moisture made the vast space feel cozy instead of dry and cool. Warmth filtered up from the heated Brazilian Cherry hardwood floors.

Darrius could see what must be communal areas interspersed with open bedroom doors. Corridors or wide hallways angled off the great room like spokes on a wagon wheel with built-in bookcases lining each one. The furniture in the great room was large and looked very comfortable in complementary colors. Groupings were arranged for conversation areas but didn't overwhelm the space. Instead, the enormous space reminded Darrius of the lobby of a fine hotel or a country club. During his career, he had opportunities to visit mansions owned by wealthy families, but none as grand as this. Still, though spacious, it wasn't ostentatious.

Slowly, they continued to stroll to accommodate the children's wide-eyed awe. They walked between Chuck and Vivian, holding firmly to the adults' fingers while ensuring that Dena and Althea were still in close proximity.

When they ventured through several wide halls where books of all types and descriptions were neatly shelved, Darrius noted that interspersed among the books were examples of blown glass figurines and pottery. Much of it he thought was lovely, while other pieces were rather raw. It led Darrius to believe that whoever purchased the pieces had eclectic tastes.

Finally, they reached a well-appointed cafeteria surrounded by glass accordion walls on two sides. On the other two walls were large, long, and tall aquariums filled with schools of beautiful freshwater and saltwater fish. It was a bright and cheerful space, with comfortable-looking furniture, and, as was in the great room, many healthy-looking vine plants hanging from the vaulted ceiling rafters. Round tables and chairs were age appropriate and sat six, ten, or twelve people. A vase centered on each table held colorful fresh flowers and greenery.

There was also a multitude of rainbow-coalition toddlers, tender-aged children, teens, and young adults than Darrius could count in a glance. Now he understood why the Montgomery-Alexander family needed a hotel in the Pennsylvania mountains and a mansion in the rural Maryland countryside to house their family. As Althea Hardyston had explained to him, the family was legion. However, what he did notice was that all the family members wore a gold necklace that spelled *FAMILY*. In addition, everyone appeared to be busy preparing for breakfast, like a well-choreographed scene at a time still shy of seven o'clock in the morning. Yet, they all seemed to settle with the sight of their parents.

Introductions were made and acknowledgments accepted when youngsters, who appeared to be about the same ages as the boy and girl, came forward and engaged the two children, leading them away from the adults. Darrius watched as Chuck, Vivian, Althea, Eve, and Dena greeted each person, from the youngest to the oldest, with hugs and kisses. Then they settled in to hear a poem one of the young boys read before breakfast commenced in earnest.

There were buffet-style stations that held mouth-watering food choices. Darrius sniffed the fragrant air and watched in amazement as the young people served themselves and took seats at various tables. Room was made for the boy and girl as Dena and Althea looked on.

Eve came to stand next to Darrius. "It seems that the cook, Melvin, has made several traditional Greek breakfast specialties and if you're not quick, you'll miss out."

"So I see. He's made strapatsatha."

"Yes, the scrambled eggs with tomatoes, olives, and feta cheese."

Surprised, he turned to look at her. "You know Greek foods?"

She shrugged, and using a cloth napkin, she picked up and handed a warm oblong plate to him, grabbed one for herself, and then guided him toward one of the stations. "Some, yes. My family visited the Greek Isles several times when we were much younger. We enjoyed the cuisine, so the head cook makes dishes from different countries from time to time. We never get bored with what he makes. Today, he made these dishes to welcome you. For example, we have sfakianopita, better known here in the states as unleavened dough and soft white whey cheese. Fill it up with all these seafood and vegetable choices and eat it as if it were a burrito."

He smiled and followed her lead. There were several more familiar Greek dishes. By the time they circumnavigated the breakfast stations in the room, Darrius's oblong plate was full to nearly overflowing, but he had a sample of almost every offering. Finally, they sat at a table where Chuck and Vivian sat feeding two babies bottled milk. To Darrius's trained eyes, Chuck and Vivian looked rather sad. However, they conversed with him, Eve, Dena, Althea, and another daughter, Samantha Montgomery. According to the conversation, it appeared that more family members would arrive later that day. It wasn't until after breakfast that Darrius was made privy to the family's apparent melancholia.

In a salon with the fireplace lit, Chuck made an announcement to his family. "Earlier this morning, KiLe died in an automobile crash on her way to the city."

CHAPTER 10

Shocked and angry, Eve started to leave the salon, but her father's voice stopped her.

"Eve, please stay. Don't leave."

"Dad, Brian shouldn't have to go through this alone."

Chuck shook his head. "He's not alone, honey. Your brothers, Vincent, Roger, and Ryan, are with him. They've gone to the crash site."

Anguished, Eve pleaded. "I need to go, too, Dad. They won't know what to look for."

Chuck frowned. "Do you think that this is something other than an accident?"

Eve shook her head and looked earnestly at her parents. "I don't know, Dad, but I can't allow any detail to be ignored. We were under a red alert when Dena went missing. KiLe wouldn't have left to go into town if the red alert were still in place. I lifted the alert to a caution yellow after finding Dena and taking her to Point of View. I believe that if I had signaled an orange alert, KiLe would still be alive."

Vivian put her hands on her daughter's shoulders and then turned Eve to look into her face. "This is not your fault, babe." When Eve would have protested, Vivian gave her a stern look and a little shake. "I believe that you did the right thing. We all would have gone about our business with caution. That includes KiLe. She knew the rules, but we still would not have been overly concerned after we were informed that Dena was all right."

Eve agreed and sighed. "I know you're right, Mom. However, I'm raising the threat level to orange until I know more about what happened to KiLe."

Vivian put a comforting hand on her husband's arm. "Eve has a point, Chuck. It wouldn't hurt to have her take a fresh look at where the accident occurred." At Chuck's apparent nod of acquiescence, Vivian turned back to her daughter. "By now, the scene may be cleared. Call one of your brothers before you go."

Eve hugged her parents before leaving the salon, pulling her phone from her back pocket.

Darrius followed her out and fell into step with her. "Lieutenant Montgomery, I feel you're concerned about this accident that occurred this morning in relation to the murder and attempted abduction in Massachusetts."

Eve nodded, but kept walking. "Yes, I am. I don't believe in coincidences. My sister saves two tender-aged children from being kidnapped. We learn that the kidnappers have been killed and their bodies burned. I also learned from FBI Agent Baker that two imposters are looking for you to discuss a case they are unwilling to divulge to another lieutenant in your department. The task force has verified that they are not who they claim to be. Still, they've been hanging around, trying to get more intelligence from other officers from your squad. They are under surveillance to determine who they are working for. Most UNSUBs would get as far away from this situation as humanly possible and cut their losses, but that's not the case. Someone is still searching for these two children.

"On the same day I bring the children here, my sister-in-law is killed in a road accident. Whoever these UNSUBs are, they intend to get these children back and have indicated their willingness to kill to get their hands on them. I will not let that happen, and I will protect my family from further harm."

"Look, Lieutenant, I don't have a family, so I'm not emotionally invested. However, I suspect your protectives instincts are strong and appropriate. Still, I understand your need to have a look to assure yourself of whether what happened to your sister-in-law is connected or an unrelated incident. That is a purely clinical approach that any detective worth his or her salt would make a critical part of the investigation.

However, I want to help in any way that I can, particularly if your theory about a connection between these incidents is correct. One of those ways is to ensure that you don't make yourself a target or put yourself in danger. So, I want to go with you.

"From what I've seen of this place, it's a fortress, and my witnesses will be safe because of who your mother is. It's my guess that you've got security on the premises that I haven't spotted yet. You use color codes for security signals. Apparently, everyone in or around this place knows what that means. Hell, you've got a frekkin' helicopter landing pad on this farm. I believe you're more capable than many would give you credit for, but I would appreciate it if you would let me go with you to provide a second set of eyes on the scene and watch your back."

Eve sighed and slowed to a stop by the north staircase to the upper level of the house. The lieutenant didn't know her, so she had to make allowances for that. "Because this is my family, it may appear that I'm running on pure emotion, but I have my head on straight, Lieutenant. I'm a former US Coast Guard captain. I've had to operate in dangerous situations in the military and because I've done a lot of undercover work as a DC cop. I have a twenty-five-person squad of detectives, undercover operatives, and police officers on my team. I know how to tamp down my emotions." Still, she considered his offer. He was right. Her family would be safe on the ranch, particularly with the Richardson Security Agency in place on orange alert. He was also right that having a second pair of eyes on the scene wouldn't hurt. The portfolio that Jenna Baker furnished indicated that Pappas was very good at his job and had solved the majority of his cases just as she had. The squad of detectives that Pappas managed was disciplined and effective, as was her team. "Okay, let's grab our coats, hats, and gloves and go."

After donning heavy weather gear, Eve called her brother, Roger, as she and Lieutenant Pappas headed out of the mansion to the helicopter. Roger confirmed that the county sheriff was still at the crash site investigating the scene. Moments later, Eve fired up the helicopter, and they lifted off. Using the helicopter's whisper-quiet stealth capabilities and following the path of the single-lane road through the rural area at tree-top level, it didn't take long for Eve to spot the sight of the accident and the multitude of emergency vehicles.

Since the roadway was blocked off in both directions, Eve easily found a spot to land. Then, putting her police badge in clear view, she proceeded toward the area where her sister-in-law's car was wedged between several large trees and was yet to be retrieved from the gully. At first glance, Eve could see that the front was smashed to the point that not even the safety equipment could have saved the driver.

Sheriff Ely Houston led with his hand extended. "Hello, Eve. Let me say that we're all sorry for your loss."

Eve accepted his hand for a shake. "Thanks, Ely, I appreciate it. What can you tell me?"

He didn't hesitate to bring her up-to-date as he led the way closer to the crash site. "Your brothers were here, but they left with the county coroner, Ruth Randolph. She took the body to the morgue."

"The body? My sister-in-law is…was a person. Her name is KiLe Hakamora Montgomery."

Chagrined, he nodded. "Yes, of course. An autopsy will be performed on Mrs. Montgomery to determine what they can about her condition at the time of the crash. The roads had been cleared and salted from the storm that passed through here a few days ago, but in spots, there was still black ice on the road. The temperature was below fifteen degrees overnight. You know this is a rural area, and there is not much traffic through here. I imagine that's why your sister-in-law chose to travel toward Washington, DC, using this route." He hesitated a beat and Eve frowned while looking into his eyes. "Uh, Brian couldn't tell us much about her…Mrs. Montgomery's state of mind before she left home, I mean. Can you shed any light on whether she was upset or having problems?"

Eve shook her head. "I haven't spoken with KiLe for the past few days. So, I can't help you there. If you're leaning toward a theory that because this appears to be a single-car crash and a suicide, you would be wrong. KiLe was completing work on her doctorate, and, as far as I know, nothing was bothering her. When I spoke with Brian yesterday, he didn't indicate that anything unusual was going on. He is usually up and out of the house before five in the morning. Most of the family gets up around five, so it wouldn't be unusual for KiLe to leave the house for the city before dawn.

"Look, Ely, in case you're wondering, Brian and KiLe were deliriously happy. They just had a second son on Christmas Day. KiLe was not experiencing postpartum depression or any other mental health challenge. Yes, she was a brilliant researcher, but she wasn't about to experience a breakdown. Her doctoral thesis wasn't giving her problems. KiLe was like a sister to us all. I don't believe she had problems she wouldn't share with Brian or any of us."

As she and the sheriff continued to talk and he took notes, Eve watched the men attempting to retrieve the mangled car from the gully. However, Darrius wandered away to take discrete pictures of the roadway leading to the crash site.

Sheriff Houston pointed his chin at Darrius's back. "Who's your silent partner?"

"He's a part of an FBI/CIA task force, so he's not here in any official capacity."

"You know that I'm required to make a record of anyone who is on-site."

With a last look at the desecrated vehicle, Eve reached out a hand to Sheriff Houston. "Thanks for the tick-tock, Ely, but I was never here." She strode toward Darrius, who fell into step with her as they returned to the helicopter and lifted off.

Once airborne, Darrius looked toward Eve and spoke to her through their headsets. "Did you see what I saw?"

She nodded. "This was no accident. KiLe's car was forced off the road. She was murdered."

The two lieutenants rode the rest of the way back to the Alex-Mont farm in silence.

CHAPTER 11

Before noon, most major television networks broke into their regularly scheduled programming to announce that basketball icon Chuck Montgomery, and his wife, Supreme Court Justice Vivian Alexander's daughter-in-law, KiLe Hakamora Montgomery, a foreign national, was killed in a single-car crash early in the morning. Of course, there were standup reports with the crash site as the backdrop, and most reporters never mentioned Brian Montgomery's name, just his famous parents. Fortunately, the paparazzi didn't catch Brian and his brothers at the morgue. However, some enterprising reporters actually got pictures of the mangled vehicle. Likely, some tow-truck driver was a few hundred dollars richer as a result.

Talking heads speculated on the cause of the accident. Their comments ran the gamut from a woman experiencing postpartum depression who took her own life to conspiracy theories about her Japanese royalty status being a burden she could no longer bear. Some zealous woman in Pennsylvania claimed that KiLe was distraught because Brian never got over his feelings for another woman.

Darrius found the stories ran from the sublime to the ridiculous. He watched most of the coverage on eight wall-mounted monitors and recorded each one. The media room was located on the lower level of the mansion and better equipped than what he used in his police precinct.

When Brian Montgomery and his brothers, Vincent, Roger, and Ryan, returned from the morgue, he was introduced to them, but chose to stay out of the way while the family discussed funeral arrangements. Darrius was surprised that Brian Montgomery was so young to be the general manager of the three Alex-Mont properties in Pennsylvania, Maryland, and South Carolina. He, nevertheless, was a handsome young man with startling blue eyes and dark blond hair.

KiLe, who actually was Japanese royalty, had been married to Brian for less than three years. They had met through Brian's cousin, Whitney Ivy Alexander. KiLe and Whitney attended the same private elementary school in Japan and became close friends throughout high school. Whitney Ivy's parents, US Air Force General Benjamin Alexander, and his wife, US Navy Admiral Stacy Greene, both high-level military attachés, were stationed in Tokyo, Japan.

Whitney Ivy and KiLe remained friends as preteens throughout their different academic programs at Georgetown University. During that time, Darrius learned they were also housemates at Whitney's parents' home in the Embassy Row area of Washington, DC. KiLe was still studying for her doctorate, while Whitney was now a successful lawyer and a partner in her aunt Vivian's prestigious former law firm. Other housemates from that time were approached by the media, but all declined to be interviewed.

Whitney was now married to Tucker Duncan Cavanaugh, a US Marine medical doctor, who practiced medicine at the Landstuhl Medical Center in Germany. Whitney and Tucker were married hours before Brian and KiLe recited their marriage vows during the Alexander family's Juneteenth Family Reunion in Goodwill, Summer County, South Carolina.

There was an extensive video catalog of family members and events. Darrius was able to dial-up videos of the ceremony and other clips that included KiLe.

She was an attractive, pint-sized young woman with an incredibly powerful singing voice. Darrius found many video clips of KiLe and Brian singing duets at local and family events, particularly with his Montgomery cousins in Pennsylvania. In addition, Darrius noted that Anderson Montgomery often sang with his older brothers, Liam, Daniel, and Pierce. They had a good sound when the Montgomery brothers sang with Brian and KiLe and seemed to enjoy themselves as they performed.

It appeared that all of the Alex-Mont children learned to play at least one musical instrument and often lifted their voices in song with various degrees of proficiency.

KiLe also sang professionally with a Washington-based college group named Changelings. Whitney Ivy's husband, Tucker, also sang with Changelings while in medical school at Georgetown. It surprised Darrius to see film clips where Whitney Ivy also occasionally played electric guitar with Changelings. There was also a rising movie star and high-fashion model, Miguel Menendez-Gaza, who is an integral family friend and shared the stage with this group of college musicians. The interconnections among the Montgomery family members and friends were quite interesting.

Darrius was also surprised to learn that Eve Montgomery was a twin. Her biological brother, Vincent, was a pediatrician and pediatric surgeon. Many twins were among the Alexander and Montgomery family, including Roger and Ryan Montgomery, both stars in the Major Baseball League.

However, it didn't take long for Darrius to discern that overarching all was the cohesive nature of the Alexander and Montgomery family collective. They may not have been bound by blood, but it was clear to Darrius that they were cemented together by mutual trust, respect, and love.

Before dinner, Dena knew that their Alexander and Montgomery families were in situ or on the way. So, she helped out in the kitchen and kept her charges insight with her other tender-age siblings, snapping fresh green beans at a trestle table in the industrial-sized kitchen. There was a large pile of the green beans that she and they had harvested from one of their hydroponics farm buildings. Along with some of her preteen siblings, the little ones gathered enough vegetables and fruits to serve upwards of a hundred people. Although profoundly sad, Dena realized that being with the children helped ward off her grief.

It was not uncommon to have large parties when family members and close friends gathered for happy events. They had suffered losses before with their first father, Derrick, Senior, their grandfather, Derrick's father, Grover Jackson, and their grandmother, Chuck's mother, Esther Montgomery. Regrettably, this would be the first time they gathered to provide moral support for the death of someone they considered a sibling. After all, KiLe was still very young, under twenty-five. Dena wiped away her silent tears as she and some of her teenage siblings continued to clean and cut up fresh produce to assist the kitchen staff.

It was hard for Dena to imagine that KiLe would not be there in person. She was such an integral part of their family. This loss would be nothing short of catastrophic for her brother, Brian. However, Dena suspected more was happening than Eve shared when she and Lieutenant Pappas returned from the crash site. They immediately went into conference with her parents and the Richardson Security Team that guarded the property.

Dena's suspicions grew when the security company owner, Slade Richardson, a svelte six-five, Arab or East Indian with enormous sex appeal, arrived. Slade was a former US Navy SEAL captain whose name in the teams she learned was Cobra Khan. As a pre-teen, Dena had a crush on Slade. He had the look of the actor Sendhil Ramamurthy. Even now, as an adult, the sight of him still stirred her childhood memories. Actually, his beautiful olive-brown skin tone now reminded her of Lieutenant Pappas, another heartstopper.

When Dena felt a little hand pat her leg, she looked down into the upturned face of the little girl she had rescued. Then, putting aside the squash she was cutting, Dena stooped to look the girl, whom they had decided to call Jane, in the face.

Dena held the girl's hands. "What is it, honey?"

Jane frowned and danced from foot to foot. Dena got the message and quickly led the girl to a restroom outside the kitchen. Because there were so many pint-sized children, the bathrooms were also configured to accommodate the little people. She helped Jane verbalize what she was doing to take care of her needs and was pleased when Jane actually spoke the words Dena had taught her. Helping Jane wash her hands, her heart nearly broke when Jane smiled at her in the mirror. The little girl turned to face Dena and pointed to herself. "Jane." Then she pointed again. "Dena."

Dena gathered that child to her for a gentle hug and said, "Kiss" before she kissed the child's cheek. Jane held Dena's face in her small hands and repeated "Kiss" before kissing Dena's cheek. Dena smiled through her tears as she slowly nodded her approval.

Darrius leaned against the wall in the hallway with his hands in his pockets. He was facing the girls' restroom near the kitchen, waiting for Dena and the little girl to come out. He thought it was progress when the child did not startle at his presence, clutch Dena's legs, and try to hide behind her. Instead, she simply looked up at him with a blank expression on her cherubic face and held Dena's hand.

Surprised, Dena frowned. "Were you looking for us?"

"I was, yes. I've been recording news clips about the accident and your family. Your twin brothers, Roger and Ryan, have also shown video clips to me of your sister-in-law from your family's extensive video library. Your media setup is very sophisticated and cutting-edge. Your brothers had to show me how to use it."

Dena shrugged. "Yes, Roger and Ryan are our family video techs. It's been that way since we were all very young. In addition, our uncle, Kenneth Alexander, owns a tech firm. He keeps updating the equipment for all of us as new technology emerges. His company, CompuCorrect, created the software and manufactured the hardware you were given in Pennsylvania. Was there something specific that you were looking for?"

Darrius shook his head. "It helps me get a sense of the victim; who she was. There was a lot of footage that included her life back to when she lived in Japan with her parents. When I learned that KiLe was a member of the reigning Emperor of Japan's family, the Imperial House of Japan, kōshitsu, also referred to as the Yamato Dynasty, I took some deep dives into KiLe's parents' history. KiLe's mother is the emperor's sister and a tenured professor at the American University in Japan. That makes KiLe the emperor's niece. However, KiLe's father is a commoner who rose through Japanese society as the owner of a biotech firm. KiLe's parents met in college in England. At about the time KiLe came to

America with your cousin, Whitney Ivy Alexander, to attend Georgetown University, her parents divorced and married other people. Apparently, the ink wasn't dry on their divorce decree before her father and mother remarried, and each had a son with their new spouse. In addition, I found that KiLe's paternal grandfather is Yakuza. Are you familiar with who they are?"

"I am, yes. The Yakuza are members of transnational organized crime syndicates originating in Japan."

"That's correct. The Yakuza are considered by law enforcement to be one of the most sophisticated and dangerous groups in organized crime."

Defensively, Dena met Darrius's eyes with a heated, level gaze. "KiLe wasn't involved with the Yakuza, and she wasn't aware of her grandfather's criminal connection until the day before she and Brian married. Because KiLe chose to marry Brian instead of some hand-picked criminal selected by her paternal grandparents, KiLe was disowned by her family. She was obedient to her Japanese heritage, and it deeply hurt her when she was accused of causing her family to lose face and disowned as a result. Nevertheless, she was in love with Brian. KiLe was not a part of her paternal grandparents' criminal world."

Darrius recognized the cold edge to Dena's defense of her sister-in-law's character and wanted to diffuse Dena's pique. "Look, Doctor Montgomery, I was not trying to implicate your sister-in-law in some criminal behavior. On the surface, it doesn't appear that her father was involved either, just her paternal grandfather. Still, it is curious how KiLe's father came up with the resources to start his biotech company. I haven't found an answer to that question as of yet. Unfortunately, I don't have a genius-level IQ, so I'm not proficient in Japanese culture."

He felt that his voice was a little more strident than he intended. Then he felt the small hand pat his leg. He looked down at the little girl's face. When he stooped to her level, she patted his face and uttered "Kiss" in a soft voice. Then she put the word to action and kissed his cheek. He had never been around children since the days that he was a child himself in the orphanage. Still, he understood her offer of solace and kissed her cheek. She gave him a slight smile and reached for Dena's hand again.

At that show of comfort, Dena released her combative stance.

CHAPTER 12

Darrius regarded Dena for a humming moment before his brain engaged. *She is so frekkin' young, but she has an air of confidence, sophistication, and tenacity I haven't experienced with any woman I have known. Yet, something about her is like an itch that I can't reach or scratch. Dena is getting under my skin and I am uncomfortable with this feeling. She is a witness I am here to protect, but I am beginning to think I am the one who needs protection from her.*

Dena raised an eyebrow at Darrius's continued silence as he stared at her. "Lieutenant, you said that you were looking for me? Was there more that you needed to discuss?"

"Uh, yes." He shook his head in an effort to reengage his brain for the task at hand. "Is there someplace where we can talk?"

"Sure. I was working in the kitchen. Let me take Jane back to continue her tasks." She moved into the noisy kitchen and seated Jane with the other children singing "The Alphabet Song" while they snapped green beans. "Melvin?" she called out to the head cook.

"*Yo!*"

"I need to take a break. I'll be right back."

"You've done enough. You can go."

"Okay, thanks. Aunt Althea?"

Althea glimpsed Darrius and smiled at Dena. "You go on. Take your time, babe. I've got this for now."

"Okay, thanks." She turned to Darrius and led the way out of the kitchen. "Let's take a walk outside. You'll see more of the farm that way."

"Sure, but I need to get a coat. Don't you need one, too?"

"Yes, we can find what we need in here." Dena opened the door to what Darrius thought could have been a high-fashioned clothing store.

"Uh, is your family into manufacturing apparel?"

"No. These clothes are what's left of last year's Chandler Stallion Collection."

"William Chandler?"

"Yes. You've heard of him?"

"I read his *Stallion* magazine and buy from his online store."

She inclined her head in acknowledgment. "He and my mother were housemates while they were in law school. He's also one of the founding members of her former law firm, Alexander, Carter, Chandler, Charles, Lightfoot, and Towson, PA. He and my parents are still best friends. We call him Uncle Bill. I think he's in Cancun this week at a bar association convention and taking meetings with young professional athletes who want his legal representation. He'll likely come home when he gets the news..." She faltered and fought mightily to gather herself. "He'll be here...soon. So, you'll have an opportunity to meet him."

Dena chose a gray Stetson and designer sunshades before putting on heavy-weather gear. They left the mansion from a different door than Darrius had seen, but it led through a barn full of cars, SUVs, Alex-Mont delivery trucks, utility trucks and jeeps, ATVs, motorcycles, and a few humongous long-distance buses. Then they went outside into the bright, sunny, but cold day. Quietly, she and Darrius strolled toward one of the horse barns. Leaning their arms on the top rung of the corral fence, Dena put one booted foot on the lowest rung as they watched the horses grazing or exercising in the fields.

Darrius hadn't been near a farm since he was a kid, mucking out stables for pocket change. However, standing here, looking at the beauty of this farm, brought back some of the warm feelings of his youth. "It's nice here," he heard himself say, unexpectantly.

"Yes. Living on the farm grounds me." She climbed up, sat on the top railing, and blew a loud, shrilled whistle. Several horses' heads came up before they began galloping toward her. She climbed down inside the corral and giggled as the big steeds surrounded her, nudging her and angling for a brisk rub or a hug. "Hello, my beauties," she crooned to one of the big palominos she called Butterscotch and then repeated the greeting naming each one. Then reaching into a covered box, she pulled out a handful of carrots and began feeding them. When they ate their fill, Dena signaled with a hand gesture. "Away!" The horses turned and galloped back toward the pasture. Then she climbed up the fence to sit on the top rung again. Once settled, she patted a space inviting Darrius to climb up and sit with her.

He did and stared off into the near distance at the horses as they galloped around the field and the wooded area beyond.

Without looking in his direction, Dena addressed him. "Do you ride?"

Darrius shrugged. "Yes, some, when I was a kid. I read in your file that you used to perform in rodeos."

"I did, yes. My first dad put me on a pony when I was about six. I loved it and rode every chance I got. My parents stressed academics, but encouraged me to follow my dreams. They and my sibs attended every event when I competed. I kept competing until I won every event and then retired when I was twelve. Now, during my summer break, I plan rodeo competitions for young people."

Darrius frowned and swung his gaze toward her. "Your *first* dad?"

"Yes, his name was Derrick Jackson. He was a famous NBA star like Chuck. They were best friends. Later, when Derrick retired from professional sports, he became a pediatrician and pediatric surgeon. That's when my mother and Derrick met and married. They adopted me and my first ten sibs. They also had one biological son, Derrick Junior. Unfortunately, our dad died of a massive heart attack the same day Derrick Junior was born, April Fool's Day. So now my brother, Vincent, is carrying on in Derrick Senior's footsteps."

"I didn't see that in your file…that you were adopted twice."

"It was a long time ago. Derrick Senior died young. Five years later, Mom and Chuck married and we held another adoption ceremony. We hold a ceremony whenever new children become our siblings. Dad and Mom have had six babies and we've legally adopted more into the family. The rest is history."

"Your parents just go around looking for children to adopt?"

Dena shook her head. "No. The first eleven of us were Derrick's medical patients. He volunteered his time and services to the orphanage where we lived. We were orphaned or abandoned with medical conditions that were very expensive to remedy. For example, Linda was five when her mother and younger brother were killed in an automobile accident that she survived. However, her hips and legs were shattered. Derrick developed a webbing system for babies and toddlers that revolutionized pediatric medicine. His treatment caused their bones to knit and muscles to form normally or be replaced by harvested bones and connecting tissues. It stretches to allow for growth, but keeps the bones from developing stress cracks. As a result of his treatment, Linda learned to ice skate and to dance. She won medals in the Olympic games for ice skating and simultaneously became a famous prima ballerina known globally as The Black Swan.

"Vincent and Eve were conjoined at the hip at birth. By the time they reached junior high school age, they were running track and winning races. Roger and Ryan were joined back to back. Now they play professional baseball for a major league team. Other twins in our family were also conjoined, and everyone is doing well because of our parents' dedication, love, and care. The orphanages couldn't have afforded the costly treatments for our conditions.

"Chuck is an emergency room doctor and general practitioner. Mom and Chuck continue to adopt abandoned children with severe medical challenges who have been recommended to them from places around the globe. Dad's hospital is one of only a few worldwide specializing in separating conjoined twins and triplets. Unfortunately, in several situations, the biological parents abandoned the babies even after they were separated. So, rather than sending them to an orphanage where their medical needs may be too costly, Dad and Mom adopted them and continue to provide the medical care they need.

"You see, Mom inherited Derrick's medical practice. He owned it with three partners for many years. Now there are twelve doctors associated with the practice. However, since Chuck is legally our dad, he can't treat us because we are his offspring. So, the doctors at Goldmahn, Fitch, Bellingham, and Jackson provide for our medical care until we age out of pediatric medicine at twenty-one."

"When will you age out?"

Dena hooted a laugh. "I'll never tell."

"What about the others? You said that not everyone had medical problems."

"That's true, but all of us were either orphaned and/or medically challenged. Friends of my parents, Doctor Raymond Phillips and his wife Denise Harris, were killed in a tsunami in Indonesia. They had six biological children who were in an American school not near where their parents were when the tsunami hit. The children did sustain various degrees of injury. Their oldest boy, Raymond Junior, was only eight when their parents died.

"Dad went to Indonesia to get the children and bring their parents' bodies back to the states for burial. My parents are the godparents of the Phillips children. Both of my fathers did their residency training at Georgetown with Doctor Phillips. His wife, Denise, was a registered nurse on staff at the hospital. A few other American children whose parents worked at the hospital lost them during the tsunami. So my dad brought them and their deceased parents home, too. Because they were all medical practitioners, many people from hospitals, medical schools, and private practices came to the celebration of life for the tsunami victims. Just as Raymond and Denise Phillips's children didn't have close relatives willing to take all six Phillips kids, neither did the other families. Those families didn't want the responsibility of taking on tender-aged children to raise. So, my parents went to court and became Guardian ad Litem for all American children orphaned because of the tsunami.

"Mom's former law firm took on the task of representing the children and settling their parents' estates *pro bono*. They established trust funds for each child. They were very young and are now about John's and Jane's ages. Dad and Mom kept them together, raising them as our siblings. We don't make a distinction between them and us."

Darrius thought *it was very selfless of her parents to do such a thing for so many. He was curious about Dena's ailment, but she clearly was not comfortable enough with him to discuss it. Still, she looked to be very healthy now with a youthful, understated beauty that was impossible to miss.* When Dena spoke, he was so embedded in his thoughts that he almost missed her question. "I apologize. What did you say?"

"You wanted to talk, remember? What about?"

"Oh, yes. Several things. I'd appreciate it if you'd give me more insight into your sister-in-law."

Dena frowned. "I thought you looked at the video clips that included her."

"I did, yes, but that doesn't tell me everything that I need to know."

"Okay, what else is there?"

"Humanize her for me. Tell me more about who she was."

Dena shrugged. "My cousin, Whitney Ivy Alexander and KiLe had been close friends since they met in a private elementary school in Tokyo, Japan. When they completed their academic studies in Japan, Whitney Ivy came to study at Georgetown's School of Law. KiLe came to earn a master's in science, technology, and international studies. Whitney Ivy's parents have a home in the Embassy Row section of Washington, DC. It's convenient to Georgetown University, so Whitney Ivy and KiLe lived there with other advanced studies students at Georgetown.

"On weekends or other events, Whitney Ivy would bring KiLe with her to visit us here on the farm or we would go into town. We all became fast friends with KiLe. She was funny and smart. That's when Brian and KiLe met. However, it wasn't until spring break of KiLe's senior year at Georgetown that a romance sparked between Brian and KiLe. By Juneteenth, they were deeply in love.

"KiLe was scheduled to be the maid of honor in Whitney Ivy and Tucker's wedding. As friends of Whitney Ivy's parents, KiLe's parents were invited to the wedding. Since KiLe's grandparents were traveling with KiLe's parents, they were also allowed to attend Whitney Ivy and Tucker's nuptials. However, after Whitney's wedding, KiLe didn't want to be forced to return to Japan to marry a man handpicked by her grandparents, who she didn't even know. Instead, she begged her parents to let her stay in the United States to take advantage of the opportunity to receive her graduate degree from Georgetown University.

"KiLe's parents refused her request because they arranged for her to continue her master's and doctorate studies at their respective alma maters, Cambridge or Oxford in England. They were of the opinion that she had lived in America for four years. So they felt it was time that she gained experience living in England. Then she would return to Japan to marry and procreate the appropriate number of offspring. Because KiLe was Japanese royalty, her grandparents arranged a lavish party for her to be introduced into Japanese society. In fact, they had chosen a date and time for her "coming out" party. They also handpicked a number of suitable Japanese men for her to choose as a husband. These men were, of course, rising stars in Japan's societal, corporate and/or the political arenas. According to her parents, she would make an appropriate helpmate for any one of them as they rose in their respective careers.

"Does any of what I've said help?"

"It does, yes."

Chapter 13

"You said that there were several things. What else do you need?"

"When your sister took us to the crash scene, I noticed a community about a mile south of here. There were also large homes, not as large as this, but surrounded by a golf course."

"I think you're referring to the housing on this farm where our workers can live if they choose to." She laughed. "Dad likes to think of this land as a ranch instead of a farm. Indeed, it is located in a rural agricultural area with no public means of transportation. So, we let him call it whatever he wants, but it is a working farm. However, it's a twenty-first-century hydroponics farm that operates twenty-four-seven and three-sixty-five. As a result, workers choose between the four six-hour shifts. Some propose to work nights and have the days free. Brian works out the assignments and schedules.

"We hire most of our workers from one of the homeless family facilities in Washington, DC. Most don't have cars, so we have housing suitable for both situations. We have all-terrain vehicles and jeeps for travel on the property and cars, trucks, and vans for travel off the premises.

"There are other amenities, such as schools and shopping for the workers' use. They also have an indoor space surrounded by the condo complex where they have a swimming pool, game equipment, certain stores, shops, parties, and other forms of entertainment. Most enjoy the communal meals the spouses prepare daily and charge a nominal fee. Some nights they have movies, group activities, or individual training, like the old-fashion forge where they make our horseshoes and other ironworks. I like to spend my time there when I have time to spare when I come home.

"The farriers or blacksmiths, who are skilled ironworkers, create custom shoes for our horses. Our farriers evaluate how a horse walks and runs and consider the animal's hoof balance when adjusting or applying shoes. Iron-working skills are still crucial even though some horse owners buy prefabricated shoes. Most of our clients and customers trust our farriers to know the right thing to do for their animals.

"Some of the workers have been here since Dad bought the property. Others have come to work here or at one of our other farms, stayed long enough to get their feet under them, and then moved on. They can transfer between the three properties. We've lost very few people, so our workers are like family members to us. My parents offer tuition help to our workers and their families at the local colleges and universities in the area or encourage the workers to go to a trade school to improve their skills and abilities. Recently, we've hired a number of vets at all three properties.

"Brian pays a good wage, and because the farm has been so successful, he gives promotions and bonuses each year in the spring and the fall. He takes time to talk with our workers so that he usually doesn't have problems crop up." She smiled wryly. "The thing is that Brian likes to roll up his sleeves and work side by side with the farm workers. There isn't a job on this property he hasn't done many times over. As a consequence of being his sibling, there isn't a job or task he hasn't assigned us to do."

"It's hard to believe that Brian handles all of these responsibilities at his age. He's what, twenty-seven or so?"

Dena smirked. "Brian was a preteen when Dad and Mom married, and we moved here. We all love living here because we have unlimited space to rip and run. Even though we all had chores, we had free time, too. There was still so much to see and do. I already knew how to ride, but Dad and Mom taught everyone else how to ride and care for our animals. We'd take all-day rides through the woods and have picnics or camp for a few days where we could go swimming. We do the same thing in Pennsylvania and South Carolina. We just had fun with our parents and learned many things about nature. Sometimes, our cousins would visit just to go frolicking through the woods and camping for a week or two. We took a lot of pictures and videos. Some of them were pretty good, and we voted on the ones we wanted to be enlarged, printed, and hung on our gallery walls. We also selected the best one to be our annual holiday card.

"Still, perhaps Brian loves farm life just a little bit more than the rest of us. He was just a kid when he told our parents he wanted to manage the farms. So, Dad taught him everything about farm life. Then, when he was twenty-one, Brian was *summa cum laude* at Penn State with a double masters' program in business and economics. He achieved that distinction while playing collegiate lacrosse, a very competitive NCAA sport, for four years. So for him, managing the farms is a no-brainer. Although he's not thirty yet, he has always loved farm life, as do all of us. He's even expanded our investment by starting tree farms on all three properties and other cottage industries used to support the farm and sell to regional vendors. You'll see Alex-Mont Ranch trucks coming and going while you're here. Most of our customers are boutique grocers and/ or restaurants. We've lived in the city, but this is better.

"I've told you more than you asked for, but is that essentially what you wanted to know?"

"Well, I was also concerned about the security measures here. As we flew overhead, this place seems extraordinarily large and open."

"You're right, there is a lot of land, most of which is still wooded and undeveloped, but I have reason to feel secure here. Brian is our expert on security measures, as is Claudia Shaffer. She's back, and her security force and her K9s are still on orange alert status."

"Yes, so I was told by your father and mother, but I didn't think this was the time to question Brian about it."

"Then, you may want to talk with Eve, Roger, and Ryan. I'm in Cambridge most of the time. I usually come home for birthday parties held on the first weekend of each month. Still, my sister and brothers know more than I do about the security setup. Because of Mom's judgeship, she has federal government protection from the Supreme Court of the United States Police. They report to the Supreme Court Marshal. There is a second layer of protection provided by Richardson

Security. Claudia handles the next layer of security. Beyond that, I'm not the best source of information."

"Okay, what about the other community on what looked like a golf course?"

"Oh, that's Havenhurst Estates. It's a private gated community about five miles from here. It's situated on a professional seventy-two-hole golf course that's contiguous to the Alex-Mont ranch property. We board horses for the residents and provide bridle paths through the wooded areas. Dad also has a race track where we train horses for local and regional races. Brian and I and several of our younger siblings usually put Alex-Mont thoroughbreds through their paces in preparation for the upcoming Native Dancer Stakes. The American Thoroughbred horse race is run annually at Laurel Park Racecourse in Laurel, Maryland, not far from us here. Since the race is open to horses aged three and older and is contested on dirt tracks over a mile distance, Alex-Mont Ranch has seven entries scheduled to participate. Although the seventy-five thousand dollars winner's purse is attractive, Dad, Brian, and I feel that the trophy alone would be more beneficial to Alex-Mont's reputation for quality thoroughbreds. The notoriety would cause the stud fees to double the winner's purse per horse. Brian and I don't make a practice of studying data or other information on the competing horses. Still, I created a mathematical paradigm demonstrating that our thoroughbreds would win, place, or show against the rest of the field. We looked forward to the challenge. The residents of Havenhurst have access to the course and also enter their horses in the races."

"I also saw several fields of cattle. Are those fields also a part of this ranch?"

"They are, yes. Brian breeds several different stock bovines, including American buffalo. We don't sell to slaughterhouses. Instead, our stock is sold to breeders who are attempting to improve their own stock bloodlines. In addition, Brian ensures contractually that our cattle get to die of old age. The same is true for some other farm animals, like the sheep, though my sister, Samantha, has them sheared and uses their wool in her textile business."

"I think I saw some of your younger siblings carrying baskets of eggs from a barn to the house. Obviously, those eggs were a part of this morning's breakfast buffet."

Dena cracked a slight smile. "*Touché*, Lieutenant. Yes, not everything has a contractual lifespan, but we sell the setting hens to other farmers and the additional excess produce which is not used on the Alex-Mont farms.

"My youngest siblings learn about the chickens when they care for eggs in incubators until the chicks hatch. They get to keep those chicks and name them. Those chicks and some turkeys we breed don't end up on the dinner table. Each of us has a raised garden where we choose to raise fruits or vegetables in soil with chicken shit as fertilizer. So, our chicks have other uses other than fried food." She laughed. "We have apple orchards in Pennsylvania and other fruit orchards in hydroponic gardens that sacrifice their lifespans for our glutenous behavior of eating copious amounts of fresh food. In addition, we have fisheries for both fish and crustation. We love seafood. So, you can imagine that the seafood does not enjoy a long life either."

"Ah, now I understand."

Dena frowned. "You understand what?"

"At your home in Pennsylvania, there were Christmas trees in tin tubs lined up in your garage. You don't chop the trees off at the root. Instead, you keep the trees alive to be reburied. That's eco-friendly. It's the kind of thing I think your family would do."

"Ah, yes, you're right. To us, it's wasteful to chop down a tree to be used for a few weeks and then discarded. So, we dig up the trees with the root ball attached, wrap them up in burlap, and keep them watered in the tubs to use in the house for Christmas. We decorate at least one tree in each common area in our home. Then, when the holiday is over, we gift the trees with the decorations in a lottery to raise money for various charities. Our extended family members and friends who come to stay for the Christmas holidays also decorate the trees along the quarter-mile driveway to our home with us."

Darrius was awed by how altruistic these people appeared to be.

Just then, two black Labradors bulleted out of a barn and raced to Dena. She knelt to receive their affection. "Hello, boys." Dena briskly rubbed them while they licked her face and danced around her. "This is Starsky and Hutch, Lieutenant. They are mostly KiLe and Brian's dogs."

The affection is apparent on her face and a bit of sadness, Darrius thought.

A shrilled whistle had the dogs stopping their play and racing toward Brian, who carried his newborn in a sling across his chest, and Vincent, who carried Brian's sleeping toddler son on his shoulder.

Dena intercepted her brothers and kissed both sleeping boys. "Where are you four off to?"

Brian tilted his head toward a nearby wooded area. "I've got some things to take care of at my cabin. It will take a few hours, but I want to get it done before the rest of the family arrives."

Dena rubbed Brian's arm. "If you want, I could take care of the boys while you work."

"Thanks, kid, but I want them with me for a while. I think they'll rest better in their beds in the cabin. I'll bring them back for dinner tonight and maybe for breakfast in the morning."

"I understand. Let me know when you need anything."

He smiled sadly at her, embraced her, and kissed her forehead. "I will. Let's ride sometime before dinner tonight, okay?"

She squeezed him to her. "I love you."

"I love you more."

Vincent also briefly hugged Dena as Brian moved on with Starsky and Hutch at his feet. "I want to examine the children, John and Jane, a little later. Roger and Ryan are working on a memorial video for KiLe's wake. Linda, Will, and their two boys just arrived from New York. Once they get settled, they will come to spend time with Brian. The grands should be here shortly. Then I'll come to examine the children. Oh, and Dad wants to be there, too. For now, he and Mom are greeting the family members and guests as they arrive at the west portico. Samantha and Quentin will take over that task. Then Mom will help assign rooms and Dad will meet with us."

"Okay. Come find me when you're ready. The children are in the kitchen. I'll bring them to the Med Suite."

Vincent tilted his head before he followed Brian into the woods.

Darrius frowned. "Where are they going?"

"Brian has a cabin down that path into the woods. He had it built many years ago and then expanded and remodeled it when he and KiLe married."

Darrius turned to look at the mansion. It sat on a knoll less than a quarter of a mile away and dominated the landscape. The impressive and massive white three-story structure had deep terraces on each level that circled each floor and were held up by large pillars. Because of its size, he imagined it could have been the prototype for the Parthenon. "Brian chose to move to a cabin instead of living there?"

"Yes, but he still has a bedroom suite in the house whenever he chooses to stay there."

Darrius shook his head in wonder and awe. "You call your home a house when it's clearly much more than that. The bedroom suite where I slept last night in Pennsylvania is more than half the size of my entire condo in Cambridge. The bedroom suites here are even larger than that."

Dena shrugged. "For us, it's home regardless of the size. Yes, it's big, but Brian's cabin isn't a one-room shack."

He shook his head again. "I apologize. I'm unaccustomed to this kind of wealth. Like you, I spent time in an orphanage. It wasn't a bad experience. The nuns were very kind to us, as were the visiting priests. We were fed, clothed, and had a roof over our heads. We never went hungry. However, I never came close to being adopted. I had a good education and was taught English as a second language. I was eighteen when I graduated, left the orphanage, and came to America to attend college on a full scholarship."

"No apology is necessary. I don't mean to sound cavalier about my home, Lieutenant. Both of my dads and my mom came from humble beginnings. They grew up on farms and worked hard for what they have. Initially, the house and outbuildings were in shambles when they found this property. The farmland was overgrown, and most of the property was a thick, uninhabitable forest. Dad is from a large family, all of whom are Pennsylvania farmers and artisans. Initially, Dad and his brothers and sisters took nearly a year to restore it to what it looked like in the early eighteen hundreds. Then, when he and Mom married and we moved in, my parents took on more renovations to accommodate all of us, extended family members, and close family friends for when they came to visit. Of course, my parents never stopped helping young ones needing medical care. So, more renovations took place. The youngest ones share a four-person bedroom and bath until we are thirteen. Then we get our own bedroom and bath suite. All of the sibs are on the second floor. However, there aren't many services, like hotels, motels, and shopping areas, because we're in a rural area. So, immediate family and guests have suites on the third floor.

"Dad and Brian developed small cottage industries as needed as a part of the sale of farm produce. You may have noticed the convenience stores and gas station across the road from here."

"I did, yes. It looks like those Cracker Barrel restaurant facades. Very rustic."

"That area is also a part of the land that Dad bought. Originally, it was just an old-fashion general store and a barbershop. Dad kept those services and then enlarged the shopping area to include his medical office, a beauty salon, a farmer's market, and a day spa. In addition, my mom and dad built a school, Alex-Mont Academy, on the farm between here and Havenhurst.

"Because we lost KiLe, Dad and Mom permitted my brothers and sisters to participate in classes remotely if they chose to do so. It also helps reduce the number of security team members needed to guard the family members and the workers' children on the school's campus while we're preparing for KiLe's life celebration.

"Dad and some of his colleagues also built and operate Physicians' Hospital, which is approximately a couple of miles west of here. They built it because there were no medical facilities in the area."

"Necessity is the mother of invention?"

"Exactly. However, the side benefit is that those by-products were also lucrative. Still, this is a working farm or ranch, as my dad likes to call it. We are a hydroponics facility and sell quality produce primarily to boutique stores and high-end regional restaurants. We grew up here and had challenging tasks. So, we know what hard work means, and we're not shy about lending a hand when and where needed. Still, my parents and all of us would be happy to live in a one-room shack as long as we could be together. Believe me, Lieutenant, we don't take for granted what we have. For those of us who were adopted, life could have been nightmarish.

"No one gave my parents anything except a lot of love, moral support, and an excellent academic foundation upon which to build their lives. Our parents do the same thing for all of us. They ensure we have everything we need to succeed in our chosen fields. They don't ask anything of us in return except to be kind, honest, and hardworking. They also encourage us never to stop being curious about everything in our orbit. As a result, failure is not an option or found anywhere in our vocabulary."

"I've noticed that you're a very closely-knit group."

"We are, yes, but don't place a halo on our heads. Growing up, we got into our share of mischief, but we learned that one of those 'Jedi mom looks' was worse than a tongue-lashing and extra chores from Dad." She smiled. "Our parents are a united front and omniscient. They kept us so busy with academics, athletics, and chores that we didn't have much time for misbehavior. So the punishment was never worth doing the crime."

"I noticed that everyone calls you 'kid.' Why is that?"

Dena smirked as they continued their walk back to the main house. "I'm the youngest girl of the original kids that Mom and Derrick adopted. Obviously, I'm not the youngest of all my sibs, but they claimed I got away with more mischief than anyone else."

"Did you?"

"You've met my mom. What do you think?"

"Not on a bet."

Dena laughed. "Yeah. Vivian Lynn Alexander Jackson Montgomery has that Jedi master persona down to a fine science. She *is* The Force, and we all know it."

Chapter 14

After Darrius and Dena returned their coats to the closet room, he noticed several preteens soaking wet and drying their faces and hair as they passed them in one of the wide halls. Darrius frowned and turned to Dena. "Do you have a swimming pool here?"

"Yes, but it's different than the one in Pennsylvania. The one here is more like a lagoon. Do you want to see it?"

"I would, yes."

"Okay." Dena shrugged and turned around to go in a different direction.

Once they turned down another couple of hallways, Darrius could feel the excess moisture in the air. When they walked through double doors, the humidity engulfed them. Before them was what resembled a smaller water park wholly enclosed in a glass-paneled dome. An exterior pool and pool house were to the left of the glass dome. Also, beyond the glass was a panoramic view of pristine snow-covered fields that led into the wooded area. The inside space was lush with large, healthy-looking tropical plants, trees, and water cascading off of rock formations strategically placed to provide alcoves where comfortable-looking pool-appropriate furniture was placed. A kitchenette ran along one solid wall to the right of the entrance. However, the vast lagoon, with a lazy river, water slides, diving boards, and other challenging water features, was the centerpiece the likes of which Darrius had never seen outside of a theme park.

Three of Dena's brothers, Spencer, Darren, and Andrew, who Darrius met at breakfast, were teaching their younger siblings how to balance on the surfboards in the rushing water. Darrius noted how they were careful with the youngsters, ensuring they wouldn't be hurt. They praised the success each child experienced and encouraged the less skillful to keep trying no matter how unsuccessful they were.

Dena shared that these three mathletes kept trying to stump her with complex math equations. Of course, they never won, but she created convoluted mathematical tests they had yet to solve. Still, they kept trying, and it appeared that both Dena and her brothers enjoyed the competition.

Darrius also noted that these three couldn't be more dissimilar in appearance. Darren was clearly Indigenous American with long black hair, high cheekbones, with a bronze skin tone. Spencer had gray-green irises and Nordic features reminiscent of someone with a Scandinavian heritage. Andrew was American of African descent. He had a medium brown complexion, golden-brown irises, and thick, curly, sandy-brown hair. All three were about the same age, solidly built and skillfully athletic, somewhere in their mid-to-late-teens.

Dena monitored the changing expressions on the lieutenant's handsome face. She could almost read his thoughts in his expressive dark eyes. When he looked down at the grass-covered surface, she sensed that he wanted to disrobe and go surfing with her brothers. Then he turned his gaze to her.

"I read about a structure like this that's built somewhere in the southwest. This is like a biosphere, isn't it?"

"I think you're referring to the University of Arizona's Biosphere 2. It's the world's most extensive controlled environment dedicated to understanding the implication, mitigation, and adaptation solutions for the resilience of our planet. It's a meso-scale Earth science facility, encompassing over three acres and houses five synthetic ecosystems encased in a glass and metal spaceframe. The meso-scale ecosystems include the world's largest controlled systems of tropical rain forest, desert, savanna, mangrove, and ocean.

"Well, this is similar to that, but clearly nowhere near as large. This structure was my first major project for my doctorate. You see, a biosphere extends from the deepest root systems of trees to the dark environment of ocean trenches to lush rain forests and high mountaintops. Clearly, I couldn't achieve all of that here in a scale model. So, the best that I could do was build an ecosphere. It's a self-contained and self-sustaining miniature world encased in glass. It's the type of environment that can be adapted for use in outer space. It's under consideration for use on SPACEHOME by the US government and certain biosphere companies. I hope that I'll hear something soon. Aerospace engineer and UCLA professor, Doctor Tate Kennedy, is on SPACEHOME now. He approves of my project. That will go a long way toward complete approval and, hopefully, implementation."

"Your parents let you do this?"

Dena frowned curiously at the lieutenant. "Uh, yes, they did. My parents don't limit exploration or creative thinking. In fact, they encouraged me to rework the pool we had here before for this new environment. It helps my sibs study the ecosystem up close and personal.

"As you already know, I teach Astrophysics and am a principal investigator at MIT Kavli Institute for Astrophysics and Space Research. Everyone in my family thinks this ecosphere is a great addition. As I've mentioned, Doctor Kennedy wants to build this type of environment on SPACEHOME and then replicate this artificial environment throughout deep space. We would be able to daisy-chain link the planets and study each one from a space station conducive to Earth's environment."

Darrius just stared. He didn't understand more than half of what this kid was talking about. Moreover, he couldn't fathom parents letting a kid redesign parts of their home to something as incredible as this. Still, he didn't have parents, so what would he know about how they would behave? He shook his head and moved on. "You know that the term ecology is from the Greek Oikos-house, logos-study."

"I do, yes, but the term was coined by German biologist Ernst Haeckel in 1869. Ecology deals with studying interactions between living organisms and their physical environment."

He turned to face her and crossed his muscular arms over his broad chest. "You were *that* kid, weren't you?"

Dena frowned. "Pardon me? What kid?"

"The one who was always the smartest one in the class. You skewed the curve for the rest of us who couldn't catch a clue."

She grinned. "I had help. I dated a German guy while I was working on my Ph.D. He was rather competitive and kept me on my toes."

"What happened to him?"

"We were up for the same position at MIT. When he didn't get the position as assistant dean, he dumped me."

"He must have been a real dunce. So, I suspect that his name isn't Drew."

Dena quirked a brow. "As a matter of fact, it isn't. His name is Alfonse." Dena realized that the lieutenant was digging for information unrelated to the investigation. She wondered why, but left that thought to move on. "You're welcome to use this area of the house at your discretion. However, once the rest of the family arrives, you'll note that it's one of the more popular areas of the house."

Darrius frowned. "Are there other popular areas I should know about?"

"Sure. It depends on your interests."

"I'm interested in many things. Do you have time to show me around?"

Dena frowned and checked the time on her cell phone. "Yes, I can do that. However, I don't want to leave John and Jane for too long. I don't want them to worry that I've abandoned them. Also, you know that Vincent and my dad want to examine them. It will be their nap time soon. I want to get them on a regular routine with my brothers and sisters who are their ages. So, we'll have to make this quick."

"If you want, we could go get them and bring them with us."

"Let me check and see how they're doing." With that, she called Althea and learned that they were doing fine. Other tender-age children had joined them, and they were making cookies for their afternoon snack. "I think we're good to go for another hour. Let's cover the lower level and then work our way up."

The first area they visited had a clear view of the underwater area around the lagoon. It had task lighting for the quiet teens who were reading or listening to audiobooks through earphones. Watching the sunlight filter through the water was calming. It was a tranquil and comfortable space if someone just needed to sit quietly and think.

Next to that space was the media room where Dena's twin brothers, Roger and Ryan, were busy putting together the memorial video to be shown as a part of the celebration of KiLe's life, which would be held the next day in the ballroom. Darrius had used the media facilities and noticed they connected to a full-scale music studio, stage, and lounge.

Next, they came to double doors and glass panels resembling a restaurant or bar. When Dena opened the doors and they went inside, Darrius laughed.

"This is a bar? Like an old-fashioned speakeasy?"

Dena held up her hand to wave at the array of wine bottles gracing the walls and those in tall wine coolers. A modern mahogany bar stretched across one of the sidewalls, and a dance floor centered the room. Individual chairs and bistro tables clustered together across the opposite wall. The space appeared to hold approximately fifty people comfortably, but more than that in a pinch. "This is primarily my parents' and grandparents' space. They, the family members in their age groups, and their close friends congregate here to have parties that usually go well into the wee hours of the morning. Unfortunately, those parties usually don't include me and my sibs."

When Dena laughed aloud, Darrius thought that the sound went straight to the space centered somewhere in the vicinity under his heart. It was the first time he had heard that sound coming from her since they had met nearly five days ago. It struck him that he'd like to listen to her laugh often.

Dena led him in and out of other spaces designated for specific enjoyable activities. There was an entire room that held costumes in many sizes. Mirrors were on the walls with tables before them where wigs and makeup were in plentiful supply. Some of the areas were occupied by her siblings, while others were empty. When they came to a game room, it was filled with activities, kids, and noise. Electronic floor-model arcade games with flashing lights and scoreboards lined up along the back wall. Still, other spaces held pool tables, ping-pong tables, Skittle ball, air hockey games, and other table games. Darrius was surprised to see several bowling lanes for both ten-pin and duckpin activities in use. When they left the madness of the game room, not a sound could be heard outside the doors.

"This is my sister, Samantha's, space." Dena knocked on the closed door.

"Come," Samantha called out, her voice shaky and full of tears.

Dena stuck her head in to see her sister leaving the arms of her guy friend, Quentin King. "I can come back later."

Samantha shook her head and wiped her tears. "No, come on in, kid." She held her arms open for Dena, and they embraced, rocking back and forth. "I apologize, kid. I'm still trying to get over the shock…" With Dena in her left arm, she shook her head to ground herself and stuck out her right hand. "Hello, again, Lieutenant Pappas."

He accepted her hand. "Hello. I remember you from breakfast this morning, but you didn't stay for long after you finished eating. So I take it that you're another one of Doctor Montgomery's sisters?"

"If you mean Dena, yes. When you say Doctor Montgomery around here, there are several people in this household you might be referring to." She smiled, as did he. *His face transformed to movie-idol splendor,* Samantha thought. "Uh, this is Quentin King, who, as of fifteen minutes ago, became my fiancé."

"Wait! What?" Dena's eyes went wide. "You went to the knee, Q?"

Quentin smiled and hugged Dena. "I did, and Samantha actually said yes."

While Dena examined the engagement ring on Samantha's finger, Quentin and Darrius shook hands.

Then Darrius looked up and around, astonished as he stood in Samantha's studio. He noted a bolt of black lace. It reminded him of the lace the nuns made and sold in his homeland.

Dena noticed the lieutenant's surprise. It was a little intimidating, she knew, for someone to see fabric everywhere, hanging on the walls, on tables, shelved in cubbies and baskets, and on desktop mockups. A loon in the corner was threaded with newly sheered wool and a half-completed tapestry in progress. Samantha had sample designs pinned to a wire that spanned the studio. Those were usually her current projects.

There were pictures of stylized furniture Darrius had never seen before and coordinated room groupings resembling fashion-forward furniture and textile coverings that he had seen in the mansion, expanding his imagination.

Darrius looked back at Samantha. "This is incredible."

Samantha shrugged. "Thanks. It's my adult playroom."

"I hope I'm not interrupting." Then, still awed by the sheer kaleidoscope of colors and textures, his eyes wandered back to the twelve-foot-long tapestries and rugs hanging from the ceiling.

"No, not at all. You're welcome to explore. Quentin and I are scheduled to relieve Dad and Mom and welcome family members."

Darrius shook his head. "Thanks, but we're short on time. It was a pleasure to meet you both." Darrius shook their hands again and he and Dena left, closing the studio door behind them. "Your sister is very creative and talented."

"Thanks. Sam enjoys what she does. She heads her own textile company. She got back from a world tour just before Thanksgiving last year."

They continued to the next double doors, but didn't knock before entering. When Dena opened the door, Darrius could do nothing but stop and stare. The shelves attached to the walls were filled with pottery at various stages of completion. Eight children of different ages sat before spinning wheels, fashioning wet clay into various shapes. Their concentration was so focused that they didn't look up when he and Dena entered.

For Darrius, this was like heaven. The scent of wet clay in the air and the sound of spinning pottery wheels had him itching to sit, wet his hands, and get to work. As he walked around the space, the colors in the different dried pottery pieces seemed to take on life.

Dena observed the light that sparked in the lieutenant's eyes. He was clearly fascinated when he picked up one piece of pottery and examined the artistry of the objet d'art that each piece purported to be.

He looked up and around before wandering the room again and speaking in a quiet voice. "I would never leave this studio. Your siblings are very talented. Their work is inspirational."

"Actually, we've all taken turns in here. My parents wanted us to be able to express ourselves in a number of creative ways. It also helped us identify things we enjoyed doing or what we may have had the talent to achieve. Unfortunately, I never gained the kind of patience this type of artistry and precision required. I did a little better with blowing glass, but not enough to stick with it. However, my younger brother and sister, Craig and Petra, who are twelve-year-old twins, are great at it. They have sold pieces at art shows and exhibits."

Darrius frowned at her. "You have a studio for blowing glass?"

"Yes, it's on an upper level because of the heat the process generates. I'll show it to you. It's probably in use, too, since our family members are making gifts for KiLe's life celebration tomorrow." She stopped and pulled her phone from her pocket to read the text message. "Uh, we'll have to do that later. My dad and brother are ready to examine the children. I have to bring them to the Med Suite."

Darrius was reluctant to leave the pottery studio. Instead, he pledged that he would make time to return later.

CHAPTER 15

Before the surgical procedures began, both Chuck and Vincent discussed what the examination and X-Ray revealed with Judge Alexander, Eve, Dena, and Lieutenant Pappas. Based on that report, the decision was made to immediately go forward with the removal of the devices for further examination.

Rather than take John and Jane to Chuck's medical office across the country road from the farm or to his hospital a few miles away, for security reasons, it was decided to treat the children at the farm's medical suite. It was as well-equipped as any treatment room in his hospital. After making the decisions, Vivian and her daughter, Eve, left the medical suite to attend to other matters. Darrius and Dena waited for the completion of the surgery.

Hours later, Dena paced the medical suite her father established in their home to treat minor ailments and injuries. Sometimes, her siblings, the household staff, or farmworkers needed emergency care for minor medical problems. However, in this case, her father and brother used the treatment area to remove the devices from John's and Jane's backs.

Darrius watched a monitor that showed the surgery underway in a sterile environment.

While they waited, Dena received several calls offering condolences for her loss. From the conversations Darrius overheard, she seemed popular and had many friends. She let some calls go to voicemail, but her face lit up when the Drew person called. Dena attempted to persuade him not to come to KiLe's funeral. However, Darrius was interested in seeing who he was and observing their interaction. So, he hoped that this Drew would still make an appearance. Darrius refused to question why it mattered but recognized that it did. She was so unique that it piqued his curiosity about the kind of man Doctor Montgomery might find intriguing.

Darrius never had trouble attracting female attention, but Doctor Montgomery didn't display any responses he was accustomed to receiving. That surprised him and pleased him. She wasn't the type of woman who let a man's outward appearance influence her. It was a sign that perhaps what interested her was what was on the inside…or maybe he just didn't appeal to her on any level. That was even more intriguing.

Darrius noticed that Dena didn't make idle conversation or participate in chitchat. Instead, she was quiet unless asked a question or received calls from her teaching assistants about class assignments or specific student questions. Darrius even got to see Doctor Dena Montgomery in action when she held a lecture session with nineteen advanced doctoral students for nearly an hour without the benefit of notes. However, even when speaking about or participating in Zoom meetings with MIT's department heads, she was precise and used an economy of words when speaking. Yet, she had a commanding personality and total control of her topic, even though she still looked like a kid who should still be in high school to him.

Darrius stood when the door opened and both doctors stepped out. Dena went to them and reached out. They both attempted to calm her concerns and led her to a table and chairs, where Darrius joined them.

Vincent held up two small clear glass containers and passed one to both Dena and Lieutenant Pappas. "We successfully removed these devices from the lower spine of John and Jane. I've never seen this specific model, but I believe it's made in Russia."

Dena frowned. "How do you know?"

Chuck took the one from Dena's hand and gave her the micro goggles he wore around his neck. "Put these on and focus on the indentations in the device."

Dena did as instructed. "Okay, I see the lettering, and I believe you're right, Dad. They look like Cyrillic letters to me. However, I'm not an expert, and I only learned to read some German words. Still, I don't understand what the devices do."

Vincent handed his goggles to Darrius, who frowned as he observed what looked to him to be about the size, color, and shape of an adult black widow spider with six legs for tentacles. "Any indication about the purpose of these devices?"

Vincent nodded. "I've seen devices similar to these used to deliver electronic shocks to the nerve system in arms, necks, and heads. The tentacles are essentially electrodes used to eclipse pain. It appears to me that, unlike their stated medicinal uses, these were used to administer pain. Usually, a pulse generator is implanted in the lower back, as these were, and an external remote control device sets the level of intensity. It's called electroconvulsive therapy or ECT.

"You see, a small electric current is passed through the brain, intentionally triggering a brief seizure. It causes changes in brain chemistry that can quickly reverse symptoms of certain mental health conditions. However, I have never heard of ECT used on four- to six-year-old children. It's monstrous to think of what John and Jane may have suffered. When administered in high electricity doses, ECT may lead to memory loss or amnesia, fractured bones, and other serious side effects."

Dena's anger was palpable. "Do you believe any serious or long-term damage was inflicted on John and Jane?"

Vincent took Dena's hand across the table. "Dad and I gave both children thorough examinations. Based on his bone structure, we believe that John may still be about five years old. Jane may be four years old, but they have been malnourished for so long that their normal growth rates could have been impacted. Still, we agree that they seem to be all right in the motor system and brain functions except for the dehydration and malnutrition they experienced before you found them. However, there is one other interesting thing that we discovered."

Dena frowned. "What is it?"

"They both have the same blood type. Rh-null,"

Dena inhaled sharply. "Like Linda and Bradley, Dad?"

"Yes, I'm afraid so. However, I stored Linda's blood, but Vincent and I didn't have to give transfusions to John or Jane. Vincent's incisions to extract the devices are less than the size of a dime. There doesn't appear to be any indication of disease involving the children at this point."

Darrius frowned. "I don't understand. What does having this Rh-null blood type mean?"

When Dena looked at him, Darrius realized that whatever this meant was extremely serious.

"Rh-null is a rare blood type, and very few people worldwide are known to have it. However, my sister, Linda, is one of them, and her biological half-brother, Bradley, is another. Several years ago, Bradley had a severe case of aplastic anemia. Linda saved Bradley's life by giving him her hematopoietic stem cells from her bone marrow."

Darrius frowned. "Linda is the sister you mentioned who is a prima ballerina and ice-skating Olympian?"

"She is, yes."

"This question is a bit off-topic, but is that what ended her career?"

Dena shook her head. "No, both Linda and Bradley had full recoveries from the surgical procedures, thanks to our dads. Linda used Derrick's webbing procedure to lengthen her career. She can still perform and does for charity events. Chuck's swift diagnosis and ability to reach out to medical specialists worldwide was the catalyst that saved Bradley.

Darrius continued to frown. "I've never heard of this."

Still angry over what these two tender-aged children must have suffered, Dena sighed. "I hadn't either until Dad diagnosed the problem for Bradley."

Chuck rubbed his daughter's shoulder to comfort her, but spoke to the lieutenant. "Aplastic anemia is a rare disease, and, as I said, bone marrow and the hematopoietic stem cells that reside there were damaged in Bradley. This caused a deficiency of all three blood cell types: red, white, and platelets. Aplastic refers to the inability of the stem cells to generate mature blood cells. It's most prevalent in people in their teens and twenties. So, Vincent and I don't believe that John and Jane will have a problem in the near future the way it happened to Bradley. It can be caused by heredity or immune disease, exposure to chemicals, drugs, or radiation. We will ensure that John and Jane are never exposed to those triggers. Normal bone marrow has thirty to seventy percent blood stem cells, but in aplastic anemia, these cells are mostly gone and replaced by fat."

Darrius stood and paced, running his right hand through his thick pelt of black hair. "What's more puzzling to me concerns two children who are not biologically related to having this rare blood."

Vincent shoved his hands in his pockets. "You're right, Lieutenant. When we checked their DNA, we established that John is Cuban and Jane is from the bayou area in Louisiana. They don't have any relatives in common. However, one or both of their biological parents likely have Rh-null blood."

"Then Doctor Montgomery…I mean, Dena Montgomery was correct. She offered that suggestion the same night she found the children in the alley."

Dena shook her head. "I did a six-month study on the migration of peoples of color in the Caribbean. Based on that study, it was a guess about where the children originated. However, I'm glad to have their origins verified by DNA results. Now we must find a way to anonymously compare the children's DNA to people in those areas to find their parents."

Darrius shook his head and put up his hands. "I would hold off on searching for their biological parents until we determine why they were taken. Did either of you discover that the children were sexually abused?"

Chuck and Vincent regarded one another and shook their heads. "No," said Chuck, "they were physically mistreated, but it didn't appear from our examinations that either child was sexually abused."

Darrius rubbed his chin. "Then, at least we can presume that the children were not used for that purpose. However, that leaves me with the impression that their abduction is related to their rare blood type."

Dena frowned. "I don't disagree with your theory, but I still question for what purpose is their blood type a key to the reason for their abduction?"

Vincent spoke up carefully. "Dena, organs are harvested all the time for transplants. I've done those surgeries myself to save a child's life. However, all of the organs I've used for transplants came through the US government's National Organ Transplant Programme or the United Network for Organ Sharing (OPTN). It's a private, non-profit organization that serves as the nation's organ transplant system—the Organ Procurement and Transplantation Network—under contract with and oversight by the federal government."

The implications slammed into Dena's brain like a body blow, no matter how delicately her brother delivered the information. Yet, her anger spiked visibly. "Over my dead body, will either of these children be harmed!"

Just then, the door to the Med Suite waiting area opened and Eve and Althea stepped in. Eve frowned, noticing Dena's heightened state as she paced with a scurrilous frown on her face and her hands on her hips. "Apparently, the surgery is over?"

Chuck nodded to his daughter, Eve, and handed the glass containers to her. "Here are the devices that we removed. Vincent established that these are gadgets that can be used to administer pain. Determining whether they are also miniature tracking devices is up to you."

Eve took the containers and smiled her appreciation to her father and brother. "Lieutenant, I want you and Dena to come with me while Dad and Vincent see to the children. Aunt Althea will stay with them until they wake up."

Vincent stood, arms akimbo. "We'll keep them sedated throughout the night and evaluate their conditions in the morning. We can keep them relatively pain-free with topicals."

Dena hugged her father and brother and then left with Eve and the lieutenant.

Darrius followed Eve and Dena. "Where are we going?"

Eve jogged down a staircase. "We want to look at the devices in the science lab."

Darrius frowned. "Science lab? You have one of those here?" He shook his head. "Of course you do. I don't know why I asked, but who is the 'we' you're referring to?" As they traversed a hall, Darrius realized that this was not part of the Alex-Mont mansion area that Dena showed to him on their earlier tour. His curiosity was further piqued when they went to a door that required a coded sign-in on the door panel and a handprint on a scanner. Dena also coded in with a handprint. Darrius was also asked to place his hand on the scanner.

Dena waited while Eve went through the necessary access coding. "We have curious young minds in our family. Although research and experimentation are encouraged, those projects are conducted under strict adult supervision. Anyone of my brothers, Spencer, Darren, Andrew, and Vincent, Dad, and I know and understand chemical reactions and the periodic table of chemical elements. So we keep this door passcoded so that it is only used if one or more of us is with our younger siblings to work on projects for class." When done, Eve gave an authorization with a series of numbers.

When the door opened, people Darrius didn't recognize met them in the interior hallway.

Eve made the introductions. "Lieutenant Darrius Pappas, this is my uncle, Kenneth Alexander, the head of CompuCorrect Global and two of his sons, Kenny and Kevin. Kenny works in CCG's research and development department and Kevin is on the product management team."

Darrius offered his hand to Dena's uncle and twin cousins. "Yes, Althea Hardyston mentioned your Silicon Valley tech firm to me." Darrius marveled at the tall, fit-looking father and sons. Like his sister, Judge Vivian Alexander Montgomery, Kenneth Alexander didn't appear to be old enough to have twin adult sons. However, except for the lighter skin tones, his sons had the look of their father. Darrius also remembered that Kenneth's wife is the current junior senator from California, JeNelle Towson Alexander.

Eve continued. "We also have my cousin and family attorney, Donald Dixon, my aunt, Admiral Stacy Greene Alexander, and one of Richardson Security's top operatives, Avilla Montenegro.

"Lieutenant, while you and I continue to focus on our original investigation, Avilla will focus more of her time on investigating KiLe's death."

Darrius shook hands with each person. He noted that Kenneth Alexander and Donald Dixon had a striking resemblance to one another.

They could have passed for brothers. Also, the admiral's impressive display of ribbons and medals on her fit US Navy uniform did not outshine how beautiful she was. Still, Darrius noticed that all the family members wore the same gold chain, which spelled *FAMILY*. Even Dena's necklace had been repaired or replaced, but he couldn't dwell on these disparate issues as he had to tune into what Eve was saying.

"Uncle Kenneth, here are the devices that Dad and Vincent removed from the lower spine of the two children Dena rescued."

Kenneth smiled warmly at his niece and kissed her forehead. "Good job, kid."

The rest of her family followed suit, hugging her and praising her skill used to save the children. Then, Kenneth and his sons donned white protective coveralls, hair coverings, and masks before entering a sterile, glass-enclosed white room. Monitors were activated and powerful cameras magnified and scanned the interior of the devices. Next, Kenneth and his sons dissected one of the devices.

Kenny looked to his father, who nodded and then to his twin, who also nodded. Then he looked up at the camera. "These devices are manufactured in Russia by a company known as Via Straker. The facility is believed to be owned by a Russian oligarch. They also contain a short-ranged tracking device."

Chapter 16

After Kenny Alexander locked the devices in a science lab vault, he joined the others in a comfortable salon on the main floor to discuss their discovery.

Dena lit the sleek, six-foot-long, hot water vapor fireplace, and warm moisture filtered into the air, taking away the chill. Then she got everyone cold water bottles from the concealed refrigerated beverage cabinet. Her uncle and cousin, Kenneth and Donald, beckoned her to sit between them on one of the sofas.

Donald Dixon took a sip of water and regarded his young cousin. "Kenny, what more can you tell us?"

Kenny shrugged. Like his father's and twin brother's, his voice was deep. "Not a great deal more. I can tell you about the engineering of those devices, but Kevin can do a deeper dive into the company and industry."

Kevin cleared his throat. "As we've discussed, Via Straker is a Russian R&D company. I mean, a diversified research and development company. CompuCorrect Global is a direct competitor of Via Straker in some industries, particularly in transportation services and power engineering. They are also into the oil and gas industry and high-level finance. We, I mean CompuCorrect Global and its subsidiaries, are strictly into the new technologies, like solar energy, geothermal energy, and wind turbines, not fossil fuels. CompuCorrect does all its banking through Uncle Gregory's New York Wall Street firm, CTI. However, we also invest in certain African banking institutions, but we don't use any banks in or connected to Russia."

Darrius spoke up. "CTI?"

Kevin looked at Darrius. "CTI stands for Compliant Trading and Investment, Incorporated. It's a brokerage house, banking institution, and business insurance underwriter."

"This is the Wall Street company owned by your uncle, Gregory Alexander, the basketball player?"

"Former basketball player. Uncle Gregory retired from playing professional sports several years ago. He received his undergrad and masters' degrees at the University of Virginia and its Darden School of Business. Before he ended his career in sports, he was a founding member of the business entity. CTI is an equal partnership between Margo Chandler, Troy Jackson, Jeremy Lightfoot, China McAlister-Goins, and Joyce Montgomery-Callaway."

Recognizing some of the partnership surnames, Darrius decided he'd investigate that information later. For now, he didn't want to delay the dissemination of this information. So, he nodded and Kevin continued.

"What is known is that the Via Straker facility is owned by a Russian oligarch. However, because of its diversity, the owner is shrouded by many shell companies. So, who is at the top of the food chain is unclear. Dad has been around longer than my brother and me," he joked. "So he might be able to provide further insight into Via Striker."

Kenneth smirked good-naturedly at his son. "Yeah, and who dunked on whom?" Kenneth grinned and both Kenny and Kevin looked properly chagrinned before he continued. "*However*, over the years since CompuCorrect began operations, various people aligned with Via Straker have contacted me to forge a partnership in our aerospace industry products. More recently, they wanted to piggyback with transponder space on CompuCorrect's geostationary satellites for long-ranged tracking. One of their proposals claimed to be a scientific research program to identify weather patterns over Russia.

"We, CompuCorrect Aerospace, denied the request like other tech firms with satellite ownership or access. CompuCorrect's refusal was primarily based on the fact that we didn't have a clear view of who we were dealing with.

"Secondarily, transponder space on our satellites could potentially give them unintentional access to US federally protected data. CompuCorrect

Global and our aerospace subsidiary have contracts with various domestic and foreign enforcement agencies. We're unwilling to share transponder space with companies with shadow interests and ownership."

Donald chimed in. "I recall discussing this company related to the Santangelo Sanction years ago."

Donald also recalled, more recently, *the murder of three people in Simon Wilde's home. One of the murder victims was international financier Calvin Chapman, the former husband of Texas heiress JaiHonnah Hawkins Baylor. Eve was the DC police detective assigned to investigate the murder and protect Simon Wilde. She uncovered evidence that certain Russians murdered the three people in Simon's home and were trying to murder Simon.*

As an internationally known, award-winning investigative reporter, Simon discovered valuable intelligence that he used to expose malfeasance through his father's Wilde Star Media and Communications Conglomerate of satellite-delivered television networks, magazines, and newspapers. They also had a substantial presence in their own social media distribution centers. As a result, several international factions wanted to silence Simon, particularly dictators and other duplicitous global leaders.

Avilla stepped into that case, as did Simon's former SEAL team, to help Eve foil the plan to murder him. Nevertheless, Eve and Simon are now in love and planning to marry in June.

For Donald, this new threat hit too close to JaiHonnah's sister and his agent, heiress LaiLoni Hawkins Logan, aka Dakota Sinclair, aka Wind Breeze. Both Hawkins' sisters were the daughters of Texas multibillionaire, Jake Hawkins. Currently, Jake is the US Ambassador to the Republic of Seychelles in Africa.

Several years ago, his eldest son, Jacob Hawkins, endangered Jake and his family by creating an international kidnapping incident involving many American businessmen and women. He was in an alliance with Tyler McKinzie Montrose, III. Jacob was attempting a hostile takeover to wrestle away BlackHawk Holding, the company owned by his father and managed by his sister, JaiHonnah, and her husband, J. Roderick Baylor.

However, Tyler Montrose III was negotiating with international terrorists to have his son-in-law, Ambassador Jefferson Logan, murdered.

Thereby, he could take control of Logan's sons and the multibillion-dollar conglomerate they inherited from their deceased mother. Because the three Logan boys resulted from an interracial marriage, Tyler Montrose III planned that they, too, would be killed before they reached the age of sixteen.

Wind Breeze thwarted her older brother's and Tyler Montrose's plans. As the instigator, Tyler Montrose was tried and convicted of treason. He was imprisoned and recently died while incarcerated. Tyler's eldest grandson, thirteen-year-old Jefferson Montrose Logan, inherited the multibillion-dollar monolith, Montrose Global.

Kenneth regarded Donald directly across Dena, Derrius noted and felt an undercurrent transmit between them. Of course, he would not have noticed if he weren't keeping an eye on Dena for her reaction to the discussion. Or, at least, that was what Darrius told himself about his continued attention to her.

He sat quietly listening to this discussion about potential multibillion-dollar trade deals and marveled at the level of insight the younger generation in this family possessed. The twins, Kenny and Kevin, looked like they were still in college or grad school and somewhere in their early twenties. Yet, they were permitted to participate in programs people twice their age had not experienced.

Again, Darrius looked at Doctor Dena Montgomery. Like her siblings and cousins, she was immersed at a very young age in academics to stimulate their brains, cultural options to create a well-rounded personality, and physical activity to hone their bodily skills. This understanding further solidified for Darrius that the Alexanders and their immediate relatives were a very supportive and cohesive group. However, the identical gold chain continued to pique his curiosity.

Donald looked around the room at his family members and then at Avilla Montenegro and Darrius Pappas. He was familiar with Agent Montenegro, but Pappas was an unknown entity. Avilla came through Stacy Greene's secret all-female Navy SEAL and Mossad-trained group. Despite her primary role as a security expert for Richardson Investigations and Security, a high-tech private security firm, Avilla remained in covert ops in the Nursery, The Nations United in Security, and the World Security Network created by the G7. In addition, Avilla still led her all-female warriors for special ops missions when required.

Admiral Stacy Greene's position is in the US Navy's Office of Naval Intelligence (ONI). The ONI is responsible for the nation's premier source of maritime intelligence. Her tasks were broadened to include real-time reporting on the developments and activities of foreign navies. To facilitate her responsibilities, she created all-female tiger teams to protect maritime resources and interests; monitor and counter transnational maritime threats; provide technical, operational, and tactical support to the US Navy and its partners; and survey the global maritime environment.

As one of the critical directors responsible for leading intelligence collection, covert operations, and counter-terrorism plans in The Nursery, Stacy Greene brought Avilla and many other females into covert and special ops when they were very young and personally trained them to be warriors.

Everyone, including Avilla, knew the significance of the San Angelo Sanction, except one: the police lieutenant from Cambridge, Massachusetts. Donald had read FBI Deputy Chief Jenna Baker's thorough dossier on Pappas. He had an impressive career in law enforcement, an open mind to new and novel problem-solving techniques, and a creative bent toward expressing himself in clay and blown glass.

Yet, he was quite a ladies' man, more like a James Bond persona and very chic in his style of dress. From an early age in Greece, the women seemed to fall at his feet. He took advantage of women fawning over his impressive physique and handsome face. Still, although he tended to date frequently, he never dated more than one woman at a time. He clearly respected the women he knew intimately, but never got close to any woman for long. When he began a relationship, he was the type of man who was looking for the next goodbye. More recently, Pappas was involved with the Cambridge police SVU leader, Alana Fulton. That was until he discovered she was in a long-term, intimate relationship with his married boss, Captain Russ Noland. That was when Pappas dropped Alana Fulton like a bad habit.

Yet Donald was curious about Pappas's level of integrity. For some reason, Pappas reminded him of himself at times during his life. Donald had many loveless liaisons until Cecile Elizabeth Jordan captured his heart and soul. She became his wife, his center, his alpha and omega, now and forever.

So, Donald was determined to discover more about the man since Pappas was, to his keen insight, impressed with his brilliant young cousin, Dena. Donald was also determined that Pappas would not add Dena as just another notch on his bedpost.

Still, the lieutenant's assets could be useful to The Nursery, as Bill Chandler's good looks and sex appeal are as a member of The Nursery's sandbaggers units. So, he would test his theory. "Lieutenant Pappas, do you have a theory about the devices?"

Darrius leaned forward in the wine-colored, wide leather chair with his elbows braced on his widely spread knees. He held his empty water bottle between the fingers of his right hand. "I have thoughts, but they are unrelated to the devices at this time."

Donald's brows furrowed. "All right, what are your thoughts about this case?"

Darrius stood, walked to a trash receptacle, and dumped the empty water bottle. Then he stuck one hand in his pocket and raked the other hand through his thick hair. "I don't believe that the case of the abducted children and the death of Mrs. KiLe Montgomery are related."

Eve frowned. "I thought that you agreed that KiLe was murdered."

Darrius stood, rubbing his chin. "I agree with you there, Lieutenant Montgomery. Yes, her death was no accident. One and, more likely, two UNSUBs, I mean unknown subjects, forced her car off the road. There were three sets of tire tracks. It appeared that Mrs. Montgomery tried to stop, but the car that must have been tailing her slammed into her from the rear and pushed her car forward at a very high rate of speed. A second car came around to her left side and crowded her to the edge of the road. They were not trying to stop her. There was black ice on the road, but only Mrs. Montgomery's car left skid marks. The other two cars didn't try to stop. Instead, they boxed her in so she couldn't speed up or avoid being pushed off the road into the gully. There were guard rails in some spots, but they waited until they reached a critical point to send her flying off the road and into the trees. If it weren't for the destruction on the car's rear and left side, it would appear that she hit black ice, skidded off the road, and went airborne into the trees."

Donald regarded the lieutenant more closely. "Then why do you believe that these two things are unrelated?"

"The timing is off. You see, my detective brought Doctor Dena Montgomery and the children to the police station less than an hour after the murder. We were on a flight out of town in less than two hours. It was after we landed in Pennsylvania that the van was discovered on fire with the perps, I mean perpetrators, inside. The UNSUBs may have gotten the information about what happened in the alley from the perps, but the children were in the station by then. The short-range tracking device would not have been able to follow them."

Kenny chimed in. "That's correct. The tracking aspect of the device was only effective within a few hundred feet of the children."

"Exactly. Of course, the UNSUBs could determine which precinct caught the case, but again, we were likely on our way out of town by the time they could figure that out. Other than the 9-1-1 call to dispatch, we didn't have time to enter anything significant in the police data system. Also, the FBI scrubbed the data from the police department's computer system in less than an hour.

"Now we have impostors looking for me, I believe, because I'm the only lieutenant in Homicide who is not in the office."

Eve spoke up. "The FBI has backdated a leave request from you, Lieutenant. Just in case someone was tracking you, a person claiming to be you boarded a flight out of Boston to Greece with your passport and credentials. He's an FBI agent who resembles you enough that no one will be able to tell the difference. He knows how to avoid the cameras, and in some locations, the FBI has ensured that the video equipment is undergoing repair or updating. So it would appear to anyone attempting to follow you that you're off on vacation to your homeland."

Darrius nodded in appreciation of the FBI's thorough work. "The FBI has covered every conceivable aspect to keep this case off the radar. So, the UNSUBs have no reason to target Doctor Dena Montgomery or her family."

Donald frowned. "I've seen the video of Dena's rescue. What about the homeowners' security cameras used to capture the murder scene?"

Eve grinned. "Altered with a bit of movie magic. It's unclear whether the person involved in the altercation is a male or female. Dena had on all-black with her sweater covering most of her face, and her Stetson covered most of the rest. At no time is her entire face visible and the children have been completely removed from the video, along with Dena's grocery bag with the bodega's logo on it. It appears that one perp shot another, some Good Samaritan attempted to intervene, and the perps got away. So, it's likely that the recently deceased perps had no idea that their caped assailant was female.

"So, whoever killed the two perps and burned them to a crisp did so because they failed to furnish the two children. The perps killed the man at the original crime scene, which tied up several loose ends about what happened to the products, namely the children."

Darrius splayed his hands. "The UNSUBs would come to a dead-end, pardon the pun, with no place to follow up or a thread to pull. Moreover, they know nothing about Doctor Dena Montgomery and the children, her flight to Pennsylvania, and her destination here in Maryland. Therefore, there is no reason to target KiLe Montgomery."

Donald tilted his head. "Except if they have satellite service access."

Darrius shook his head. "There was heavy cloud cover in advance of the nor'easter. Even when we flew out of the remote airfield, we climbed through the thick clouds. So, even if satellites were passing directly over Cambridge, they would not have been able to penetrate the heavy cloud cover."

Donald leaned forward in his seat, resting his elbows on his knees, steepling his fingers. "Good point. Eve?"

She slowly nodded, seeming to come to the same agreement. "I believe that Lieutenant Pappas may be correct."

Donald regarded his young cousin. "Okay, Dena, you were closest to KiLe academically. Tell us what you know of her research."

"KiLe was brilliant. She was offered an opportunity to join a group for advanced studies in science and technology."

Donald interjected, holding up a finger. "I believe that invitation from Mensa came as a result of your recommendation, didn't it, Dena?"

Dena shrugged. "Yes, I'm a member. The group KiLe joined worked under the auspices of Mensa. It's the largest and oldest high-IQ society in the world. We're a non-profit organization open to people who score at the 98th percentile or higher as KiLe did on standardized, supervised IQ and other approved intelligence tests. As you may already know, Mensa is comprised of national groups and the umbrella organization, Mensa International. KiLe was at the top of her group academically." Dena shook her head. "I don't think the other students competing against KiLe for top honors were willing to kill her to get her out of the way."

Kenneth cocked his head to the side. "You studied there and wrote mathematical theories for what, two years?"

"It was more like eighteen months, Uncle Kenneth. I helped KiLe through her minor in Science, Technology, and International Affairs offered by Georgetown in connection with the School of Foreign Service. It was KiLe's passion to work in the international arena. Since the program is designed to provide policymaking training to students with a strong math and science background, KiLe felt that she perfectly fit the requirements. All students majoring in a program offered by Georgetown's Department of Biology, Chemistry, Computer Science or Physics are eligible to pursue the minor. The interns were focused on Science and Technology in the Global Arena, Principles of Microeconomics, International Relations, Energy; Business, Growth and Development; Biotechnology and Global Health; and Science, Technology and Security. The internship counted toward KiLe's master's degree program and she nailed it with flying colors. She was in the top one percent of the program. It also guided her doctoral study.

"KiLe was happy and intrigued by the possibility of having only a few more months to receive her doctorate. She felt that perhaps this would help convince her parents to accept her decision to stay in America to complete her education. It hurt KiLe that her parents disowned her, but she was not sorry for her decision to marry Brian. She was over the moon in love with him and their boys she loved fiercely. She read stories to them about their Japanese heritage and was teaching them to speak Japanese."

Eve nodded. "Okay, we'll pursue both cases along separate tracks and re-evaluate the facts as more intelligence becomes available. Lieutenant Pappas has the lead on the Massachusetts case and Avilla has the lead on KiLe's murder here in Maryland."

"Good." Donald rose from his seat and eyed Avilla. She knew what he expected of her. "Keep us informed." He was impressed with Pappas and, as he glimpsed Stacy Greene Alexander, he noticed her nod in apparent agreement. Pappas had no idea that he was being vetted for a possible offer to join The Nursery. This salon was chosen because it was wired for sound and video. Slade Richardson, Simon Wilde, and Bill Chandler were watching this discussion from different remote locations as a part of the vetting process. Donald expected to receive a thumbs up or down from Avilla, Slade, Simon, Stacy, and Bill. If all were in agreement, Pappas would unknowingly undergo further scrutiny, likely from Bill Chandler.

Bill asked for another trainee since his law practice was so large now that he spent most of his time away from Washington, DC, his home base. He wanted to train someone new to take on more of his covert activities globally, and Donald agreed to Bill's proposal. To his way of thinking, Donald believed that Darrius Pappas was shaping up to be a candidate for Bill's trainee. Bill was on his way, and they would discuss Pappas when he arrived at the farm.

Eve and Darrius nodded as the meeting began to break up, and the people left the room.

For some reason, Darrius felt Donald Dixon was more than just the Alex-Mont family's attorney. He had a warrior's bearing and an edginess that defined him as potentially dangerous. Though outwardly, he resembled a well-dressed, physically fit attorney, there was something that made Darrius feel that this Donald Dixon could command legions.

Darrius turned to find Dena in the departing group, but she was moving rapidly with her cell phone to her ear. He wanted to ask her to continue their tour of the lower levels of the mansion. However, Avilla Montenegro got his attention by easing up in front of him, blocking his view.

"Lieutenant, let's remain here and discuss what you witnessed at the roadside accident."

She moved to the tufted wine-colored leather sofa, crossed her impressive legs comfortably, and patted the seat beside her, designating a space for him to sit.

With no opportunity to follow Dena, his protected witness, he sighed and moved toward the sofa, prepared to brief the case to date. However, he caught Agent Montenegro's salacious once-over and recognized her appreciative view for what it was: pure lust. He was accustomed to women coming on to him, and, if he were in the mood, he accepted their overtures for one-night stands. Avilla Montenegro's physical attributes were generous and alluring and fit his usual type. She looked to be of Mediterranean extract with a head full of thick black curly hair that framed a face that should be on the cover of fashion magazines. His eyes were drawn to her dark, expressive eyes to a fleshy mouth that begged to be ravished.

Everything about Agent Avilla Montenegro screamed hot, wet, sexual pleasure. Yet, his thoughts went to the kid, Doctor Dena Montgomery.

CHAPTER 18

Dena quickly went to her bedroom suite on the second floor. First, she put on her black leather chaps, a Christmas gift from Brian and KiLe, over her jeans. Then, after grabbing and fitting on an old pair of riding boots on her feet, she picked up her mud-brown Stetson from a shelf in her walk-around closet. Next, she searched for and found an old floor-length brown duster, a pair of riding gloves, and an orange and brown wool scarf her Nana Sylvia had knitted for her several years earlier.

When Dena reached the garage barn door, Brian was riding up on one of their thoroughbreds, Star Gazer, and leading another of their thoroughbreds, King. She took the lead from him and fluidly boosted herself into the saddle. They had to hold back their mounts as they trotted carefully around where farmhands were working. Nevertheless, their horses had the spirit to race. That was likely why Brian chose them for their outing. When they reached open fields still covered with a few inches of fresh snow, they let them trot. Then, since they couldn't easily see any rocks, gopher holes, or fallen tree limbs among the waist-high winter wheat and weeds, they headed to the seventy-two-hole professional golf course at Havenhurst Estates to let their horses have their heads. The horses moved as if a gale-force wind lifted them across the open fairway. Because of the snow, the golf course was closed for a few days. Brian and Dena weren't racing against one another. Instead, they shared their grief with a hard, fast ride.

KiLe and Dena were close. Since Dena already had her doctorate, she helped coach KiLe through her research. They had become close friends as well as sisters-in-law, and they were about the same age.

Dena keenly felt KiLe's loss, so when Brian pulled Star Gazer to a stop and let out his grief in a howl, Dena did the same. Then, they dropped the reins, opened their arms wide with their faces turned up to the heavens above, and freed their pain in tears and cries while the horses started running again.

Deep in the woods on one of the bridle paths, they dismounted, sat on a fallen tree, and linked arms. Dena laid her head on her brother's muscular shoulder, and he placed his head against the crown of hers.

"Brian, I know there is nothing I can say or do to make KiLe's loss less painful, but I want to try. What can I do for you?"

"You're doing it, kid. Just being here for me helps. You and I like to ride regardless of the temperature or the weather conditions. I needed to break away for an hour or two. Then, I realized that I shouldn't go alone. I didn't want to worry the family unnecessarily. That's why I called you. Getting on a horse and going for a ride with you helped.

"After Vincent, Roger, Ryan, and I left the morgue, I kept thinking about the laundry that had yet to be finished. KiLe and I did all the housework together. We danced when we dusted and swept and mopped the floors. We could clean the kitchen and bathrooms with no sweat, but we both hated to do the laundry. So, we let it pile up until the boys and we were almost out of clean clothes, sheets, and towels.

"Last night, after we read to the boys and put them to bed, we started doing the laundry while we relaxed in the whirlpool tub. Still, there was so much of it that we didn't finish before we went to bed.

"We were up early this morning and planned to finish the task, but KiLe jumped my bones, and we got busy before the boys woke up. Then after we showered and dressed for the day, KiLe, with one hand on her hip, shook a finger of her other hand at the washing machine and fussed because she said that it ate the boys' socks." Brian smiled at the thought. "She was so cute when confused and frustrated with appliances or inanimate objects. She never had to use that type of equipment until we married. She's always had someone to do her laundry, cooking, and cleaning for her. Even when she lived in Georgetown, Anna handled those household chores for the students.

"So, before I left to take the boys to school, I had to disconnect the drain hose, and low and behold, there were three tiny pairs of socks stuck in the drain. If she hadn't made a fuss over the missing socks, the washing machine or the tub might have overflowed and flooded the laundry room. Then I really would have had a mess to clean up.

"However, KiLe laughed like a loon and jumped my bones again before I could get up off the floor." Tears slid down Brian's face and froze on his cheeks. "By the time she let me up off the floor, and I finished reconnecting the hose, we were both running late. KiLe said she didn't plan to be at school past noon because she wanted to spend some quality time with the boys today. So she planned to finish the laundry when she got home and then pick up the boys early from school. I asked her to call me when she got home, and I told her I'd come home to help finish the laundry and put the clothes away.

"This ride helped me clear my head for the next steps and stages of grief. Everyone is pitching in to help me through this initial shock. Right now, I don't know what to think or feel. Still, I've got to pull myself together for my boys. KiLe would want me to be there for our sons. In any event, I'm not naïve. I know the grieving process won't end just because I finished a task that KiLe and I started. You and I were still very young, but we watched Mom go through the heartache of losing Derrick. It took many years for mom to open her heart again and accept Chuck's love. Even now, I don't think that mom and Chuck have stopped grieving for Derrick's loss."

"Like you and KiLe, Mom and Chuck have a forever kind of love. Still, you're right. It took Mom five years to be able to open her heart to Chuck and fall in love again. Chuck was Derrick's best friend, but he was in love with Mom before he introduced Mom to Derrick. He was still in love with her for all those years after Derrick's death. KiLe would not want you to be alone, Brian. She loved you too much to want to see you suffer. If it were you we lost instead of KiLe, would you want her to go on and find happiness again?"

Brian lifted tear-drenched eyes to Dena and nodded. Then he enclosed her in a tight squeeze, kissing her forehead. They continued to talk and shared their sorrow.

Over an hour later, the sun was going down in the west when Brian and Dena returned to one of the horse barns. First, they unsaddled their mounts, stored their gear, and inspected their horses' hooves, using a pick to clean out any debris from under their shoes. Stable hands then took over the feeding and currying of Star Gazer and King. Finally, Brian and Dena linked one arm around each other while walking toward the mansion. Halfway there, they stopped and kissed each other on both chilled cheeks.

"Thanks, kid, I needed that."

"So did I, brother mine. We'll see you and the boys for dinner?"

Brian nodded and then peeled off with his hands dug in his pockets, following the path to his cabin. Farmhands offered their condolences, but otherwise didn't bother Brian with work-related issues. Dena watched him go and wondered whether she should go with him. However, her emotions were still raw, and Brian didn't need to carry her grief, too. So, she continued to stroll toward home.

Although it was getting dark, Dena wasn't quite ready to go inside. She put one booted foot on the split-rail fence that boarded the rise overlooking the lake in front of the main house. Breathing deeply from the icy-cold air scented with pine trees, she stood watching headlights from the mobile homes pull in and park around the opposite side of the lake. Before long, Dena knew that their extended Alexander, Jackson, and Montgomery families would be there by the morning for the celebration of KiLe's life.

When Dena heard footsteps approaching, she turned to see her maternal grandparents, Bernard and Sylvia Benson Alexander, jogging up the rise toward her. Following them were her cousin, Whitney Ivy Alexander-Cavenaugh, and her US Marine physician husband, Tucker. In no time, Dena found herself engulfed in warm hugs and many kisses on chilled cheeks.

Dena beamed at the foursome and wiped away her tears. "You've been out jogging, I see."

Her grandfather, Bernard, tall and fit, tucked her under his arm for an additional squeeze. "We didn't get to run earlier today before leaving

South Carolina to drive here. By the time we arrived, it was getting dark, so we didn't go that far."

Sylvia shrugged. "We needed to stretch after such a long drive, but we only did ten miles round trip. We were starting back when we ran into Whitney Ivy and Tucker."

Whitney's sad smile was evident on her gorgeous light *café au lait* face. "Tucker and I just got in from Germany and needed a good stretch, too."

Dena reached for her cousin's hand. "I'll bet you flew one of the jets here rather than take a commercial flight."

Tucker smiled, his movie-idol face, with deep blue eyes and dark blond hair, mesmerizing. "Have you met my wife? Whitney Ivy makes every opportunity to take her Cessna up for an hour or two at least once a week. We could have hopped on one of the military transports, but oh, no, not *my* wife. Have plane, will travel."

Whitney grinned. "I need the stress relief flying my jet allows me."

Dena frowned. "How is your law practice going? You must be busy learning to practice law in a foreign country."

Whitney sighed. "I'm loving it, but you're right. It's been challenging since I opened the foreign branch office for Alexander, Carter, Chandler, Charles, Lightfoot, and Towson, PA." She laughed, still excited about her career. "When the senior partners asked me to join the firm and focus on international law cases, just like Aunt Vivian did before becoming a judge, I was thrilled. I also took on some of the casework for Aunt Vivian's friend, attorney Thomas Ashton Marshall. He's of counsel to Alexander, Carter, so it's a good fit for me."

Bernard nodded. "I remember Thomas Marshall from when Vivian Lynn had cases before the international court in The Hague."

Sylvia smiled at her granddaughters and Tucker. "I remember him, too. Mr. Marshall is always in the news. Isn't his wife the judge who stepped into Vivian's judgeship at the Appellate Court level when Vivian was selected for the Supreme Court?"

Whitney Ivy smiled at her grandparents. "She is, yes. Judge Kristen Catherine Bryant-Marshall. She and Aunt Vivian were at Spelman together, and Aunt Vivian was instrumental in getting Mr. Marshall and Judge Bryant together. Now they have three children: two boys and a girl."

Bernard smiled at his granddaughters. "I remember meeting Thomas and Kristen at the party for Chuck's birthday."

Whitney Ivy smiled. "Yes, Granddad, they've been friends with Uncle Chuck and Aunt Vivian for many years. I've learned a lot about international law working with Thomas Marshall. That specialty involves multinational organizations, international courts and tribunals, and humanitarian issues. In addition, I've had to master new languages and court procedures quickly. So, I've been busy while Tucker is working at the hospital."

Dena cocked her head and scrutinized her cousin. "Really?"

Whitney Ivy eyed Dena curiously. "Yes. Why, Dena?"

"Have you learned to speak Russian?"

Whitney Ivy laughed and spoke a sentence in Russian. "I handled a preliminary case for Mr. Marshall against a group of Russian businessmen. So I've also learned to read and speak Russian. When Mr. Marshall came to court, his reputation preceded him. The Russians opted for a settlement rather than go up against him."

Dena smiled. *Wow!* You speak Russian very well. It's such a harsh-sounding language that I hope you didn't just curse me out."

Tucker laughed. "No, she just said let's go inside because it's as cold as a witch's…uh, you know what out here. Some things get lost in the translation."

Dena smiled. "You speak Russian, too, Tucker?"

"I do, yes. I get Russian patients at the military medical center in Germany, too. So Whitney Ivy and I are learning to speak and read German, Russian, and other languages together. Sometimes, Whitney Ivy and I will only speak to each other in another language for a week or two. It comes in handy for both of our careers. Now, I don't often need a translator when talking with a patient about their care."

Whitney Ivy added, "I've also worked for the Judge Advocate General's Corps, also known as JAG or JAG Corps. It's the legal branch or specialty of the military concerned with military justice and law.

Officers serving in the JAG Corps are typically called Judge Advocates. Being multilingual also helps when I take on cases as a JAG lawyer. The military tribunals are structured differently from the American court system. Plus, in my role in the international arena, the cases I litigate are usually contract-related, where I practice civil law.

"On the other hand, in the military tribunals, I can be assigned to take on prosecutorial trial work or defense work in criminal cases anywhere in the world where we have military bases. That means I have to defend or prosecute a case involving other countries. So those assignments give me experience in both the civil and criminal parts of the law, as well as speaking different languages.

"Because Tucker is a captain in the Marines, we discussed the ramifications of my volunteering to work for the JAG Corps. Still, seeing that my parents are both in the military, it was something to consider. Tucker's dad is an attorney, and we discussed it with him and Tucker's mom. We did the same with my parents and everyone gave me the green light. So, Tucker and I decided that volunteering my time with JAG is one way for me to serve my country, just as my parents and my husband do."

Tucker reached for Whitney Ivy's hand and drew her close to him for a quick kiss.

When Whitney Ivy looked up at her husband, Dena could see the deep abiding love shining in their eyes for one another. They were married only a few years and were still in their early twenties. Just as the love shone in her grandparents' eyes, she had seen the same chemistry in her parents' love affair and marriage. Her parents also held hands most of the time. This type of intense energy was what Dena wanted when or if she ever found her own life partner.

Whitney Ivy continued. "I'm busy, yes, but I've hired five attorneys. One of them is Roland Harrington. He and I were in law school together."

Dena gave a nod. "I remember him. Isn't he one of your former housemates, too?"

"He is, yes. He graduated in the top one percent of our law school class. I was lucky to get him to join me in Germany. The others I've hired are from different countries. They are valuable because we have cases to litigate in countries where they have experience."

Dena frowned. "Roland Harrington is from somewhere in the US Midwest, right?"

Whitney Ivy's brows beetled. "Ah, yes. Minnesota. You've got a good memory, cousin, for someone we call The Absent-Minded Professor."

Dena shrugged, grinning. "Not so much. I remember him because he had a thing for KiLe. One weekend before she and Brian married, Roland took KiLe to visit his home and parents because she hadn't seen much of the Midwest part of the country."

Whitney Ivy had an ah-ha moment. "You know, I had forgotten about that. I asked him to run the shop in my absence. He knew why Tucker and I were coming to the states so suddenly, but he didn't mention that he previously had a crush on KiLe."

Dena quirked a brow. "Maybe he's involved with someone else?"

Tucker nodded. "He is. She's a new OB/GYN specialist, Doctor Leslie Grant. I think she's from someplace like Idaho, Iowa, or another farming state. They seem to speak the same language and hit it off quickly. They met when a group from the medical center and Whitney Ivy's staff attorneys, about fifteen of us, went skiing when Eve and Simon came for a visit. Simon and his family ski at different resorts several times during the season. He knew of this great place on the slopes in Meissen in the Allgäu region of the Bavarian Alps. It is a beautiful country.

"Leslie and Roland are very good on the downhill slopes. We've also done some cross-country skiing. Simon recommended that we try Austria next because it offers the largest choice of skiing areas. So, we've formed a ski club and plan to visit several places like the Sölden ski resort. Next, we plan to go skiing after Thanksgiving, closer to the end of November. We hear that Val_Thorens can be a good option. You ought to come with us, Dena. Whitney Ivy told me that you and your guy friend, Alphonse, used to go skiing regularly in Switzerland at the Saas-Fee, Glacier Les Diablerets, the ski resort of Engelberg, and the glacier area in Laax."

Dena nodded. "We also did the runs on the Diavolezza glacier near St. Moritz. However, we're not in touch these days."

Bernard rubbed his granddaughter's shoulder. "Dena, you and Drew Hamilton are still close, aren't you?"

"We are, Granddad, but Drew is new to skiing. The slopes that Tucker and I mentioned are for skilled downhill racers. We've gone to the Poconos for long weekends, but Drew has to gain a lot more experience before he takes on the slopes that we usually ski in Europe."

When Sylvia drew her body tighter against the frisky, cold wind, Bernard put his arm around her shoulders and guided the group into the house as they continued to talk.

No one noticed Lieutenant Pappas on the balcony, within earshot of the conversation, as the family members continued to converse.

As soon as Dena entered the crowded great room, she stood on her toes and searched for Eve among those sitting or standing in groups, drinking wine, eating hot or cold hors d'oeuvres, and talking.

When Dena didn't spot her sister there, she weaved through her relatives in the common areas, several sitting rooms, the library, the den, and other open spaces on the primary level. Though often stopped for a quick chat or a hug, she didn't linger. Instead, Dena was on a mission. When she snaked through the connecting corridor to the anteroom adjacent to the ballroom, she found Eve. She was with their parents and other siblings at the wide, tall double-entry doors, welcoming newly arrived relatives. Quickly, Dena shouldered her way through the burgeoning crowd to whisper in Eve's ear.

Eve looked into Dena's eyes for ponderous moments before she nodded and got their mother's attention. "We'll be back shortly, Mom."

Vivian looked over Eve's shoulder and reached for and held Dena's hand. "It's a good thing you did going for a ride with your brother. He said it helped him pull himself together."

"The ride helped me, too, Mom. While I'm here, I hope we can ride together again."

"I'm glad to hear it." Then Vivian turned to acknowledge more family members as they approached the receiving line and nodded her consent for Eve and Dena to leave.

Rather than carve a path through the crowd of relatives and servers, they slipped into a secret staircase from the anteroom to the second-floor family bedroom level of the main house. It was the way servants moved unnoticed in the early 1800s. There were warrens like this throughout the house, and the Alex-Mont children used to have fun, traveling between floors unseen or playing hide-and-seek.

When Eve and Dena stepped out of a seemingly solid wall panel, Darrius jumped and reached for the weapon he wore at the small of his back.

"What the fuck!" Darrius frowned and ignored the mirth Eve and Dena attempted to quell. He stuck his head inside the stairwell and noticed that it didn't stop on the second floor, but continued up at least another level. Then Darrius turned back to the sisters, eyeing them closely. He shook his head and huffed. "Yeah, no, the Alex-Mont kids weren't angels."

Both Eve and Dena shrugged before Dena asked, "Were you exploring?"

"No, I was looking for you. I've been looking for you since the meeting broke up hours ago." Of course, he didn't need to mention that Avilla Montenegro wanted to take him to her bed to get better acquainted. He surprised himself when he turned down her proposal. She was undoubtedly in the group of women Darrius usually found attractive and enjoyed having a one-night stand in their beds. Yet, for some reason, he didn't *rise* to the occasion. He didn't think it had anything to do with his budding relationship with Gail Henley. However, as he gazed at Dena, he began to wonder. He didn't mention that he overheard her conversation with her grandparents and cousin, Whitney Ivy. He noted that Bernard and Sylvia Alexander were a handsome pair, but Whitney Ivy Alexander was drop-dead gorgeous. The more people he met in the Alexander and Montgomery families, there didn't seem to be anyone other than attractive relatives. Even more intriguing was that they were not arrogant about who they were or what they had achieved. He had never met a more selfless group of people in Greece or America before.

"I didn't know that you were looking for me, Lieutenant. Next time, call or send a text to me. I usually can be reached that way."

"If I had your cell phone number, I'd do that."

"Yes, that might be helpful." She held out her hand for his phone. When he handed it to her, she put her contact information in it and handed it back to him. "There you go. Why were you looking for me?"

"You're still my witness, so I'm responsible for your protection."

Dena strained to keep from laughing and sobered. "Okay, I apologize for not keeping in touch. I've been out riding horses with Brian. So, I need to shower and change for dinner. I'll be in my room for the next thirty minutes or so, and then I'll be in the ballroom. I'll make a point of looking for you as soon as I come downstairs. Until then, I have Eve to protect me. Does that work for you, Lieutenant Pappas, or do you want to stand sentry outside my bedroom door?"

He smirked at her, but his blood warmed when he thought of her wet and warm in a shower. So he nodded, checked his cell phone for the time, and set his alarm. "I'll see you in the ballroom. If you're longer than thirty-five minutes, I'll come looking for you." Then he walked away, leaving Dena Montgomery with a curious frown on her face. *Yeah, let her think about that*, he thought and grinned.

"Well, well," Eve crooned and ran her tongue over her teeth as she watched the lieutenant walk away. "I think you have an admirer, sister mine."

Dena shot her a disbelieving snort, "Yeah, right," and continued toward her bedroom suite. She began disrobing the moment she entered through the door.

Eve pulled her phone from her pocket, toed off her shoes, and reclined on Dena's bed. "So, what are you telling me about Whitney Ivy?" She began answering and sending text messages while she waited for her sister.

From the bathroom, while Dena showered and washed her hair, she told Eve about her conversation with their cousin. She also mentioned Whitney Ivy's and Tucker's abilities to read and speak Russian. "Whitney Ivy handled the preliminary trial work for Mom's friend, Thomas Ashton Marshall, on one of his cases. She dealt with Russian attorneys in court."

"Okay, so what does that have to do with the price of butter in China?"

"Well, Whitney Ivy is very good with research and details. So, I wondered whether she could figure out who is behind Via Striker and who bought the devices embedded in John's and Jane's bodies."

Eve frowned, considering, and momentarily stopped sending text messages. "You may have a good idea, but it's above my pay grade in this family. Though, I used to have the hots for Mr. Marshall when I was maybe a preteen. Were I you, I'd ask Donald or Uncle Kenneth about it before approaching Whitney Ivy." Eve resumed sending text messages.

"You're probably right, but this may be important. On the other hand, I don't want to do anything that might put Whitney Ivy or Tucker in harm's way."

"Yeah, especially after that lunatic tried to kidnap Whitney Ivy."

"You're right. I don't think Tucker will ever forget that his former commanding officer abducted Whitney Ivy, drugged her, and was about to send her out of the US in a shipping container."

Dena came out of the bathroom, wearing a robe with her hair wrapped in a terrycloth towel. "I don't think any of us will ever forget that we could have lost Whitney Ivy."

"Yeah, that's why we go into lockdown when a necklace is broken. Remember, that's how Aunt Stacy found Whitney Ivy when she purposefully broke her necklace."

Dena raised an eyebrow at her sister. "You're not going to let me forget that, are you?" She bent forward and began combing and brushing her hair with a small hand-held blow dryer attachment.

Eve laughed as she continued sending text messages. "Not on a bet, sister mine. You have a genius-level IQ, but you earned the title The Absent-minded Professor for very good reasons."

"*Ha Ha.* I'll talk with Donald and see what he thinks."

"Good move." She looked up at Dena. "You should leave your hair loose."

Dena frowned at Eve as she began to braid her hair starting at the crown of her head. She let her arms drop. "Why? I usually braid my hair when it's still damp."

"Yes, I know. Look, come sit on the bed and let me do it."

Dena continued to frown at her sister, but she did as instructed. Moments later, Dena stood and looked in the mirror. Her hair was naturally curly, thick, and wavy. Eve parted her hair on the right and swept it from the crown of her head to the left. It hung down over her shoulder. She shrugged. *It doesn't look bad,* she thought, but it waved and curled down to her waistline. Still, it was long and thick. It was a bother when it was loose like this and she hated to have to fool with it. That was why she kept it braided. It was less to worry about that way.

Eve handed a soft gray sweater-knit dress to Dena. "Here, put this on."

Dena's frown deepened. "Why?"

Eve sighed. "Just do it, kid, and hurry up. I told Mom that we'd be back shortly."

Dena huffed, but again did as she was told. Finally, however, when Eve wanted to pluck her eyebrows into shape and put makeup on her, Dena put her foot down and refused to do any of it. Still, Eve grabbed her face and put lip gloss on her mouth. Dena gave her sister the evil eye while she put on a pair of ox-blood-colored boots with skyscraper heels Eve insisted that she wear. It was not her idea of something to do. She groused because she'd be forced to walk on these stilts for hours while seeing to their family's comfort.

When Dena stood up, Eve beamed, pleased that her sister looked more sophisticated than she did wearing her usual favorite Western-inspired apparel. Then, Eve turned Dena around to look at herself in the full-length mirror.

It isn't a bad look, Dena thought, but she threw up her hands in resignation. Eve was a force to be reckoned with under ordinary circumstances, the toughest one of her sisters. So, Dena decided to suffer through the evening as Eve dictated.

Chapter 20

Darrius stood in the crowd, sipping an exceptional white wine and chatting with Dena's sister, Samantha, and her fiancée, Quentin King. They discussed the places she had exhibited her textiles in various Greek cities and what she found intriguing about his home country. Samantha was a fascinating woman who he found to be very personable yet confident. Samantha had a subtle sweetness about her and an understated beauty. He thought she differed significantly from Eve's and Dena's styles and statures. Yet, he could sense how they fit together as siblings.

Quentin King was an engaging conversationalist, too. He headed King Advertising, one of the largest agencies in the country. Darrius had heard of Quentin's younger brother, Samuel King, who ranked number one in men's tennis the previous year. However, Darrius hadn't heard that Samuel had retired from professional sports and opened a tennis school in San Diego, California. It rang a bell with Darrius because it was the part of America where he was considering relocating. Quentin had quite a bit of good information about that part of the country.

Then Linda, Samantha's older sister by ten months, joined them. Linda had a different style than her younger sisters, but Darrius easily recognized that she was a dancer. Although her body was slender, her musculature was pronounced. Still, it was hard to believe that she had given birth to two boys. He thought her body was perfection. That was until he noticed Linda and Samantha look over his shoulder and raised their eyebrows.

Darrius turned and almost didn't recognize the woman who approached them with Eve. For a ponderous moment, he didn't breathe, but just stared and swallowed hard. Dena didn't look like a kid anymore. Rather, she still reminded him of a come-to-real-life Barbie Doll in the body-hugging long knit dress. Yet, on the other hand, she could be walking the international runways in fashion-forward apparel. One shoulder and arm were bare, but the other had a sleeve covering her shoulder and arm down to the back of her hand. There was no bra strap and no imprint of panties on the body-molding, soft, gray knit dress. Dena still had that loose-jointed pace, but her gait was as sexy as a striptease dirty dance in the come-get-me booted heels. What he noticed was that she wasn't even trying to attract attention.

Nevertheless, heads turned as she passed through the crowd. Her long, thick, dark, waist-length hair curled and waved madly around her left shoulder, breast, and down her arm and back, leaving her right shoulder bare. When she reached him, Darrius breathed deeply of her exotic scent. He couldn't determine whether it was her shampoo or some perfume she wore.

Dena couldn't figure out why the lieutenant always seemed to stare at her as if she were a curiosity. She frowned and was about to speak when she felt a hand on her waist.

"There you are." Drew Hamilton drew Dena in for a kiss on her mouth and a tight squeeze. "When I arrived, your dad said I had just missed you and Eve." He leaned forward and kissed Eve's cheek. "I am so sorry for your loss," he told the four sisters.

So, this is Drew Hamilton, Darrius thought as he sized him up. With Dena's and Drew's arms hooked around each other, Darrius could see how they likely fit together like a hand in a glove. Dena was tall, but Drew looked to be a full head taller than her, even though she wore skyscraper-heeled boots. He was a very muscular man with boulder-sized shoulders and upper arm muscles, pronounced six-pack abs, a narrow waist, a high tight butt, thick thighs, and long muscular legs. Still, his physique was consistent for a young man his size. Yet he didn't have a bulky build for a man who spent a lot of time in a gym.

Moreover, his clothes fit him to perfection. His brown complexion matched Dena's, and his short beard enhanced his good looks, like a youthful Idris Elba. Well, he had been curious about Drew Hamilton, but for some reason, he wished that Dena had convinced Drew not to come. He wasn't sure whether Dena and Drew were lovers, but it was clear they cared deeply for one another.

Eve studied Lieutenant Pappas's reaction to Dena and Drew as they chatted about Drew's search for commercial property in the Boston area. However, Linda and Samantha kept the lieutenant engaged in conversation. During her career as a prima ballerina, Linda danced in several theatres in Greece. Eve noticed that Pappas was into the conversation, but his eyes frequently strayed toward Dena.

Linda's husband, Will Hamilton, who was also Drew's brother, joined the conversation with Dena to discuss the areas Drew visited with Alexandra Andrews.

"Thanks for a hook-up with Alexandra and her mother, Dena. The weather hasn't cooperated, but they virtually showed several properties to me. Once the streets are passable, we'll get out to see the ones that look promising."

Will clamped his hand on Drew's shoulder. "You got Alexandra Andrews' name from Dena?"

"I did, yes. Alexandra's mother and Vivian went to Spelman College together."

With his arm around his wife, Linda, Will nodded, smiling. "Good link-up, Dena. From what Drew tells me, Alexandra is an outstanding real estate agent. You and Drew make a great team."

Drew grinned. "You're right, Will. Dena is the best." He squeezed her to him and kissed the top of her head.

Dena grinned and looked up at Drew. "Hey, it will be great having you in town. I'd love to be able to work out at *INDULGENCES II.* Of course, I'll need the family discount package."

Drew smiled at Dena. "I think that can be arranged, but it's going to cost you." He wiggled his eyebrows, like Groucho Marx, making her laugh. "Still, I know I'd like living there. I've only lived in The Apple. The Boston area is different, but I like it. I particularly like the Back Bay, Beacon Hill area. I think, based on the home values in that area, a facility like ours would be well suited."

"It's a good choice. Land values around there are growing rapidly."

"They are. However, there is an old high school property that closed years ago. It's city-owned property, but I have to check the zoning and ordinances for the area. It's boarded up and overgrown, but I think it would be a great place to put **INDULGENCES II**. It's a large property where we can put ample parking spaces and create a facility that may be twice the size of our New York City facility. The only thing is that it will take a lot of work. I'd like to ask your uncle Gregory to give me a financial analysis, Dena. I want to ensure that the amount of monetary juice this facility may need will be worth the squeeze."

Dena looked up and around and easily spotted her six-foot, ten-inch uncle in the crowd. She got his attention, and he made his way to where she stood.

Gregory Alexander rubbed his niece's right bare shoulder. "What's up, kid?"

"Uncle Gregory, Drew needs your expertise on a property in Boston's Back Bay. Would you break out some time to speak with him about it?"

"Sure, Drew. Sit with me during dinner, and you can give me the preliminary information."

"Thanks, Gregory. I appreciate this."

"You're welcome. It's not an imposition. It's what I do."

Dena frowned while looking around the crowded area. "Uncle Gregory, where is Aunt Angel?"

He smirked. "I'll give you three guesses and the first two don't count."

"In the kitchen," Dena, Samantha, Linda, and Eve chorused simultaneously and laughed.

"You're right, but where else would a Le Cordon Bleu-certified chef be while preparing a family dinner for a wake?"

It's as easy as that, Darrius thought as he half-listened to Dena's conversation with the Hamilton brothers and her uncle. They made things happen with a few well-placed words. Now the possibility existed that Drew Hamilton would be moving to the Boston area and likely living with Dena while he completed the construction of his fitness center.

Darrius also noticed that the four girls who grew up together, starting as toddlers, were very easy with one another. They were a touchy-feely family. They seemed to need to hold on to each other in some ways. It seemed natural for them to hug or kiss cheeks, hold hands, and rub backs or shoulders. *Maybe*, he thought, *it has something to do with the rather solemn occasion. Yet, underlying their casualness is a sense of profound sadness.*

Darrius had observed the same behavior between Chuck and Vivian Montgomery and her parents, Bernard and Sylvia Alexander. He was also introduced to Chuck's parents, Steven and Harriet Montgomery. Darrius liked old American movies and thought Steven could have passed for the actor Sam Elliot, with his commendable voice, shoulder-length white hair, and mustache. His wife, Harriet, had a striking resemblance to the actress Dorothy Dandridge. He was surprised to see that Chuck's parents were an interracial couple until he was introduced to Chuck's twelve siblings, all of whom were white. There were interracial marriages between Chuck's siblings and two of Harriet's six biological children, who were Black. That led Darrius to conclude that Steven and Harriet were married later in life and didn't share biological offspring. Yet, they melded together around their shared grief over the loss of KiLe Montgomery. They shared great and funny stories about the KiLe they had come to love as much as they loved their siblings. She was an integral part of the family collective.

Through conversation, Darrius also learned more about Dena's siblings other than the four girls, an interesting and eclectic rainbow coalition of unique personalities. Though he and Dena did not participate in the same conversations, she was never out of his sight. He stayed within arm's length of where she stood. He noted that certain family members wore identical gold chains. Something about that still puzzled him and lodged unsettled in his thoughts.

When the six bells chimed, the eight tall double ballroom doors automatically opened. The crowd deposited their empty wine glasses, small finger-food plates, and napkins on trays outside the ballroom doors. Then they began meandering from the anteroom into the beautifully decorated interior space for KiLe's wake. Life-sized pictures of KiLe flashed and dissolved on the wall-mounted screens in different settings and poses. Darrius thought her smile was infectious in each image. Roger and Ryan had done an admirable job, creating a picture gallery of KiLe's life and setting it to music. Instrumental classical music played with the changes in each image. The sound reverberated quietly in the background through strategically placed speakers mounted high on the walls.

Modern crystal chandeliers dripped twinkling white light patterns on the ceiling and walls, while large fans slowly turned, keeping the area comfortable for the guests. Sizable, vibrant green palm fronds spread throughout the enormous space, bracketing the ten-foot-tall double French doors that led out to the covered veranda and the wall space on the opposite side of the ballroom.

Fresh white roses with trailing green ivy in clear crystal vases graced the white tablecloths with white tapered candles, adding a nice soothing glow to the ambiance. Each table had green ribbons dissecting the round shape into twelve spaces, allowing ample seating. The chairs were sturdy and draped in white satin slipcovers with sunburst bows on the back.

The smell of great, mouth-watering food permeated the air. As with the other meals in the house, Darrius noted that stations were strategically situated so as not to cause traffic jams or waiting lines. Selections could be made from both sides of each station. Other tables held gleaming white oblong plates, cloth napkins, and silverware. Bottles of red and white wine were available from four different bars provided by white-jacketed servers.

When everyone stood behind their seats, Chuck Montgomery's voice offered a blessing. "Be free, be strong, be proud of who you have been, KiLe Hakamora Montgomery…Move beyond form, flowing like water, feeding on sunlight and moonlight, radiant as the stars in the night sky."

Dena waited until the lieutenant finished making his food selection before she approached him. "Lieutenant Pappas, would you care to join us at table six?"

Surprised, Darrius' brow rose. "Yes, thank you. If you don't mind, I want to select a glass of wine before I sit."

"Okay." She looked around for the closest bar. "Let's try this one."

They moved together, and as they approached, one of the servers, a handsome young man, looked up and smiled at her. "Your usual, Dena?"

"Yes, please. Thanks, Joshua."

"You're welcome. Okay, one Pouilly-Fuissé coming up." He played his fingers over a computer keyboard. "And for you, sir?"

"Louis Jadot Beaujolais, if you have it."

Joshua smiled. "Yes, sir. Any particular vintage?"

"No, I'm open to whatever you have."

"Of course." The bartender again played his fingers over a keyboard, and two small bottles slid through a door in the bar. Then he filled their glasses in less than one minute and handed their drinks to them.

They moved toward the table where Darrius expected to find Drew Hamilton and Dena's uncle, Gregory Alexander. Instead, he noticed Eve, Avilla Montenegro, Donald Dixon, Kenneth Alexander, and Stacy Greene sitting with people he didn't recognize. However, Dena put down her plate, silverware, and wine and immediately made introductions. "Lieutenant Darrius Pappas, I'd like to introduce you to Doctor Cecile

Jordan Dixon, cousin Donald's better half. You've already met my uncle Kenneth, and this is his better half, Senator JeNelle Towson Alexander. Also, Stacy Greene, who you've already met, is the better half of my uncle, Benjamin Alexander."

"I'm beginning to see a pattern here," Benjamin joked. "Why are the women in our family considered the better half?"

"Can you deny it, Uncle Benny?"

"Not if I want to sleep on the couch for the rest of my life."

Everyone laughed, and then a man swooped in and kissed Dena's mouth.

"Okay, what's the joke?"

"Hi, Uncle Bill." Dena grinned as William Chandler put down his plate of food, wine, silverware, and napkin before circling the table, kissing cheeks, hugging bodies, or shaking hands. When he finished making the rounds, he grabbed a chair from against the wall and squeezed in next to Dena. When he settled, she introduced Darrius. "William Chandler, this is Police Lieutenant Darrius Pappas. He's working on a case with Eve."

Bill extended his hand. "A pleasure to meet you, Lieutenant Pappas." Bill didn't reveal by so much as a change in his countenance that he had reviewed a complete dossier on Pappas.

Darrius stood to shake Bill's hand and thought that the actor Matt Bomer was almost the spitting image of William Chandler. In addition to his clothing line, Darrius knew that Chandler was an actor, high-fashion model, and gifted attorney in the sports and entertainment industries. "The feeling is mutual, Mr. Chandler. Doctor Montgomery said that you might be here. I subscribe to and enjoy your *Stallion Magazine*."

"That's good to know. I hope you buy from my advertisers and my clothing line, too," he joked. "Every penny counts." Bill said a quick prayer, crossed himself, and tucked into his plate of food. "Are you Greek, Lieutenant?"

"Yes, born and raised in Koufonisia, Greece."

"Ah, yes. That's in the archipelago, right?"

Surprised, Darrius smiled at Bill. "Yes, south-southeast of Naxos and west-northwest of Amorgos."

"Yes, I know the place. We've done some photoshoots for my magazine *Risqués de Voyager* in the Lesser East Cyclades. There is this uninhabited area known as Keros, which is a protected archaeological site. There are many ancient Cycladic art pieces that have been excavated in the area. As a result, we had a helluva time getting government permission to do the photoshoot in that area, but it has miles and miles of stunning pristine waters and beaches. The water was so clear that I could see the shadow of our boat reflected at least twenty feet deep on the white sandy bottom.

"Have you done any modeling?"

Darrius shrugged. "Only a couple of times when I was in college. The men's and women's swim teams modeled for calendars used for fundraisers."

Bill wiped his mouth with his napkin. "I'll be here for a couple of days. I'd like to get you in front of a camera. You'd make a great model for my summer edition of *Risqués*." Then he rose from his seat to go back to one of the stations for more food.

Stunned, Darrius stopped eating in mid-bite, wiped his mouth with his napkin, and looked at Dena. "Whoa, *Risqués de Voyager* is Chandler's gay trade magazine, isn't it? I know it's trendy, but all of the male models are nude." Darrius frowned at Dena. "He's joking, right?"

She put down her fork and wiped her mouth, stifling a grin. "I don't think so. The photos in *Risqués de Voyager* are very sophisticated, like pictures of art. Uncle Bill has a very long successful career as a high-fashion model. He's done many nude studies in iconic places around the globe. Male nudes are the norm in Greek art, aren't they?"

"Yes, but historians have stated that ancient Greeks kept their clothes on mostly—and so have I."

Dena released the grin. "I read somewhere that new research suggests that art might have imitated life more closely than previously thought. For example, wasn't nudity a costume used by artists to depict various roles of men, ranging from heroism and status to defeat?"

"Well, yes, in ancient Grecian art, there are many kinds of nudity that can mean many different things."

"Yes, I believe it was Jeffrey Hurwit, a historian of ancient art at the University of Oregon, who said that 'Sometimes they are contradictory.'"

For a ponderous moment, Darrius just stared at Dena. Then he shook his head and sighed. "Yeah, you were that kid." He picked up his fork and continued eating while Dena laughed at his dejected expression.

Eve hid her smile behind her napkin at Lieutenant Pappas's surprised expression. He, obviously, didn't want to make a nude showing in a gay magazine. She wasn't sure why her cousin Donald asked her to ensure the lieutenant sat with them during dinner, but she never questioned his motives. In any event, it was a task easily accomplished by asking Dena to invite him to share the table. Also, Eve was asked by several of her single female cousins about Pappas, so he would have received any number of invitations to join a table for dinner. Eve knew that a sure bet was for Dena to extend the invitation. Lieutenant Pappas would not have turned Dena down to sit elsewhere.

Eve thought it was also interesting to see Dena bantering with the lieutenant. Usually, Dena didn't engage with the male species unless it had something to do with complex math or science theories. Of course, Dena had a close relationship with Drew Hamilton, but Eve didn't think it went much beyond friendship, with occasional benefits. Still, from what she could see, Lieutenant Pappas was beyond intrigued by Dena. The thing was that Dena was clueless about her high level of attraction to men. Dena was a very pretty woman who did not know it, or even if she did, she wouldn't care.

CHAPTER 22

Throughout the day, Darrius heard helicopters landing and taking off. Eve explained that, because of the rural location of their home, some of their Alexander and Montgomery relatives were being shuttled in from various airports in the area. Those flights took only a matter of minutes instead of hours traveling on the still icy rural roadways. More would come in early the following morning by air or recreational vehicles. The helicopter sounds had dissipated during dinner, except for one he had heard about ten minutes ago.

He was returning to his seat after a second trip to a food station when he noticed six men…no, five men, and a diminutive woman enter the ballroom. Though dressed casually, they looked to be straight off Ukraine's battlefields. Darrius put his hand on his gun holstered at the small of his back. However, the face of the man leading the pack seemed vaguely familiar as his blue eyes searched the ballroom as if seeking a target.

Then Darrius heard Eve emit a strangled cry before she rose from her seat and hurried toward the newcomers. Eve went into the arms of the bearded man for a thorough kiss, and the others crowded in around her.

Dena stood and touched Darrius's arm. She knew he was reaching for his weapon, and although the people who entered the ballroom looked like dangerous criminals, only the *dangerous* part was correct. "It's okay, Lieutenant. That's Eve's fiancée, Simon Wilde, and his camera crew."

The face, though bearded, now resembled someone Darrius recognized from televised US news and world reports. Simon Wilde was a young man about his age, but as famous as Anderson Cooper, Lester Holt, or

Richard Engel. Yet, if this entourage were simply Wilde's camera crew, he'd eat his jockstrap. Each one of the people warmly embraced Eve, too. Darrius watched as the group went to where Brian sat with his parents and grandparents. Again, there were warm manly hugs, firm handshakes, and short, intense conversations.

Then Simon looked up and around and followed Eve's pointed direction toward Dena. He broke away from the crowd and crossed the ballroom, holding Eve's hand. He swept a giggling Dena up in one arm and kissed her nose before he set her on her feet again. "Okay, kid, here you go." He dug into the left back pocket of his jeans and handed a sheet of tattered paper to her with a smudged list of names.

Dena threw back her head, laughed through her tears, and held the piece of paper on one edge. "Okay, brother-in-law-to-be, you done good. I can work with this list of your groomsmen for the wedding, although I will likely need a hazmat suit in the process."

He grinned conspiratorially at her and affected a deep Irish brogue. "I'm good with that, Dena, me darlin', just so long as I get to marry your pretty sister. Although, since I met your deadline early, couldn't we speed up the wedding date to say, uh, this week on Saturday? I saw all of the RVs when I landed. It looks like the entire Alexander, Jackson, and Montgomery family members be here already, me love. So, if we could be about convincin' 'em to stay through the weekend, I could manage to get the entire Irish Clan Wilde and the Scottish Clan Henderson here by Friday night. Then we can start the Irish Céilí, and, by Saturday morn, Eve and I say the marriage vows while we're still high as Georgia pines. We can put on our tap shoes and do the River Dance, have the Celtic Men sing "You Raised Me Up," and then be sent off on a yearlong honeymoon."

"Not on a bet, Buckaroo, even with your sneaky Irish and Scottish blarney. The save-the-date announcements took most of the Christmas holiday to address, and they were mailed on January second. From all the responses we've received, we need an outside venue to hold everyone who plans to attend this Céilí-meets-Juneteenth celebration as it is. Juneteenth is already a ten-day event, but fortunately, I'm not on that planning committee. Still, at this point, I think that a football stadium might not be large enough to hold your wedding with the six other weddings scheduled on the last Saturday of the event. So then we'll send you and your new bride off good and proper on Sunday morn after the Sunrise Service."

"Aw, come on, Dena. Give a brother-in-law-to-be a break. I want to marry this wonderful woman before she has a chance to change her mind."

Dena smirked. "Vivian Alexander Montgomery, Harriet Jackson Montgomery, and Sylvia Benson Alexander are sitting at the table you just left. If you're quick and want to use that Irish charm on them to change the date and the plans, you can turn around, march back there, and plead your case to our mother, The Judge," she laughed maniacally, "and our grandmothers. If you are successful, then you can call your mother, The Senator, Veronica Henderson Wilde, and your grandmothers, Maureen O'Shaughnessy Wilde and Victoria Kenton Henderson, and lobby them to change the date."

"What, and get my head handed to me on a platter with Faber beans, rice, and a nice chianti? I love Eve more than my next breath, but the women in these families rule."

Eve cheekily grinned. "Yep, pal-of-mine, and always will, so don't forget it." She popped him on his butt and winked at him.

Simon leaned down and salaciously kissed Eve's mouth.

Her eyes gleamed, and her smile was beatific. "This is mid-January, babe, so we only have five months and counting."

"Still not soon enough for me." Simon grinned back and then looked up. He extended his right hand. "You must be Lieutenant Pappas from the Cambridge Police Department. Eve mentioned that you two are working together on the joint task force investigating a couple of murders and kidnapped children Dena rescued."

Darrius accepted Simon's hand for a shake. "That's correct. Lieutenant Montgomery has been gracious with her time and experience on this case. Likewise, all of the doctors Montgomery and the immediate Alexander and Montgomery family have been very generous with their hospitality."

"Perhaps later, with Eve's permission, we should talk. Of course, everything will be off the record, but I've some experience with cases involving criminal cartels, particularly the Russian oligarchs."

"That would be appreciated. I remember you did a live presentation a couple of weeks ago on the Russian border with Ukraine."

"I did, yes. According to Ukrainian and Western officials, US Intelligence agencies have assessed that the Kremlin has drawn up plans for a military operation involving up to one hundred seventy-five thousand troops."

"That's quite an undertaking. I'd like to know more about that."

"Good. For now, I want to grab something to eat and talk with family relatives. If it's all right with you, we'll make time to talk after dinner." Simon made a tip-of-the-hat gesture and walked away with Eve toward a table where his crew members were already sitting and eating.

Darrius sat, as did Dena, and he tucked into his still-warm food. Most of her relatives were up selecting seconds or desserts from the buffets or visiting with their relatives at other tables. The white-jacketed servers provided digestifs, from amaros and fortified wines to brandies, whiskeys, and herbal liqueurs. Darrius also noted that coffee cups had replaced empty dishes. "Your family must do big events like this fairly often. I didn't notice anyone clearing the table of the used dishes. They are very efficient."

"We love to entertain family and friends for any and all occasions. Dad has this big March Madness event and watches every basketball game televised anywhere in the lower forty-eight.

"Mom's friend, attorney Cheryl Lawrence Brock, started the Women's Empowerment Workshop of twelve successful female friends. Each year in September, they select a group of twelve at-risk teenage girls to help them focus on their self-respect, improve their academic careers, and understand their worth to society. The workshop holds events twice a month with the twelve teens at homes and businesses inside the I-495 Beltway area around Washington, DC, and into Maryland and Virginia. However, the sponsors are available to the girls twenty-four-seven. Then before school starts in the fall, they hold a cotillion here in the ballroom to celebrate the girls' success.

"My father and brothers, and their friends, do the same thing with twelve at-risk teenage boys. It's been in operation for ten years, and now there are Men's and Women's Empowerment Workshops in major cities throughout the country. A high percentage of the young women who have come through the program Cheryl Lawrence Brock started are very successful in their own right. Many of the young women have started workshops, too."

"Is that success true for the teenage boys, too?"

"It is, yes. You see, outside of our family, my dad's friends are mostly in the sports and entertainment industries. So, given who the high-profile male sponsors are, it wasn't difficult for Dad and my brothers to help convince twelve teenage boys each year to stick with the workshop program."

"So, what else do you do as a family?"

Dena shrugged. "We celebrate all holidays here in the United States or abroad. Thanksgiving is usually held in Goodwill, South Carolina, with our extended Alexander family."

Darrius snorted a laugh. "Christmas must be a madhouse."

Dena grinned. "It is, and we love it. We usually spend at least a part of the Christmas holidays in the mountains at Point of View with our extended Montgomery and Jackson families. By then, if the weather cooperates, there is good powder in the mountains to go skiing every day.

"Generally, we travel out of the country three or four times during the year, for spring break and again for Easter. Derrick owned a small island in Bimini, off the coast of Florida. Mom already owned a sailboat that was Derrick's before they married. She keeps it docked in a marina in Washington, DC. We use it to sail on weekends to an ocean-front home in Virginia or sail to the island at least a couple of times during the spring and summer. Or we fly if we don't have a lot of time. The island can only be reached by sea. Chuck and Mom often go for long weekends or a week as a retreat.

"There is a sailboat regatta held off the coast of Buenos Aires, Argentina, each year during the sailing season around August. For several years, we used Mom's J-Class sailboat in the races. However, because there are more of us now, Chuck commissioned a new, larger J-Class sailboat, ***Hoop Dreams,*** for the regatta."

She grinned. "Uh, our immediate family also holds birthday parties on the first weekend of each month, and we include those who work on the farm. However, the biggest event is the New Year's Eve Ball we hold each year and invite family and friends. No matter what the event is, this ballroom, the gymnasium, or the car barn get a lot of use, depending on what's planned."

"You celebrate a birthday for more than one day each month?"

"As you've seen, there are a lot of us. At least three or more of us have birthdays each month of the year. So, those who have a birthday that month decide what they collectively want to do to celebrate. It can be something held here on the farm or somewhere else. It's a three-day event starting on Friday afternoon and ending after Sunday dinner."

"When is your birthday?"

"September. Now, would you like something more from the bar?"

He smiled at her and shrugged. She was quick. She knew he was asking for her birth date and year, but he let it go. Still, he had to smile. His birthday was also in September. He'd bet real American folding money that she was a Virgo: practical, loyal, gentle, and analytical. However, to the best of his knowledge, he was a Libra, born on or about the thirtieth day of the month. That was when the nuns said they found him in the Chapel Rectory. They believed he was only hours old when they heard him crying. He shook off the memory and tuned back into his conversation. "Are you having something?"

"I am, yes. Why don't you join me?" She rose from her seat and moved to one of the four bars.

Darrius followed, but he had to look away from her formfitting knit dress. It had a slit up the back to above the back of her knees. It molded around her body like sealskin and was a killer to any male with a heartbeat. The sway of her hips on the dark red stilted boots had the blood draining into the nether region of his body.

Unaware of what she caused Darrius to feel, Dena smiled at the bartender. "Joshua, may I have a glass of Tuaca?"

Joshua witnessed the lieutenant's dilemma. "Certainly, Dena."

Darrius frowned. "Tuaca? I've never heard of it."

"Really? Tuaca is a naturally flavored brandy liqueur originally produced] by the Sussex families of Brighton, England. Linda's biological half-brother, Bradley, introduced me to it. It's a sweet golden brown blend of brandy, citrus essences, vanilla, and other spices."

"Ah, would you let me introduce you to Chios mastiha? It's a Greek liqueur made with Masticha Chiou, which is a resinous sap harvested from Schinias trees. Although Schinias trees are found in other Mediterranean countries, the plant only produces resin on Chios because of the island's unique microclimate."

Dena shrugged. "Sure. It sounds intriguing."

Darrius turned to the server. "Do you have it?"

The server played his fingers over the computer keys, then nodded and smiled. "Yes, of course."

Dena grinned. "Okay, Joshua, please let us have two glasses of each."

After collecting their drinks, they returned to the table to sit, sip, and chat. "So, you come from Boston here or wherever the birthday event is held each month?"

"That's correct. It keeps us all connected. No matter what else is going on, we're there for each other. We also hold Zoom get-togethers on the fifteenth of the month."

"You obviously don't get bored with the routine."

Dena shook her head. "No, for us, it's like breathing. We like to share what's going on in our lives with one another. We're friends as well as relatives."

Darrius frowned. "I just noticed that your younger siblings aren't in the ballroom."

Dena shook her head. "Oh, no, chaos would reign if the twenty-and-under sibs and cousins were in the ballroom now."

"Okay, so that makes you older than twenty years old."

She smirked. "Maybe. However, more than half of my relatives who are already here have brought their children with them. For example, Uncle Kenneth and Aunt JeNelle have nine children. Kenny and Kevin are the oldest. Uncle Benny and Aunt Stacy have seven children, two sets of triplets in their teens, and Whitney Ivy. She's married, but she and Tucker, her husband, don't have children yet. My mother is the middle child of five, and, between my two dads, Derrick and Chuck, we number thirty-plus. Uncle Gregory and Aunt Angelique have three children, all under the age of six. Then there is Aunt Aretha, the youngest of Mom's siblings, who is not married yet. So that accounts for my mother's siblings.

"My dad, Chuck, has twelve siblings, all with children of various ages, from babes-in-arms to adults with children of their own. Then my first dad's family, the Jacksons, have five siblings. Each one is married with offspring except Uncle Troy. He's the baby of his family and not married…yet. Then, of course, that doesn't account for all of the cousins, like Donald and his twin brother, James, who both have more than five children. Or my maternal granddad, Bernard. He is out of a family of thirteen, just like Chuck." She laughed. "Remind me to show the family trees to you. They're in the library, but we would need a great deal of time to go through them. So, my nearly forty sibs and the cousins are enjoying themselves and their meal in the dining hall. It would be a tight squeeze with them in the ballroom. Also, each of the older cousins has responsibility for one of the youngest ones."

"Ah, so you have aged out of pediatric care."

Dena stared a moment and then laughed. "I see what you tried to do there. Again, I'll never tell." She wondered why he cared about her age.

"Okay, but I won't give up on figuring it out. However, tell me why almost everyone in this ballroom and your siblings wear identical gold chains."

"The chains are gold-plated titanium. They symbolize our family unity around a set of twelve principles. Have you ever heard of The Wish-Fulfilling Tree?"

Darrius shook his head. "No, what is it?"

"Essentially, it's believed to be the Tree of Life. The Sanskrit word for it is Asritakalpalateeka. Sanskrit is a classical language of South Asia. It belongs to the Indo-Aryan branch of the Indo-European languages and arose in South Asia after its predecessor's language had diffused there from the northwest in the late Bronze Age. Sanskrit is the sacred language of Hinduism, classical Hindu philosophy, and historical texts of Buddhism and Jainism. It was a link language in ancient and medieval South Asia. While transmitting Hindu and Buddhist culture to Southeast Asia, East Asia, and Central Asia in the early medieval era, Sanskrit became a language of religion and high culture for the political elites. As a result, Sanskrit had a lasting impact on the languages of South Asia, Southeast Asia, East Asia, and the African continent, especially in their formal and learned vocabularies.

"However, The Wish-Fulfilling Tree is also spoken of in the King James' version of Revelations. It is purported to have twelve kinds of fruit. Each kind of fruit represents one of the twelve principles nourishing us. So we benefit from the fruit from our family tree. We continue to adhere to a set of twelve principles passed down through many Alexander family generations. They purport to guide us in how we live our lives and interact with others for the common good."

More intrigued, Darrius asked about the principles while sipping his drinks.

When Dena settled more comfortably in her chair, crossing her left leg over her right knee, the movement didn't go unnoticed by Darrius. He swallowed and choked.

Dena patted him on the back. "Are you okay?"

He caught his breath and cleared his throat with difficulty. "I'm okay." However, his voice was hoarse and a bit raspy with its lowered timbre. "The drink went down the wrong pipeline. Go on. These principles sound interesting."

"Okay, if you're sure, you're all right."

He nodded and coughed to clear his throat completely.

Dena eyed him, concerned, but continued. "The family principles are that:

"We strive for and maintain unity in the family, communities, nation, and human race.

"We define ourselves, create for ourselves, and speak for ourselves.

"We build and maintain our communities together, make our sisters' and brothers' problems our problems, and solve those problems together.

"We build and maintain our careers, stores, and industries and profit from them together.

"We use our collective vocations to build and develop our communities to continue our ancestors' traditions of love, peace, and harmony.

"We leave our communities more beautiful and financially sound than when we inherited them.

"We believe in our family, our parents, our teachers, our leaders, and the necessity to improve ourselves to reach higher levels of understanding.

"We honor ourselves and treat everyone with love, kindness, and respect, always learning to appreciate another point of view.

"We each wear a never-ending gold chain as a reminder of what this family stands for and what we are challenged to achieve and protect.

"We honor and acknowledge our ancestors' struggles, making a good life possible for all of us.

"We stand for something and will not fall for anything. Those who have fallen, we will collectively lift up.

"We are the links to an unbroken chain stretching back through the ages to the beginning before the Middle Passage. We will never falter or fail."

Surprised, Darrius just stared for a moment. "You recited those principles as if they were the Pledge of Allegiance."

Dena shrugged. "For my family and me, the twelve principles are a solemn pledge about how we live our lives. Do you live your life by a code of ethics?"

Darrius folded his arms, frowning. "I never thought about it. Yes, there are things that I will or will not do, but it's on a case-by-case basis."

"Then you have principles. However you define those principles, they are how you live your life. We make our principles a daily part of our lives and we make the pledges to one another. Do we all adhere to these principles all of the time?" She shrugged. "I really couldn't say. However, I can only adhere to my promise to the best of my ability and never falter or fail. I hold on to the chain that binds us together, and by doing so, I never lose the feeling of what our family means to me. If it were not for them, I would not be happy with who I am.

"Are you happy with who you are, Lieutenant?"

Darrius didn't have an answer to that question. *Of course, someone with his background wasn't expected to achieve much. The nuns created his name, and he was christened Darrius St. Nicholas Pappas. St. Nicholas being the patron saint of Greece. However, with the nuns' help, he survived and succeeded against all odds.* As Darrius thought about it, he realized that *over the thirty-plus years of his life, he had experienced fun moments or good times, but was he happy with himself? Happy wasn't a word he often used or associated with his life.*

As Darrius scanned the ballroom and saw the many gold chains, he could believe that the Alexander relatives believed in their principles as fervently as did Dena. Or they wouldn't have the chains on display. However, there were Montgomery and other extended family members who were not Americans of African descent who also wore the gold chain. He wondered about their reasons for adhering to the Alexander family's principles and traditions. There seemed to be more to the reason for wearing the chain than Dena stated. It was a minor point that kept intruding on his thoughts. Although it wasn't relevant to his mission, Darrius wanted to know the answer to that question.

CHAPTER 23

The following morning, Darrius stood in the ice-cold rain, holding a wide black umbrella over his and Dena's heads. They were surrounded by the rest of the Alexander, Jackson, and Montgomery families, who wore black clothing with a white rose on each lapel. They watched as Brian, his sons, parents, and grandparents were lifted off in a helicopter carrying KiLe's remains in an urn. They were headed for Monroe County, Pennsylvania, where KiLe's remains would be spread around a mountaintop lake she loved. It was the place where Brian had built a cabin on pontoons for them as a wedding gift for KiLe.

Darrius learned that Brian and KiLe spent their honeymoon there and often returned to spend quality time alone together. Apparently, the mountaintop lake could only be reached by helicopter, so only a limited number of people could attend this final resting place for KiLe Montgomery.

Still, Darrius couldn't fathom the number of people in attendance. They were all immediate and extended family members. Very few close family friends were in attendance. Darrius felt honored to be among those invited to participate. Yet, there appeared to be more than twice the number of family members who attended the wake for KiLe the previous night. Dena warned him that this would be the case. There were so many faces in this United Colors of Benetton family that he didn't recognize. Yet, Darius admitted to himself that he had never experienced a celebration of life as beautiful as the one held for KiLe Hakamora Montgomery.

At daybreak, the family members, including the children, were assembled in the ballroom. Everyone wore unrelieved black clothing and shoes, and the women added a twelve-by-twelve-inch square intricately designed piece of black Chantilly lace covering their heads. The lace reminded Darrius of the bolt of black lace he saw in Samantha's studio.

A six-foot oblong sweetgrass basket of sufficient size to be a casket sat on a white festooned cloth-covered table in the center of the ballroom. It was surrounded by white roses, baby breaths, and dark green ivy. An extensive array of funeral flowers sent to the family sat on a raised platform. The family members moved around the basket, adding small gifts to the interior. Some added glass or pottery pieces, handwritten notes, and cards to the growing pile. There were also flowers, or pictures, or small books. Darrius noticed that Brian carried both of his sons, and the nearly two-year-old Cord Montgomery added two pairs of small socks and one pair of socks that must have been Brian's to the woven basket.

When he asked Dena Montgomery the reason for the socks, she said it symbolized that Brian and their two boys would always walk with KiLe in her next life. Darrius felt that it was a surprisingly warm and loving sentiment.

Darrius followed the religious and philosophical Buddhism and Shintoism service conducted by two Buddhist Priests, which lasted an hour. The service order was beautifully embossed in gold filigree script on a single white card. KiLe's picture was on a stylized tree on the front, surrounded by flowers and twelve kinds of fruit.

However, Darrius barely had time to absorb the quiet ending of the religious aspect of the service. Before the service ended, Whitney Ivy Alexander, her husband, Tucker Cavenaugh, and her teenage triplet sisters, Shannon, Sharon, and Sierra, came to the stage. They were joined by the Montgomery brothers, Anderson, Liam, Daniel, Pierce, and KiLe's band members, Changelings. All wore black leather with one white rose on their lapels. They all moved silently to their instruments. Tucker and Whitney Ivy Alexander Cavenaugh and the actor Miguel Menendez-Gaza connected electric guitars to the amps, and then all stepped to the microphones. As the eight oldest Montgomery teenage males lifted the sweetgrass basket and carried it out of the ballroom, KiLe's potent voice and those on the stage ripped off the solemn occasion with a rip-rousing rendition of Bonnie Raitt's "Let's Give Them Something To Talk About."

Darrius enjoyed most current-day music and played it while working on his clay creations. However, he had never heard an electric guitar sing the way Tucker, Whitney Ivy, and Miguel took their instruments and the intro to a whole new level of proficiency. Then their voices blended effortlessly with those of the others, whose voices harmonized both solemnly and robustly. Yet, when Whitney Ivy took the lead and climbed even higher in her incredible vocal range, Darrius couldn't believe his ears. She sounded better than the incomparable Whitney Houston that it blew his mind. Yet, he had heard that voice on his high-end sound system on every disk copy of Ivy's sensational singing group in his collection. However, the group was very private and never appeared in public without wearing costumes to disguise their appearances. They released at least two albums each year, but would only perform for benefit concerts with others, never alone. Now he believed he knew why. Whitney Ivy and her triplet sisters were the internationally well-known group, and they wanted to lead their lives unencumbered by the glitz and glitter of public performances and notoriety.

It was such a shocking difference from the peaceful celebration that it took moments for Darrius to adjust. Nevertheless, it seemed an appropriate conclusion, like the procession leading away in a New Orleans jazz funeral pageant to celebrate the beauty of life after death, except the song wasn't "When the Saints Go Marching In." Yet, when those on stage went *a capella* on the last stanza of the refrain, it was so emotional that there wasn't a dry eye to be found. The crowd began clapping to the beat and singing along. Darrius was unfamiliar with the words to the song that Whitney Ivy belted out. Nevertheless, he felt his eyes misting while an unexpected smile rose on his face, and he found himself clapping along with the others. He never met KiLe Montgomery, but he was beginning to feel her loss as deeply as those related to her.

Dena informed him that "Let's Give Them Something To Talk About" was the first song Brian and KiLe sang as a duet on stage at a Friday night fish fry in Monroe County. It was also the first time KiLe ever heard or sang the song, but she did such a great job that it became Brian and KiLe's love song.

While the relatives ate breakfast and listened to recorded music KiLe had once performed with the band Changelings, the sweetgrass basket with its send-off gifts was taken to the crematorium. KiLe's body was laid to rest in the basket of offerings, wearing the gown she wore on the day she and Brian were married. Once KiLe was cremated in the basket, the remains were returned to Brian in a clay urn one of the Alex-Mont in-laws designed.

As the helicopter disappeared from view, the relatives began their farewell hugs and kisses. Cars were delivered two abreast under the *porte cochére* at the front of the ballroom. Linda Montgomery Hamilton and her husband, Will, headed the line of nearly forty siblings seeing their relatives off with hugs and kisses. Some planned to see one another on a family vacation to Seychelles, and all vowed to attend the annual Juneteenth family reunion celebration in Goodwill, Summer County, South Carolina.

Darrius kept Dena, John, and Jane in clear view as they participated in the farewell procession leaving the farm. Earlier, some enterprising reporter attempted to infiltrate the grounds, but was quickly and easily found and detained by Claudia Shaffer's K9s and a security force of former military agents. The reporter got nowhere close enough to take even long-range photographs. The county sheriff and several of his deputies were there to handle traffic control, but also took the reporter away to be processed and jailed for trespassing on private property. Most relatives had no knowledge of the reporter's attempted breach of the property. Only he, Eve, and Avilla were brought into the real-time discussion by Claudia and Richardson security.

Darrius watched as the last cars, vans, trucks, SUVs, and RVs snaked down the driveway and pulled out of sight. Then the sheriff's deputies allowed the traffic to resume regular flow. All through the departures, shuttle helicopters left for the different airports. Many of them went to the small airport where Eve landed the Cessna nearly a week ago. As Darrius watched, farmhands were already laying straw or hay over the grassy area around the lake where relatives had parked their motor homes for the night. The cold rain had made the grassy area a marshland. Now, ducks or geese floated on the peaceful lake while the workers laid new grass seeds and restored the muddy puddles to a nicely landscaped scene overlaid with straw.

Dena shepherded John and Jane into the main living space and took seats. However, it didn't take long for other tender-aged children to come and lead John and Jane away, accompanied by older siblings. Eve and Simon sat on one of the sofas, holding hands, while Darrius and Dena sat facing them across a cocktail table.

Simon covered his yawn on his now nearly beardless face with his hand. "I apologize, Lieutenant Pappas, for fading on you last evening. Jet lag usually doesn't take me down easily, but we chased stories all over the Middle East and got very little sleep. Then we had to wrap up our projects quickly and double-time it back to the states when we heard about KiLe."

"Understood. Lieutenant Montgomery contacted me and explained. Do you have time now to tell me about your encounter with the Russians?"

Simon looked at Eve, who nodded and squeezed his hand in encouragement. He huffed and ran his free hand down his face before speaking. "Last year, a Russian tiger team was sent to kill me while I was out of the country on an assignment. First, they killed three victims in my home. Eve was one of the homicide detectives brought in by the DC Police Department to investigate the case. Days after I returned to the country, there was a drive-by shooting unrelated to the homicides, but we didn't know it then. Still, I was shot three times. Eve took me into protective custody at a safe house on an island off the coast of Maine. Again, we didn't know it at the time, but when the Russians killed the three victims, they put tracking devices in my clothes and shoes. I took some of those clothes and shoes with me when we left for the island. Subsequently, they found us on the island and made another attempt to assassinate me, but again, Eve saved my life." He squeezed Eve's hand and grinned at her. "So, I decided I'd better marry her since she has this uncanny ability to save me. She resisted, but I brought in the big guns, her parents and mine, and we finally wore her down together."

Frowning, Darrius searched his memory. "I don't recall hearing about any of this."

Simon shook his head. "No, Eve kept all of her investigation on radio silence. Together with Avilla Montenegro and my former US Navy SEALs team, they took down the Russians who are now doing a long stretch at undisclosed Black Sites, where they gave up names and other critical intelligence."

"Why were they trying to kill you?"

"I would answer your questions, Lieutenant, but we need to be in a SCIF to discuss it. It's not that I don't think that we're secure here, but I don't take chances with Eve's life or that of her family."

"A SCIF?"

"Yes, a Sensitive Compartmented Information Facility used for handling mission-critical intelligence."

"I've never used a facility like that."

Simon shrugged. "It can be any accredited area, room, group of rooms or installation where sensitive compartmented information may be stored, used, discussed or electronically processed."

Darrius looked at Eve. "What about your science lab?"

She shrugged. "It's a secured room, but I don't know whether it would qualify as a SCIF. Still, you're welcome to use it. I don't think anyone is using it now." She pulled out her phone to check. Then she shook her head and looked from Simon to Darrius. "No one is in there, and no one has coded in to put a name on the schedule to use it."

Simon stood. "Okay, why don't we use that for lack of a better venue?"

Darrius and Eve both rose, but Dena stayed seated.

Darrius noticed. "Aren't you coming with us?"

Dena shook her head. "No, I'm going to spend time with John and Jane. Now that Aunt Althea has left to go home, I need to more closely monitor their progress. Vincent has hospital rounds, but since Dad is with Brian today, he wants to inspect the children's incisions. He wants to guard against infection."

"Okay, I'll find you after, but please don't leave the property."

Darrius smiled at her and left to follow Simon and Eve.

Eve coded in and then had Simon and Darrius place their hands on the scanner. When the door opened, Eve stepped back and let the men enter the science lab. "I know you'll probably have to discuss things I'm not authorized to hear. So, I'll leave you two here and ensure that no one can come in and disturb you. Simon, use your grandmothers' birthdates in reverse to code out."

Nodding, he leaned down to capture her mouth again. "I'll find you when we finish. I need time with you…uninterrupted time. Does that work for you?"

She smiled. "It does, yes. I need time with you, too."

Pleased, Simon let Eve close and lock the door. Then he moved into a small space with two sofas, a coffee table, and a monitor on the wall. They sat, and Simon activated the screen. "There are things I cannot share with you, but I'll tell you what I can."

When they took seats across from one another, Darrius nodded his understanding.

"Okay, this took place last year while I was on assignment." The monitor digitized, and Simon keyed in a series of numbers. Wilde Star Communications' logo, a green four-leaf clover, came up on the screen, overlaying the world globe. "I was meeting with my contacts when three militants opened fire on us. We were inside a joint Afghan-US military base in Kandahar Province here." He used a penlight laser to point out the specific regions on an electronic topography map. "Two of the militants were reportedly Russian soldiers." He left out the fact that he and his Tiger Team returned fire, killing two of the assailants and wounding the third, who managed to get away using smoke bombs. "It occurred just after we got word sanctions were placed on a top Afghan Taliban bombmaker we were trying to find to interview." Actually, they were there to capture or eliminate the bomb maker, and they accomplished their mission. The man was now buried in the sandbox, the code name for Afghanistan. "I did a stand-up, talking-head report of the situation, filed my report for my newspaper column, and then headed for Pakistan." In short, it signaled that the mission was accomplished, and they were moving to the next target.

"About twenty days in, I interviewed disenfranchised people in the Tirah Valley located in Khyber, Kurram, and Orakzai agencies in the Khyber Pakhtunkhwa province of Pakistan. It's a smaller part straddling the border to the north. It lies in Nangarhar Province, Afghanistan. Tirah lies between the Khyber Pass and the Khanki Valley. It is inhabited by the Afridi, Orakzai, and Shinwari tribes of Pashtuns. I have good contacts there and arranged to meet with them. However, I came on militants attacking a Pakistan Army position in the Khyber Agency. I didn't want to jeopardize my contacts or camera crew, so we laid low for a couple of days in the mountains. It's the federally administered tribal areas here." Again, he used the penlight laser. "At least ten Pakistani soldiers and more than twenty militants were killed while we were nearby. We got film footage of the massacre. The next thing we knew, a suicide bomber targeted the Lashkar-e-Islam militant group in Khyber Agency, killing at least twenty people. We got film footage of that too. Lashkar-e-Islam is a Sunni-Deobandi Islamist group chiefly concerned with implementing Sharia law. It's led by Mangal Bagh, but the group has been weakened recently in its Khyber Agency stronghold.

"A contact, an Afghan general, told us that the Taliban had a sophisticated method to infiltrate Afghanistan's security forces. We were able to verify that intelligence from two other reliable sources. First, the Taliban installed rogues inside the army in well-placed positions. They receive special training and, as a result, we learned that the Russians were the ones pulling the strings.

"You see, troops in tanks, waving Soviet flags, rolled out of Afghanistan as Moscow withdrew from its costly decade-long war with the mujahideen guerrillas. The Kremlin called the Afghan conflict a political mistake. Now Russian lawmakers, and isn't that a contradiction in terms, are trying to make a one-hundred-and-eighty-degree turn on that assessment. After the Soviet forces pulled out, various mujahideen factions, known as the holy warriors, took control of the country and began fighting among themselves. That continued bloodshed between the warlords gave rise to the radical Taliban movement.

"Since America has pulled out of Afghanistan after devastating the Taliban leadership, the Russians see an opportunity to infiltrate the weakened country's political infrastructure. Recently, the Russians hosted a peace conference for Afghanistan to bring together government representatives, the Taliban, and international observers. The Russians claim that it's a bid to jumpstart the peace process. However, my investigation revealed that this is a clear move for the Russians to attempt another more covert infiltration of the country and simultaneously expand Russian control on several borders.

"It surprised me that more than forty-five hundred Russians left their country to fight with the terrorists in the Middle East, North Africa, and other regions against American and allied forces. The Russian Security Service effectively prevented militants from getting into Russia and stopped Russians from going to those regions where the militants were railing against the Russian dictatorship. It is concrete evidence that Russian government factions are working against us while professing to be supportive of the Afghan efforts.

"What's even more concerning is the growing relationship between Russia and China. Those relations, also known as Sino–Russian relations, refer to the more covert international relations between the People's Republic of China and the Russian Federation. Diplomatic relations between China and Russia improved after the dissolution of the Soviet Union and the establishment of the Russian Federation.

"Some time ago, with the collapse of the Soviet Union, that de facto US-China alliance ended, and a China–Russia rapprochement began. The two countries declared that they were pursuing a 'constructive partnership.' Then they progressed toward a 'strategic partnership,' and more recently, they signed a 'treaty of friendship and cooperation.'

"The delicate balance here is that the two countries share a land border demarcated many years ago. They signed the Treaty of Good-Neighborliness and Friendly Cooperation, which was renewed recently for five more years. On the eve of a state visit to Moscow by the Chinese leader, the Russians announced that the two nations were forging a 'special relationship.' The two countries have enjoyed close relations militarily, economically, and politically, while supporting each other on various global issues. However, Russian commentators have increasingly raised concerns about China's ambitions and influence in Central Asia, which had historically been under the influence of Russia. As a result, there has been debate over whether the bilateral strategic partnership constitutes an alliance."

Simon omitted from the conversation that he and his Tiger Team spent a great deal of time undercover on the border between Russia and China. They had picked up critical intelligence there that they had yet to impart to their handlers, but they would do so the next day at a safe house in Washington, DC.

"My upcoming exposé will highlight the Russian's covert plan and hopefully advance intelligence gathering on the movements of recruits, tap their cell phones, and find out who they are in contact with outside the army infiltrating Afghanistan. About seventy members of the NATO-led force were killed in more than forty insider attacks in recent years. It won't be long before the NATO allies will be forced to commit covert agents to countermand the Russians in countries other than Ukraine."

"I've followed your newspaper column and believe you're one of the foremost experts in that area. Any intelligence on a company known as Via Striker would be appreciated. It's the only conduit we have so far to figure out who kidnapped John and Jane and inserted the tracking devices. Unfortunately, this company may only be the manufacturer of the product. So, we still may have to go further to find out who purchased the product and whether other children have been outfitted with the same type of device. The bottom line is finding out why these children were kidnapped in the first place. Until we have answers to those questions, Dena's, John's, and Jane's lives may be jeopardized."

Simon appreciated the lieutenant's comment. "I've promised Eve and Dena that I'll look into Via Striker. I haven't heard much about them before now, but I will, going forward. Eve said that she and Dena have enlisted the aid of their cousin, Whitney Ivy, to see what she can dig up about the company. Between the two of us and other law enforcement factions, we should have a clear picture of why John and Jane were abducted. However, it is generally believed that this situation is related to their rare blood type. Getting at facts about Russians with the same rare blood type may be problematic. I'll investigate whether there is some Russian database that may have that information."

Simon thought of contacting his active-duty SEAL Team member Kaseem Ally Ghailani. He was still shadowing the NGO, Doctors Without Borders. Several international teams of doctors, nurses, and other medical professionals floated around the area serving the small, remote villages. They would know who had rare blood types and whether any efforts were underway to kidnap children with that rare blood type.

Simon also knew that if Whitney Ivy were involved, her mother, Admiral Stacy Greene Alexander, code name: Explorer One, would be on alert.

Chapter 24

"Okay, Dad, we'll see you on Sunday." Dena disconnected the call and turned on the sofa, sitting tailor-style to look at her sister Eve.

Eve frowned. "They're not coming back today?"

"No, Brian stayed at the cabin with the boys after KiLe's ashes were spread. He wanted a little alone time with his boys and his memories. So, Granddad Bernard and Nanna Sylvia suggested that they and Dad and Mom stay at Point of View until Sunday when Brian said he'd be ready to come back here. Granddad Steven and Grandmom Harriet agreed, but they said that since they live there, if Dad and Mom needed to come home soon, they would keep an eye on Brian."

"Maybe he should work from Point of View for a while. Then there would be fewer memories of the crash than he would experience here."

Dena shrugged. "He could do it, but I don't think he has that much of KiLe's breast milk with him for Kyle. She had about a three-month supply saved in her freezer, but I don't think Brian took that much milk with him."

Eve looked at her watch. "Since Simon and Lieutenant Pappas are still talking in the science lab and John and Jane are down for an afternoon nap, what say we go raid the kitchen and get some lunch?"

"Yeah, let's do that." She linked arms with Eve as they meandered toward the kitchen.

Eve nudged her sister in her ribs. "What do you think of Lieutenant Pappas?"

Dena frowned. "What do you mean?"

"Do you have an impression of him?"

She shrugged. "I don't know. I suppose Lieutenant Pappas is competent, but you'd know more about how to judge his law enforcement acumen than I would."

"I noticed you spent time talking with him during the wake."

"You asked me to invite him to sit with us. He didn't know anyone except a few of us, and we sat together at the same table. So I thought that was why you asked me to make the offer."

"You still seemed to be engrossed in conversation."

"He was curious about our family principles and the gold chains."

Eve stopped walking. "Why was he curious about the chains?"

"Perhaps seeing so many people wearing them, he didn't understand the meaning."

"You didn't tell him the purpose of the chains, did you?"

Annoyed, Dena frowned at Eve, reinserted her arm in Eve's, and continued their stroll to the kitchen. "Don't be daft, Eve. You guys may call me the Absent-Minded Professor, but I'm not senile. I told the lieutenant how the principles guide our lives, and the chain symbolically binds us together as peoples of color were enslaved and chained together through the Middle Passage. He didn't question me any further after that."

"Okay, but I'll bet that wasn't enough to cure his curiosity. He's quick, and according to his record in law enforcement, he's a powerful thinker."

Dena shrugged. "Well, he does know delicious after-dinner liqueurs. So I'll give him that."

"The way he looks at you, I think he'd like you to want to give him much more."

Dena laughed. "The way that so many of our female cousins dropped by the table, I don't think he has any trouble attracting women."

"He doesn't trip your trigger?"

Dena's brows drew together. "No. I mean, he's handsome and all that, but—"

"But what?"

Dena whined. "I don't know, Eve, but there is something about him that makes me think that he's not happy with who he is or that he's not satisfied in his own skin."

Eve's eyes widened as they reached the kitchen doors. "Well, that's profound."

Dena huffed out a breath as she went into the kitchen. "Hey, Melvin?"

"*Yo!*" A tall, thick Black man called out in a deep baritone voice, a former Marine with boulders for muscular arms and a bald head. He was single, and never married, but seemed to have no trouble attracting the ladies, particularly their grandaunt Althea.

"Two of your girls missed lunch today. What can you do for us?"

He groused. "Go sit down at the table. I'll bring you something to feed your faces. You're too skinny as it is. You don't eat enough to fill a fly's belly. All the time running hither, thither, and yonder and not eating *my* good cooking in *my* kitchen. Don't think that your grandaunt Althea didn't tell me that you're not eating her good meals either. I ought to take the both of yous over my knee and tan your hind parts! That's what I ought to do! I teach you how to cook, but do you do it? Oh, no! You just want to run around the streets and eat in highfalutin restaurants in foreign cities like Washington, DC, and Boston! *Ha!* I'll tell you; I cook better than anybody in those froufrou places! Raised you two on wholesome, good old American country food fresh on the farm, just like your daddy and mama had growing up. Didn't hurt them none, did it? Your daddy is almost seven feet tall and as fit as a fiddle. Well, except that Vivian. I tried everything to put meat on that child's bones. After having all them pretty babies, she should be fattened up like a Thanksgiving turkey, but oh, no. She's as bad as you two! Thin as a rail, she is!"

One of Melvin's minions carried a heavy tray to the table where Eve and Dena sat sipping iced green tea. Melvin took each dish from the tray and placed them in front of Dena and Eve. "Now, you girls eat every bit of this soup I made fresh today with real tomatoes and basil. These hoagies have real farm-fresh meat and vegetables on them. None of that processed fake meat in my kitchen, I'll bet you. They'll go real good with these homemade potato chips, these fat dill pickles, and these slices of chocolate and lemon swirl cake." He put the food down before them and walked away, still fussing.

Eve and Dena just grinned and tucked into their food.

"Hey, Melvin?" Simon called out.

"*Yo!*"

"You got anything left from lunch for two hungry men?"

Eve and Dena laughed like loons as Melvin started his litany all over again. Simon and Darrius were sent to the table to wait and found Eve and Dena chowing down.

Then Samantha came in carrying their latest baby brother, Lincoln Travis Montgomery. He was wide awake and cooing at his hands.

Dena looked up and raised her hands, clenching and releasing her fingers to get a hold of their new baby brother. "Oooh, gimme, gimme, gimme. I haven't had a chance to see him today."

Samantha carefully put Lincoln in Dena's arms and went in search of the breast milk Vivian had stored.

Dena opened the blanket a little wider and marveled at how big he was getting when he wasn't quite a month old yet. "Hello, sweet boy." She smiled at the big gummy smile she received in return.

Melvin returned to the table with essentially the same lunch he provided for Eve and Dena. "Humph, humph, humph! I'm going to have to get that big boy a turkey leg to nibble on." He smiled at the grinning baby.

Darrius looked on, admiring the beautiful tableau Dena made holding the baby. He had never been around babies except for a few times when he was still a detective. On one occasion, he was called out to investigate an emotionally challenged woman's attempt to kidnap a baby in a grocery store. The mother had her newborn in the grocery cart and had turned away to select peaches. She turned back in time to see the woman unstrapping her baby and attempting to lift the child from the seat. The mother had to fight off the woman, and a scuffle ensued. The store manager tried to break it up and got hit in the face more than once. Between the store's security officer, the beat cops, and Darrius and his partner, they finally sorted it out as to whom the baby belonged. The store security cameras clearly indicated that the emotionally challenged woman stalked the mother and child, waiting for an opportune time to snatch the newborn. Darrius made the arrest, and the woman ended up confined to a mental institution.

He watched Dena and felt that she would make a beautiful mother. The baby grabbed Dena's braid and pulled hard, attempting to bring Dena's hair to his open mouth. When Dena unclenched his fist from her braid, Lincoln began to cloud up and fidget. Her singing had him settling down and smiling again, his arms and legs in constant motion as if he wanted to sing, too.

Samantha sat beside Dena and handed the eight-ounce small bottle of breast milk to her. Lincoln hungrily latched on to the nipple and suckled. Before he drained the bottle, his eyes were closing. By the time Dena burped him, he was sound asleep.

Darrius had to shake his head, unsure why an image of Dena nursing his child at her breasts was lodged in his mind. He had never thought of marriage or having children before. He felt that he would be a confirmed bachelor all of his life. He enjoyed women entirely too much to settle for only one.

Chapter 25

When Dena heard a helicopter lift off, she turned over in her bed and glimpsed the clock on the nightstand. It was four-thirty in the morning, and she had only been asleep since two. She had difficulty shutting down her brain about so many things zigzagging through her thoughts.

First, Brian's decision to spend time alone with his boys at his cabin in the mountains bothered her. She knew he was hurting, but she had never had a reason to worry about him. Brian was always a solid rock for the rest of them. However, since the loss of their father, Derrick, nothing had rocked Brian to his foundation like the loss of KiLe. Dena knew it was selfish, but she wanted him home, where he was surrounded by everyone who loved him. She had to believe that her parents, particularly her mother, would know what to say or do to help him. Mom had suffered the sudden loss of her first husband, Derrick, and understood what a blow it was for her. Mom and Derrick had—or were in the process of adopting—eleven children when Derrick suddenly died. He died in the hospital nursery, holding Derrick, Junior, an hour after his birth. Dena hoped their mother would be better positioned to help Brian shoulder the weight of raising two boys alone. Brian was young, but he was a big brother to all of them. They would be there for him if or when he needed them.

Next, there was her continued concern about the protection of John and Jane to consider. Last night had been a week since she found them bound and terrified in an alley. They were doing remarkably well, but they had a great deal of ground to cover to bring them mentally and emotionally to the maturity level of their age group. Fortunately, her younger siblings started the academic and emotional process. Her sister, Eden, the first child born after her parents married, proved to be an excellent teacher at age thirteen.

First, Eden had all their tender-age siblings singing the Alphabet Song before they could talk or walk. She also had them singing the "This Old Man" song. Then last night, as Dena helped John and then Jane bathe, Jane was humming the tunes, so Dena sang along and used hand gestures to help reinforce the meaning of the words. Next, Dena didn't know if it was the pictures on the front of the books, but John had a stack of books he wanted her to read to him. While the other three boys John shared the bedroom with went to sleep after listening to the first few books, John stayed awake through the reading of each one. Then, surprisingly, he dropped off to sleep with a smile.

So John and Jane were learning, and as Dena suspected, they were very bright. They were also very watchful and attempted to do everything the other tender-aged children did. It only took a few days for them to acclimate to the routine of rising early, grooming themselves, and then heading to the kitchen to help set up for breakfast. They became proficient in folding napkins and placing them on the table before one of the older siblings placed the silverware on them. For lunch, they put paper placemats on the table, and for dinner, they folded the napkins like flowers and put them in the empty water glasses.

John and Jane also went to the chicken coop to gather eggs and to the hydroponics barns to gather fresh fruits and vegetables with the older siblings. They were fascinated by the fish and crustaceans on the aquatic farm. Althea said most of all, John and Jane seemed to enjoy smelling the flowers and picking fresh ones for the tables.

Aunt Althea taught them where to find fresh fruit snacks if they were hungry between meals and how to pronounce the words for apples, oranges, pears, peaches, and bananas. Generally, Dena was pleased with John's and Jane's progress. However, she knew they needed a more intensive education program. Later today, she would need to contact Doctor Paris McAlister, the dean of Alex-Mont Academy. Because they lost KiLe, her siblings weren't required to attend their classes. However, they would be expected to return to regular classroom training on Monday morning.

Still, Dena knew she would have to return to conducting her classes in person. For the time being, she was giving her lectures remotely via Zoom. The administration was aware that she had lost a family member. So they gave her wide latitude in participating in the department's day-to-day operations. Because she couldn't sleep last night, she started working on the dissertations her students had already submitted to earn their doctoral degrees. She was pleased with the first seven cases, coursework, and original dissertations. Some opted for the oral defense of their theories, while others preferred the written comprehensive examination.

Dena had more students who were submitting requirements for master's degrees. They had fewer course requirements than those who entered doctoral-level programs. Still, doctoral-level coursework included some classes in the chosen field with a strong focus on research methods and design. Because most of her Ph.D. student candidates would eventually become professors, doctoral-degree students were required to teach undergraduate classes. Dena's six TAs, or Teaching Assistants, were doing just that. They were conducting her classes, which allowed Dena only to give her lectures. Her TAs began doing their research with her as their advisor in the first or second year of study. For some, from the third year on, they focused on original research and writing their dissertations. Dena and other professors, including her former guy friend, Alphonse, in her department, were advising new student applicants on their research concepts and proposals.

Her department required that the doctoral-degree applicants pass a comprehensive examination in their chosen subjects at the end of the first or second year. Each year, Dena designed new exams. She was pleased that all her TAs passed and advanced to the candidacy phase. Next, they submitted their finished dissertations to the special committee Dena chaired. Finally, she and her committee members reviewed a host of submissions and prepared questions the students would be required to answer about their research methods and conclusions.

Dena worked on that after getting John and Jane to sleep the previous night. She worked with her students for the duration and expected their dissertation defense to go smoothly. Once her committee approved the final submissions, Dena felt she would be proud to award her candidates the Doctor of Philosophy (Ph.D.) degree. She remembered how she felt to have her entire family there to witness the results of her hard work. They were so proud of her because she was still in her middle teens when the Ph.D. was bestowed. Since then, she had done post-doctoral studies and has been pleased with her progress. Dena had a lot of work ahead of her, but the care and safety of John and Jane and Brian's emotional challenges were paramount in her troubled thoughts.

A new day was beginning, so she got out of bed and cared for her needs. Since the weather wasn't cooperating, Dena put on her running shoes, shorts, and t-shirt and headed for the gym. She hadn't exercised for several days, so she thought spending time in the gym would help get her mind on track to tackle her concerns. Just as she turned a corner toward the gym, she literally bumped into a soaking-wet Lieutenant Pappas. "Oops! Sorry, blind corners can be deadly."

He backed up. "Yes, they can be. Good morning."

"Oh, yes, good morning." Dena kept her eyes on his. He had a towel around his neck, but the rest of him was beautifully bare except for a pair of briefs and flip-flops. "Uh, I see you found your way to the lagoon."

"Actually, one of your younger siblings…I think her name is Petra… she showed me the way. Lieutenant Montgomery, your brother, Vincent, and sister, Samantha, were already exercising in the water. You really get up early around here."

Dena shrugged. "We don't consider five in the morning early. You have to remember that this is a working farm. This time of the morning is when we're most productive."

"I understand. When I was a kid, I used to do farm work to make pocket change. Uh, you look as if you're off to exercise."

She looked over her shoulder and nodded rather than look at his body. *Why did Eve have to put the potential idea that the lieutenant might be interested in me in my head? Now I have difficulty looking into his eyes without thinking of Eve's prophecy.* "Uh, I am, yes. It's pouring buckets of icy rain or sleet outside, so I'm going to the gym to run."

Darrius grabbed the ends of the towel and frowned. "The gym?"

"Uh, yes, it's that way." She tilted her head to her right. "It's behind the car barn."

"Do you mind if I join you?"

Dena shrugged, but continued to look up into his eyes. "Uh, sure. If you'd like."

Darrius fell into step with Dena. He was surprised to pass a lighted room with one end glassed-in where Ryan or Roger, he still couldn't tell them apart, and Derrick Junior were playing a spirited game of racquetball. He slowed to a stop and watched while the bright blue ball ricocheted off one wall or the other at dangerously high speeds. Yet the two brothers didn't miss a volley. Since they were both dripping with sweat, Darrius presumed they had been at it for a while, and neither showed signs of slowing down.

Then Petra and Darren came up the hall, greeted them, and turned on the lights before entering a second racquetball court.

Dena's voice interrupted Darrius's concentration on the game.

"You're welcome to stay and watch, Lieutenant." She pointed toward a couple of rows of bleachers against the opposite wall from the racquetball courts.

Darrius slowly shook his head and turned to look at her. "No, I still want to see this gymnasium." Once again, he fell into step with her. They turned a corner, and a split second before the hall lights went out, casting them in pitch blackness, Dena's hand reached out and pushed him against the wall. Darrius then felt himself being grabbed from behind and immobilized. Someone clamped a hand over his mouth and then the next thing he knew, night-vision glasses were clamped over his eyes. That was when he stopped struggling and watched Dena defend and attack five people who were not in the wide hall fifteen seconds earlier.

As he relaxed, someone whispered in his ear, each type of move Dena perfected.

"That's kung fu. She's attacking two assailants and now she's upped the dance to judo. See how she senses where she is in relation to her attackers? Now, she's stepped up because there are three that she must defend against, but she's moving to keep everyone inside her spatial area. See, there she goes. Dena knows where she is and where others are. Nicely done," the voice crooned, pleased. "There you go. Now she's transitioned up and into karate. Ouch! Ace is going to feel that chop to his liver for a while. Mmmm, nice Tae Kwon Do moves, very aggressive, yet she hasn't lost her focus. Ah, nice. She did a smooth move into jujitsu, but here comes the kill shot."

Darrius watched as a smaller person moved in on Dena and, with a baton in hand, jabbed Dena low on her back.

"Glasses off! Time?" someone called out just as the hall lights came on again.

Dena paced in an eight pattern, with her fists jabbed into her hips and breathing hard.

Simon Wilde stood with his feet apart, arms akimbo, and back straight, observing Dena's agitated pacing. He said nothing, as did the other former SEALs. They merely waited out Dena's pique and didn't have long to wait.

"I know, I know!" She huffed out a breath, stopped pacing, and folded her arms.

Simon and the others circled her, dropped their arms, and forced her to do the same. Then, slowly, they bowed as Dena turned and bowed to each person who had challenged her. When she completed the circle, she looked up into Simon's eyes. "I got too comfortable with the challengers' height and failed to defend from below."

Simon agreed and showed his pleasure with her recognition of her vulnerability. "What have we said about your hair?"

"Not to give an attacker an advantage. Pulling my braid takes my mind off focus."

"It can also be used to garotte you."

Dena nodded her understanding. "Still, I didn't expect to be attacked in my own home."

The SEAL known as Spinner shook his head. "Uh-uh, kid. You know better. You always have to be alert to everything around you. I saw you push the lieutenant back out of the way the second you sensed danger. You leaned directly on your senses in a finger snap and knew it was a test. What clued you in?"

"I smelled the warm moisture on all of you. If you had just come in from outside, I would have felt the cold sleet that's falling."

The SEAL known as Cargo challenged. "Unless?"

"Unless you had been in the house for a while. However," she stressed. "I know my siblings' scent, and I can tell you who's who blindfolded. All of you have hugged me often enough that I can distinguish who is who among you. Then the final conviction fell into place because none of you were hurting me. That's when I relaxed too much."

The lone female SEAL known as Mama grinned. "I was in your space several times, and you didn't sense or smell me. So, for the next few days, you'll train to perfect what you've learned before we move on."

They meandered toward the gym as a group, still talking about the fifteen-minute test Dena had just completed. Darrius sensed that she was not pleased with her performance, though no one accused her of failure. From what he witnessed through the night-vision lenses, Dena had responded exceptionally well to being suddenly attacked in her home before five-fifteen in the morning. Were he at home, he wouldn't have rolled out of his bed before seven and later than that if he weren't alone, since he didn't have to be at roll call before eight. Darrius admitted to himself that at this hour in the morning, he would be blindingly groping for the Keurig to get his eyes open. From his perspective, Dena Montgomery was an excellent warrior. However, he questioned whether he could have done half as well as she had.

CHAPTER 26

After breakfast, Darrius sequestered himself in the quiet space below the lagoon. The sign on the doors to the room read: ABSOLUTE QUIET IS SPOKEN HERE. It was the most peaceful place he'd ever visited. It was like visiting an aquarium and watching the water creatures in their habitat. In this instance, the water creatures were humanoids. Even with the dim light filtering through the water, it gave a cathartic tension-easing experience. If he didn't look up, he would have believed that he was the only person in the space. He didn't hear anyone else breathing. Yet, others were spread out on the comfortable furniture working on laptops or iPads with earbuds. Some were just laying on cloth-padded benches with their eyes closed, absorbing the silence.

The atmosphere made it easy for Darrius to concentrate on his tasks. Given his information, there was someplace he felt might yield valuable data. First, he searched and found a wealth of information about Rh-null blood and read everything he could find about it. Then, when he felt sufficiently informed about the various illnesses resulting from human blood types, he switched tactics. He searched for over an hour and proffered that Kenny or Kevin probably could have accessed these details in half the time. Yet, there it was on the dark web. One Russian source was searching for Rh-null blood. Darrius believed the query came from someone else using a database search engine in a computer lab that could be based anywhere in the world. Still, he pressed on, but his skills weren't sufficient to trace the data stream.

So, he sent a text to Dena, outlining his search results and what he needed. Her response was immediate. It provided a map with instructions on reaching a computer lab in the mansion's second-level labyrinth. Following the instructions, he ran into the teens: Andrew, Darren, and Spencer. Other youngsters were in the lab, but three stations were available. Darrius didn't try to listen to the geek speak, but he watched on a wall-mounted monitor when the teens keyed into CompuCorrect Global's satellite search engine. He was surprised when the screen opened to an orange alert, then changed to green before it cleared. The scene was a view of a beach in early morning shadows. Several people were apparently jogging on a sandy beach, as the view of the scenery kept shifting from side to side. There were several different heights of those silhouettes ahead of the camera view. Water was rolling onto a shore on the right. So Darrius thought these people were jogging south as the light brightened from the left, which was the east.

When Kenneth Alexander's face appeared on the screen, the beach scene continued to be in the camera's view behind him. Considering the time difference between the east and west coasts, it was very early in California.

"Good morning, guys."

All three teens spoke. "Good morning, Uncle Kenneth."

Then Andrew took the lead. "It looks like we caught you running on the beach."

Kenneth smiled as he ran. "You did, yes. We're on the return end of a five-mile run. We're almost home. What's up?"

"Lieutenant Pappas needs a trace and trap on a DW moving target. We need your permission to access the bogie."

Kenneth nodded. "Okay. Good morning, Lieutenant. Give me a second to provide shield coverage for the search."

"Good morning, and thank you for the assist." Darrius felt it was unnecessary to say or do anything more than wait and watch. Kenneth seemed to have slowed to a walk while the rest of his family ran on. Darrius noted ten silhouettes that would account for Kenneth's nine offspring and his wife, JeNelle, the US Senator.

When the screen changed again, rows and rows of computer code streamed across the screens. Darrius noticed that the three teens seemed to be reading each line as their eyes rapidly moved along each row. It seemed so much like Chinese hieroglyphics to Darius, but the teens' fingers began to move across their keyboards quickly.

Spencer looked toward Darrius. "Uncle Kenneth has given us each access, so we just logged in to the Dark Web, but we're shielded. So we will each take a different approach to the trap and trace. Uncle Kenneth will join the search if we haven't figured it out before he showers and has breakfast."

Darrius frowned. "Shielded?"

Spencer nodded. "Yes, we can move around without being seen or sensed. We can also see other operators and the source data, but they can't see us. So what we're looking for is the source of the inquiry. If it's another search engine, that will take time to access and search. Even then, if the person's name isn't associated with the inquiry, then we may not be able to trace it. We may only be able to access the inquiring operator."

Andrew shrugged. "Perhaps there is a bank account number we can trace."

Darren shook his head. "That's hacking, and Uncle Kenneth would ground us for the rest of our lives if we did that."

Spencer nodded in agreement. Then there was the geek speak between the three of them again, but they kept searching for the source of the elusive inquiry. Their younger sister, Petra, must have finished what research she had been working on at an adjacent computer station. She was now standing between Andrew and Spencer, pointing to what continued to look like gibberish to Darrius. However, whatever it was apparently made perfect sense to her and her brothers. They were nodding in agreement at whatever she was saying.

Darrius admitted to himself that to see youngsters who were likely half his age speak in a language he didn't understand made him feel ancient. Before long, a monitor lit up beside the ones in operation, and Kenneth's twin daughters, Marcella and Michelle, came online.

"Hey, Triple Threat." One of the girls grinned.

Spencer nodded with a big smile. "Hey, Marcella, what up?"

"Dad had to take a call from Aunt Stacy. He asked us to peek in and see where you were."

Spencer nodded. "Petra's not logged in, but she's been suggesting places to search."

Michelle laughed. "Yeah, like any of you have been on the DW before."

Darrius sat listening to the cousins make suggestions and add codes, traps, and traces. Thirty minutes later, the screen whited out, and the teens took their hands off their keyboards.

Spencer turned to Darrius. "Uncle Kenneth wiped us out. He's doing the search himself, and he likely doesn't want us to see what he's going to do."

Darrius sighed. "Okay, guys. Thanks for the effort. I apologize for taking up your time."

"You're welcome, but this wasn't a waste. We hadn't been permitted on the DW before, so we learned some things we didn't know. Learning something new is never a waste."

Apparently interested in the outcome, the teens chatted among themselves. Before long, Kenneth came online. "You were mostly moving in the right direction, but I had to get government approval for a higher-level trap and trace."

Petra's eyes went wide. "You found it, Uncle Kenneth?"

Kenneth nodded. "Given a little more time, you would have found it, too, Petra. You all did good research. Now, go away and get back to whatever you were doing. I'm closing the VPN to the site. I've got to speak privately with the lieutenant."

"Thanks, Uncle Kenneth," they all chorused and waved as they logged off and filed out of the computer lab.

Once they were all gone, Kenneth sighed. "This is a difficult situation, Lieutenant. The person inquiring about children with Rh-null blood type is a Russian businessman. His son is deathly ill. He has offered an extraordinary amount of money for information leading to donors, but I don't know whether he authorized the abduction of the two children or the murders. From what I've been able to determine, he is a desperate father trying to save his son's life. He is currently in Boston, Massachusetts, with his wife and child. The child is a patient at Mass General under the care of a Doctor Vaughn Brooks, a hematologist and surgeon. Vaughn studies the cause, prognosis, treatment, and prevention of blood-related diseases. He is one of the foremost authorities who specialized in this aspect of medicine, which involves treating diseases that affect the production of blood and its components of the blood and bone marrow. Our family knows Doctor Brooks very well and many of his relatives. You see, Doctor Brooks is also my niece's, Linda's, doctor and the doctor for her biological half-brother, Bradley Connor Smyth."

Lieutenant Pappas shook his head in stunned surprise. "I know something of this. Doctor Charles Montgomery mentioned that Linda has Rh-null blood and donated stem cells to her brother, who also has Rh-null blood. Linda's donation of bone marrow stem cells saved Bradley's life."

"That's correct. Bradley's blood lacked any antigens in the Rh system. In your research, I see that you discovered that twelve to fifteen active donors worldwide have Rh-null blood. More have the antigens but do not advertise that they have this rare type and are not donors. Linda and Brad have become donors. That's why Chuck stores a quantity of their blood for donation. However, I did not access the child's medical records. The Health Insurance Portability and Accountability Act or HIPAA rules are in place. Therefore, I don't know the child's medical condition specifically, only that it's grave. I only know that much because it was a condition of the financial award. The father is offering millions in Russian currency. That constitutes even more in American dollars. A note of urgency is attached to the Dark Web inquiry. However, Bradley, who we call Brad, may be able to get that information legally."

Darrius frowned. "How can he access information that you can't? I don't understand."

"You see, while in college at Cambridge in England, big business and government entities hired Brad to hack their systems legally to determine where they are vulnerable and find ways to close gaps in their firewalls. Sometimes he's hired to trace other hackers and report them to various law enforcement officials, like the FBI or CIA, the British MI5, and the Israeli Knesset. He has even worked for NSA and Homeland Security. Brad has an ongoing contract with Interpol and other entities he's prohibited from mentioning. So he has nearly unlimited access to databases, especially on the dark web. Major, multi-national corporations, including my company, CompuCorrect, hire him. Mass General is one of his clients, too, and since Doctor Brooks is his physician with hospital privileges there, Brad may be able to talk with the boy's parents through Vaughn or the hospital's administration."

When the computer lab door opened, Darrius looked around and was surprised to see Supreme Court Justice Vivian Alexander Montgomery enter. He always felt he should stand in her presence, yet she always made him feel comfortable around her. So, when he began to stand, she waved him back into his seat and took a seat next to him.

Vivian smiled at the lieutenant. He seemed not to know what to do when she entered any room. If he was around long enough, and she believed that he would be because of her daughter Dena, she'd have to fix that. She couldn't have him popping up like a jack-in-the-box whenever she came near him.

Kenneth smiled. "Ah, good morning, sister mine. I was about to mention that you would be joining us to provide a little legal advice."

"Good morning, KJ. I read your text message, and you're essentially correct." Vivian turned to Darrius. "Good morning, Lieutenant. KJ is my family's nickname for Kenneth James. As he mentioned, my brother sent a text message to me concerning what he found out about a deadly ill boy with an Rh-null blood type. KJ believes that you would likely want to interview the boy's parents, who are Russian, to determine the extent of their knowledge about John and Jane and the murders associated with your case.

"Yet, you would have to observe a strict separation of information given how you've become aware of their son's condition. Because this information needs a legal opinion, Kenneth asked me to provide advice on the topic. You may have heard of the term: Chinese Wall. It's essentially an ethical wall or an information barrier protocol within an organization designed to prevent the exchange of information or communication that could lead to conflicts of interest. In this instance, a Chinese wall would be established for inquiries made by you through Doctor Brooks to the boy's parents to protect his HIPAA rights. Doctors and hospitals are generally required by law to safeguard patient information and ensure that improper use of medical data does not occur.

"You could raise questions about the boy's health without revealing who you are and why you're asking about his health. However, if this becomes a police action, everything about this case will be available under the discovery rules in a court trial. As I understand it, nothing illegal has taken place in the discovery part of this case. However, from this point on, you would need a search warrant issued by a judge in Massachusetts to facilitate your investigation."

Darrius nodded his understanding. "Yes, I believe that you're right. First, however, I need to have a few of my detectives follow this up or return to Cambridge and personally conduct the investigation."

Kenneth nodded. "You'd know best how to proceed from this point going forward. I don't believe that I need to divulge more information for you to continue your murder investigation. You're in possession of the information you can share with your FBI contacts and, if necessary, with the CIA."

"Thank you, Kenneth. You've provided valuable information that will likely lead to discovering who kidnapped the children, which is within the FBI's purview, and who murdered the two assailants found burned to death in the van. The FBI's Jenna Baker has been following the two impostors posing as police officers. With this new information, she may be able to take them into custody and find out who employed them."

"You're welcome, Lieutenant. I'll sign off for now. Let me know if you need my help again."

Darrius nodded. "I'll do that. Goodbye."

"Goodbye, Lieutenant. I'll talk with you later, Vivian. Love you."

"Love you more, KJ. Goodbye."

When the screen cleared, Darrius offered his hand to Vivian. "It looks like I'll be returning to Cambridge, but I'd appreciate it if you would allow John and Jane to remain in your custody until I can ensure they are no longer in danger of being kidnapped."

Vivian nodded. "Already in the works. Chuck and I requested to be named Guardian Ad Litem for the children from the Chief Justice of the Massachusetts Superior Court. The request has been granted. John and Jane will remain with us until we complete a search for their parents. If none are found, we will adopt them. Rest assured, Lieutenant, we will take good care of them. They seem to be acclimating well and learning by leaps and bounds."

Darrius nodded. "Yes, they are. However, I still have your daughter's safety to be concerned with until the perpetrators are arrested, tried, convicted, and incarcerated."

"Yes, Chuck and I are aware of this. Still, Dena needs to return to her duties at MIT. So, we're sure her safety will be a high priority on your action items."

"Yes, I will ensure that she has police coverage until this matter is concluded."

Vivian did not doubt that the lieutenant would keep his eyes on Dena for alternative reasons.

Chapter 27

Dena pulled off her heavy weather gear and hung it in her condo's walk-around cloak closet by the front door. Sitting on a bench, she pulled off her boots and stuck her feet in a comfortable pair of Birkenstock slides. It had been a long day, but a very good one. She had been back almost two weeks when she got the call from Lieutenant Pappas. His case had wrapped up. The criminals who had caused John and Jane to be abducted from orphanages were now in custody. The Russian businessman had not hired the criminals to kidnap the children. Instead, the perps were opportunists of a criminal cartel looking to extort more money from the businessman in exchange for John and Jane. However, the young Russian boy's health improved with Linda's and Bradley's help. They had both donated stem cells from their bone marrow. After an extensive search for John's and Jane's families, they only found that both children were orphaned. So, Dad and Mom started proceedings to adopt John and Jane, and the children were doing well. Dena sighed. Her life was back on track, yet she couldn't seem to settle.

Drew stuck his head out of the kitchen space. "Is that you?"

Dena pasted on a tired smile and went into Drew's arms for a warm hug. He was wearing sweaty workout gear.

Drew tightened his arms around Dena and kissed the top of her head. "You've had another long day."

With her arms around Drew's waist, she nodded with her head against his damp chest. "I have, yes, but it was productive."

"You've been burning the midnight oil and your candle at both ends since you returned from Maryland."

"I've got to finish my review of three more dissertations, and I'll be done. After that, no more late nights or early mornings."

"Then you're on schedule to complete your reviews before spring break?"

"Yes, sir, I will, and then we are off to Seychelles for two glorious weeks." She kissed his chin and went into the kitchen for water. "Mmmm, something smells good."

"Before I worked out, I went to your favorite bodega and ordered two types of soup from Mr. Armegos. I also bought the brown bread his wife, Alice, bakes and fresh field green salads."

"That sounds perfect. I didn't make time for lunch today. Do I have time to soak in the tub for maybe thirty minutes before we eat?"

"Yeah, go for it. I have to shower and I have some work to finish, too. I've put the food in the warming drawers, and it should be ready in about thirty minutes."

"How is the real estate research going?"

"Thanks to your uncle Gregory, it's going extremely well. He's taught me how to research the master plan for the communities I'm interested in and how to compare the costs versus the benefits for each area. This is stuff I didn't learn while working on my master's degree at City College. I should already know this stuff, but I was totally clueless. Your uncle should be a professor at the college level. He provides commercial data, analytics, and insights for businesses. and offers a wide range of financial products and services for risk and financial analysis, operations and supply, and sales and marketing professionals, as well as research and insights on global business issues. He serves his customers in government and industries, such as communications, technology, strategic financial services, retail, telecommunications, and manufacturing markets. The company's database contains over four hundred million business records worldwide."

"*Ha!* Don't tell Uncle Gregory that. He just might take you up on it. Aunt Angelique would string you up by your gonads because she thinks Uncle G is too busy as it is. He's got his Risers Basketball Junior League in forty-two cities and counting, his partnership with the Wall Street brokerage house, and his South Carolina regional bank. Then during the college basketball season, he does the color commentary for conferences in the NCAA."

Drew laughed. "I see your point." They continued to chat while they went to shower and soak.

Darrius knew that it was a foolish idea, but he was going to do it anyway. He had closed the murder case. The perps pleaded guilty to receive a lighter sentence, and there wouldn't need to be a trial. So, he wanted to celebrate, but there was only one person he wanted to thank for all of her help…Doctor Dena Montgomery. He hadn't spoken with her since she returned to Massachusetts shortly after he did. Yet, he couldn't get her out of his mind.

Impulsively, he had stopped by her office only to find that she was in a lecture hall with a bunch of energetic first-year students. From the wings, he watched her invigorate her students to the point that they were lined up in three rows straining to get the complicated mathematical paradigms she raised right.

Dena grinned. "All right, folks, here is the clue: The essential principle of this paradigm is executing a series of mathematical functions. The abstraction's central model is the function for some specific computation, not the data structure. Data are loosely coupled to processes. Give me the functions and their implementation."

Darrius shook his head, thrilled that he wasn't in Dena's class. Still, he had never seen a class full of teens so juiced, but Dena had them eating out of the palm of her hands. She made learning fun. He wished he could have stayed and spoken with her after the class ended, but he had to return to his office.

However, he didn't have to contrive a reason to see her tonight. Instead, they had something to celebrate. He didn't know how it happened, but he believed his connection to Dena Montgomery led to today's interview with Avilla Montenegro and Slade Richardson, owner of Richardson Security and Investigation. Slade offered a position as an agent for the investigative side of the company. Avilla's team was still working on the KiLe Montgomery murder case, so he would have an opportunity to see Dena. The salary was mind-bending and more than persuasive. He would train for a year on Avilla's team and then for a year on the security side of the business. Then he would have a choice of where he wanted to call his home base and his specialty area. Now he wanted to thank Dena for facilitating this incredible opportunity.

Darrius paid for the Disaronno Amaretto Liqueur and whistled a tune as he got into his car. As luck would have it, there was a parking space in front of Dena's condo building. Then just as he was going to the door to call up to her condo, someone came out of the building. Seeing the badge on his belt, the young couple smiled and held the door open for him. His luck had held when a middle-aged woman was going to the top floor where Dena also lived. She eyed him boldly and suggestively as the elevator rose. Then, pulling a business card from her designer purse, without a word passing between them, she stuck the card in the breast pocket of his shirt. He figured her for a cougar in training. Then Darrius found himself at Dena's front door, hoping she wouldn't mind that he stopped by uninvited.

However, when a barefoot Drew Hamilton opened the door with a Velcro terrycloth towel around his waist and a rug-sized towel around his naked shoulders, Darrius knew his luck had just run out. Hamilton was dripping wet and looked like he had just left the shower to answer the door. The gold necklace that read **FAMILY** stood in stark relief against Drew's brown skin. Darrius didn't realize that Hamilton might still be staying with Dena, but not by a flicker of an eyelash did Drew seem disturbed by his presence at Dena's door at eight o'clock in the evening.

"Hello, Lieutenant Pappas. Please come in. I imagine that you're here to see Dena?"

"Uh, yes, I uh, didn't know that she…I mean, that you…. Look, I can come back at another time."

Drew frowned. "No, that's not necessary, Lieutenant. She's here. Dena's been soaking in the tub since coming in from her classes. I'd better get her out of there, or she'll have vertigo. Please, if you don't mind, hang your things in the closet while I tell her you're here. Make yourself comfortable. This shouldn't take long."

Drew was swiftly off, leaving wet footprints while drying his hair and body before Darrius could stop him. So, Darrius did as instructed, hung up his things in the ample closet, and followed the wide hallway past a powder room. He continued beyond tree-sized plants with tiny twinkling clear white fairy lights and into the wide, deep, open-concept living and dining spaces. More healthy-looking, tall leafy green plants were interspersed under unique, directional ceiling lights on wide-planked, gray barnwood floors. Beyond the living and dining area was an ultramodern kitchen with high-end appliances. It lacked upper cabinets, but open shelves held an assortment of dishes and inverted stemware below the shelves. A glass-fronted door had the word Pantry etched vertically in the smoky glass panel. Instead of cabinets, art was also arranged in a unique pattern across the kitchen wall

Placing the gift liqueur on an intriguing wrought-iron side table shaped like a stylized horseshoe, he slowly scanned the room. High art gallery walls held large, fascinating oil paintings. Russell Greene created some he recognized. One, in particular, a nearly life-sized abstract portrait, was clearly of Dena with her horses crowding around her in a field. While he studied it, he remembered the joy he witnessed on her face when she whistled for her horses at the Maryland Alex-Mont Ranch.

Music played from hidden, strategically placed speakers. The lights were low, and the smell of good food was in the air. Darrius felt that he should just leave the bottle and go. However, rivetted by the uncluttered space with its minimalist furniture, he quickly became absorbed. He recognized the pieces as being designed by Dena's sister, Samantha. Yet, it was cozy with a color scheme that brought together the paintings and the furniture. The nighttime moonlit view through the balcony doors brought the Charles River into the room's decor. Taken together, the space and the decor were ultra-chic, yet warm and welcoming. It was not at all what he expected, but as he scanned the space, it seemed to fit Dena to a T.

There was a glass-partitioned space through which he could see what appeared to be an office. Books were neatly arranged on ceiling-to-floor sapphire blue shelves, and a glass desk held a unique lamp and a small waterfall. Safire blue sofas faced one another with a squat narrow silver figure-eight table between them. On a back wall behind the desk was a collage of family photos shot in black and white. A three-foot-high, six-foot-long landscape photograph depicted the Alexander family member seated on bleachers at their previous year's Juneteenth reunion in Goodwill, Summer County, South Carolina.

First, however, Darrius wandered into the office to view the picture on the front wall more closely. There was a large, round photo of Dena with all her siblings laying on the floor in a circle. Their shoulders were touching, and they were grinning up at a camera above their heads. Thin clock hands pointed out the time in the center of the photo. Darrius imagined that the next time they took this unique photo, John and Jane would be in the picture, too. He looked at each face and marveled at the delight they shared.

Dena frowned as she wrapped her wet body in a white terrycloth robe and slipped her feet into terrycloth slippers. She was confused about why Lieutenant Pappas was there to see her. The murder case was closed and John and Jane were safe. The bounty hunters who vied for the millions of dollars to find children with Rh-null blood were incarcerated, having accepted a plea bargain for a reduced sentence for felony murder.

Still, it was good that Drew got her out of the whirlpool tub because she had drifted off to sleep. Quickly, she had stepped into her shower to wash her hair and the soap from her body. Then wrapping her hair in a towel, she stuck her hands in her pockets and walked toward the family room. The lieutenant stood in her office, observing one of her favorite photos. Moving up to stand beside him, she stood quietly and appreciated the picture again for the joy it brought her. Simon gave each of them a copy of the photo for Christmas, and she could stand and look at her family members forever.

"I can't imagine what it took to get all of you together to take this shot."

Dena laughed. "Simon didn't even try. He secretly took pictures of each of us and did a cut-and-paste job to make it appear that we were all together when this was shot. He really is very talented."

"I never would have guessed that's how he did it. I also saw the oil paintings with you and some of your horses."

Dena nodded. "Russell's work is phenomenal."

"For such a young man, he perfectly captured your essence." Then, turning his head, he watched Dena as she sighed and smiled. "I'd like to capture your spirit in clay."

Frowning, Dena met his gaze. *He is serious*, she thought. "Why?"

With his hands in his pockets, and his eyes steady on hers, he shrugged. "I'd like to express my appreciation to you and your family for your extraordinary hospitality."

"That's not necessary, Lieutenant."

He nodded. "It is for me. You see, I've never experienced anything like your family."

Dena frowned. "I don't understand what you mean. We may be larger than most families, but we're not unusual in any other way."

"You don't see your family from the outside. You all blend like a finely woven tapestry. Like Samantha's textiles. Different threads are woven together to make a beautiful mosaic. Everyone brings something to complete the picture. Even with John and Jane, your family absorbed them as if they were naturally born as Alexander Montgomery offspring. You've made them feel safe, protected, and loved. You share everything with those who come into your orbit. You're there for each other in ways I didn't understand. No one has to be asked to pitch in. You each do whatever comes next until a task is finished." He shook his head. "All of you were shaken to your core by the loss of KiLe, but you put your grief aside to be there for Brian and his boys. You stand up for one another no matter the circumstances. You may not all agree on a particular idea or direction, but once a decision is made, you're a united front. Your parents and grandparents are the hubs of your immediate family. They ensure that each of you has whatever you need to exceed your own goals and desires. Then your extended family reinforces and strengthens your bonds. The only framework I can imagine accounts for your closeness likely stems from your twelve principles."

Dena shrugged. "You're right. The principles are the glue that binds us together. However, I've never looked at my family from the outside. I've been a part of the collective almost all my life. You're also right that we fiercely trust, respect, and love one another."

"So, you'll let me share my insight with you and yours?"

"I'd be honored."

For humming moments, they stared into each other's eyes. Had it not been for Drew's voice calling them to the table for dinner, neither knew what the next few moments would have portended.

Shaking his head to bring his thoughts away from capturing Dena's mouth against his, Darrius cleared his throat. "I should go. I didn't mean to interrupt your evening."

Drew shook his head. "You should join us, Lieutenant. It's just a simple meal of soup and salad."

Dena, a bit off-centered herself, echoed Drew's invitation. "If you'll give me a moment, I need to dry my hair."

"Go ahead, Dena. I'll entertain the lieutenant until you return."

Dena nodded and hurried off to her bedroom suite, completely confused about what had just happened. As soon as she closed the door, she called Eve.

"Hey, kid, what's up?"

Dena rushed around her dressing room, pulling on a pair of leggings and an oversized bright yellow sweater. "I don't know."

Eve frowned. "So, tell me in words of one syllable in a short sentence, what happened?"

"Lieutenant Pappas is here."

"'Here,' as in your condo?"

"Yes, we just had what I consider a moment."

"I gather you felt as if he wanted to devour you in one bite."

Dena huffed as she bent forward and began to dry her hair. "Don't be silly, Eve. This is not a soap opera or one of our cousin Adelaide Jackson's romance novels from her Firelight Love or Hearth Heat series."

"Yet, somehow, he made you feel something romantic, right?"

Dena slowly nodded as she continued drying her hair. Finally, she stood straight as her hair cascaded around her and fell to below her waist. "He does. Uh, I mean, he did. He wants to do a sculpture of me as a gift for the family."

Eve laughed. "Well, he didn't ask you to come to his place to see his etchings."

Dena rolled her eyes. "That's a romantic euphemism by which a person entices someone to return to their place with an offer to look at something artistic, but with ulterior motives. I don't think that's what Lieutenant Pappas has in mind. You and Simon must be rereading Horatio Alger."

Eve laughed conspiratorially. "As a matter of fact, we were reading our cousin's latest steamy Fireside Romance novel, *Regrets*."

Simon stuck his face in front of Eve's and grinned into the camera. "It's a great book! Uh, very descriptive and stimulating."

Dena scoffed. "As if you two need something to get you in the mood."

Eve palmed Simon's face and moved him aside. He grabbed her wrist and kissed her palm. Still, while smiling at Simon, Eve spoke to her sister. "Go with it, Dena. I told you weeks ago that he was intrigued by you. I believe that he's somewhat of a lady's man, but hey," she shrugged, "why not see whether you feel something more than just curiosity about him?"

Dena pursed her mouth and gave her sister a malevolent stare. "Coy, I'm not, Eve. I can't think fast enough for foreplay."

Simon stuck his face in front of the camera again. "He's interested, Dena."

Dena frowned. "How do you know that, Simon?"

"I'm a guy. I know these things. Just be yourself, kid. If he does anything you don't like, I'll just kill him and then bury him somewhere no one will ever find his body." He grinned.

Dena laughed. "Somehow, I believe you."

"In a New York second, babe. Count on it."

She grinned. "You've taught me how to handle my light work. I've got this."

Both Eve and Simon winked at her before the call ended.

Chapter 28

Drew Hamilton ladled piping hot New England clam chowder into a warm soup tureen, carried it to a narrow buffet table, and placed it on a hot plate. When he returned to the kitchen, he repeated the process and added tomato and basil soup to a second tureen. "Are you a sports fan, Lieutenant?"

Darrius leaned against a kitchen cabinet with his hands in his pockets, his feet crossed at his ankles, and watched. "No, not really. I imagine you are since you operate a sports facility."

Drew grabbed a bag of fresh spinach from the refrigerator's crisper, rinsed and then spun it before adding it to a salad bowl with cut raw vegetables. He added white raisins, chopped nuts, sliced red apples, and dried diced apricots to that mixture and tossed them together. "Actually, I prefer shooting pool, if you can call it a sport. After college, my brother, Will, played baseball in the major league for more than ten years before he retired and opened **INDULGENCES**. My oldest brother played basketball overseas in several different countries for about twelve years before he returned to the states. I didn't want to try to compete with their prowess in either sport. So, I chose something other than a team sport."

Darrius frowned. "I didn't know that you have another brother."

"Had. He and his wife were killed in a car accident several years ago. Their two children, Eugene and Violet, are twelve and ten. They live with Will and me now."

"Oh, I'm sorry for your loss."

"Thank you. Would you mind getting the silverware from the drawer behind you? This salad is ready, and the bread is in the warmer. What type of dressing do you like?"

"Balsamic, if you have it."

"We do, yes. I prefer it, too. So, I noticed you brought a bottle of something with you. Is it a gift for Dena?"

"Yes, I almost forgot. I want to thank her for facilitating a job offer I received from Richardson Investigations and Security."

Dena came into the kitchen space and regarded Drew and the lieutenant. "I overheard what you said, Lieutenant, but I had nothing to do with the Richardson job offer."

Darrius frowned. "I thought it may have had something to do with the investigation involving John and Jane."

Dena shook her head and shrugged. "It may have been related, but the recommendation probably came from Eve or Avilla Montenegro. I haven't spoken with Slade Richardson or any of his operatives about you."

Still, Darrius handed the gift box of Disaronno Amaretto Liqueur to Dina. "I didn't know whether you've tried this before."

Slowly Dena shook her head while reading about the liqueur on the pretty gift box. "I haven't, no. We'll have to have some after we eat." She handed the box to Drew.

"This says that it can be served hot. I'll bet it would go well over vanilla bean ice cream."

Dena laughed. "For you, everything goes well with vanilla bean ice cream."

Drew grinned as he put the box on the eight-foot countertop and removed the loaves of brown bread from the warmer. "Soups on!"

An hour and a half later, Drew, Dena, and Darrius leaned comfortably back in their chairs at the dinner table. They were finishing the ice cream with the heated liqueur.

"That was a very nice meal. You're a good cook, Drew."

Drew laughed. "Uh, I tossed the salad but didn't cook the meal. Instead, I picked up the food from Dena's favorite bodega, Armegos, a few blocks away. Every once in a while, Dena will get a wild hair and make a meal, like soup or spaghetti, that we can eat for a week, but otherwise, we eat out or order in. Unfortunately, Dena's been working early and late so often recently that we're down to making sandwiches."

"Well, I did make a pineapple upside-down cake when I came back."

"Yes, you did, but that didn't last long, did it?"

Dena pursed her lips. "Well, it was good."

"Yes, it was, but eating it for breakfast, lunch, and dinner wasn't good for either of us." He smirked. "Now, if you two will excuse me, I have some work to complete." Drew stood from the table, as did Darrius.

"Thank you for dinner."

They shook hands. "You're welcome, Lieutenant. It was good to see you again." Drew made his way into the office. Once he entered, the glass partition went opaque.

Darrius frowned. "Well, that's a neat trick."

Dena shrugged. "It cuts down on distractions. Would you like coffee?"

"I suppose I should. The liqueur is more potent than I realized."

"If you feel incapacitated, you're welcome to spend the night."

In your bed, he thought, but still couldn't determine whether Dena and Drew were lovers. Throughout dinner and lively conversation, they were warm and caring toward one another, but not overly so. Darrius was so embedded in his thoughts that he didn't notice that Dena carried some of their dinner dishes to the kitchen and started the coffee maker. He stood and helped with the remaining dishes and silverware. "Uh, Drew is an interesting man. Obviously, you two are close."

Dena nodded as she stacked their dishes in the dishwasher. She looked up into Darrius's eyes. "Yes, to what sounds like questions to me, lieutenant. Yes, he is an interesting man, and yes, he and I are very close. His brother and my sister are married with two children. So, we're friends and family. Beyond that, the basis for our relationship is between us and not open for discussion."

Well, that put a fine point on things, thought Darrius, as he finished helping clean up and accepted a mug of hot, black coffee from Dena.

She filled a mug of her own and moved to sit on the sofa facing the balcony doors and the Charles River. Tucking her long legs under her, Dena sat tailor-style, facing the lieutenant. "Lieutenant, did you really stop by to express your appreciation because you thought I facilitated your job offer, or was there an ulterior motive?"

A bit surprised, Darrius studied Dena's face. She had brought him up short again with her apparent insight. Nevertheless, he could be nothing but honest with her. "Both thoughts are true, but, ultimately, I wanted to see you again."

She deadpanned. "You want to sleep with me?"

Darrius stood, stuck his left hand in his pocket, raked his right hand through his pelt of dark hair, and paced. For humming moments, he said nothing before turning and regarding her as she sat with her fingers linked, observing him. "You know, when you put the statement out there like that, it sounds opportunistic. Of course, any man in his right mind would want to sleep with you, but since I've gotten to know you, for me, it's become more than a fling."

Dena nodded contemplatively. "Thank you for being honest with me, Lieutenant. I'll be just as honest with you. I'll admit that I've thought about you as a sexual partner. You're handsome, engaging, and would likely know how to handle yourself and me between the sheets. I do not doubt that I would likely enjoy you. Still, for me, I can't spare the time. I have goals and objectives I need to fulfill. Anything I did with you would be short-lived and likely meaningless. It would not even amount to 'a fling.' I don't want to waste your time or mine. So, although I won't offer you my body, I will offer my friendship. Perhaps, if we become friends, maybe later, at some point, we will add occasional intimate benefits to the equation."

Dena rang the doorbell outside Darrius Pappas's condo building. She thought it was a nice blush-colored brick structure with black trim around the windows and doors. Deep front balconies and intricately designed black wrought-iron railings gave the place a modern edginess. Identical railings bordered the sidewalk and framed the landscaped yard with benches under matching live oak trees. Turning her back to the glass-fronted doors, she surveyed the neighborhood. His home was situated on a lovely tree-lined street in the Strawberry Hill section of

Cambridge. However, parking spaces were nearly nonexistent. That was why she had ridden her Ducati today. The roads were clear of snow and ice, a blessing in mid-March.

"Yes?"

When she heard Darrius's voice, she turned back to the speaker panel. "Hello, Lieutenant. It's Dena Montgomery."

A buzzer sounded and the glass door opened with an easy pull. Dena already knew that the lieutenant lived in a two-bedroom, two-bathroom condo on the second floor. His door opened just as she began to climb the steps up one flight from the small lobby. He wore a light gray Brazilian Jiu-Jitsu BJJ Gi with a purple belt, and, as usual, his feet were bare. His clothing surprised her. She didn't know that he was a student of martial arts.

Darrius smiled at Dena. It was late, but Dena was on time. He had been home from work for a while, working out and preparing for her visit. Immediately after work, his team threw an impromptu farewell party for him at a local cop restaurant and bar, The Padlock. He had mixed and mingled for a few hours with fellow law enforcement officers from several jurisdictions and friends he had made in Cambridge. He was surprised to see a goodly number of women he had dated were also in attendance. Still, he didn't regret accepting that it was time to move on. His time with the Cambridge Police Department ended today. He turned in his shield, gun, and Cambridge Police Department credentials. Hopefully, his departure would also put an end to Alana Fulton's constant calls and text messages. That was partly why he had waited to tell his squad he was leaving. It also allowed Captain Russ Noland time to vet several candidates for his position. Because of Alana, Darrius didn't think Noland would be sorry to see the back of him.

Dena returned the lieutenant's smile as she reached the second-floor landing. She was anxious to have these sittings over and done. Later tonight, she and Drew would board a flight to England and join her family to fly to Seychelles for two weeks of sun, sea, and sand. Then, with all her other tasks completed, she could spend more time working on her plans for the summer rodeo in Monroe County, Pennsylvania.

This would be her third and final visit to his condo. On the first occasion, he took pictures of her. On the second occasion, he had her pose in different positions while standing, sitting, or laying on a bed while he did abstract drawings of her. After each sitting, they went to dinner at a local restaurant. Dena admitted to herself that they were slowly coming around to being friends without the undertones of sexual innuendo included in the mix. It was a much more comfortable relationship for her, and she felt she could relax more around him.

Darrius closed his front door after Dena entered. "You're right on time. I just finished setting up. Here, let me have your coat and hat."

Dena handed over her outerwear and went to stand by the fireplace to warm herself. Then, while rubbing her hands together to warm them, she watched Darrius walk away. He was built like a Greek god with enormous sex appeal. Yet, Dena still had mixed feelings about him and what to do about those feelings, if anything. Still, she couldn't deny that she was curious and had lost sleep thinking about him. "It's frigid outside today, but it's only a few weeks before we'll see the flowers bloom through the snow layer." Looking around the denuded space, she shook her head. "Wow, you must be just about finished packing."

"I have, yes. I'm not taking anything except my clothes, shoes, and personal items. My pottery equipment and certain other possessions, like my bed linen and towels, will be stored until I decide where I want to live. I'm leaving my furniture, dishes, and silverware in place. Your friend, Ms. Andrews, will manage the short-term rentals with the condo furnished. She assures me that this is a good location, and she can keep it rented because of its proximity to the various college and university campuses."

Dena nodded. "Drew is very happy with her work."

"So he told me when I had dinner at your place."

Dena turned to wander the room. She thought not much would change in his home, except he would no longer be in Cambridge. Nevertheless, she wasn't sure how to feel about the possibility of not seeing him again. The idea bothered her, and she wondered whether this should be the time to test the waters, so to speak.

"It's really warm and—"

Darrius returned from hanging Dena's things in his closet and nervously rubbed his hands together. "I, uh, wanted to knock the chill off the room before we got started." Then he noticed that Dena's eyes were riveted on a piece of ceramic pottery that he considered his best work ever.

Moving toward a shelf that held some of his completed pieces, Dena focused on a striking black ceramic vase with intricate ribbons of gold filigree around the top rim and a wider band around the base. It was so beautiful that it eclipsed her ability to breathe for several moments. "Oh, Darrius." Her voice was as soft as a moan of pleasure. "This is exquisite. When did you do this?"

He lifted it from the shelf and held it out to her. "I had it fired earlier in the week. It came out of the kiln yesterday."

Dena shook her head like a kid and put her hands behind her back. "Although I want to get my hands on it, I can't hold it. It's so lovely that I'm shaking right now."

Darrius beamed his obvious pleasure at her reaction to his work. She didn't know that when finished, this piece would be his gift to her. It somewhat allayed his uncharacteristic nerves, but the next steps were critical to completing this piece and another that he was having fired for her family. However, he thought as he returned it to the shelf, he had to tell her what was on his mind.

Dena frowned at Darrius, noticing his apparent uneasiness. "What is it? What's wrong?"

He placed the pottery on the shelf and then looked into her eyes. "I admit that I like when you can read me so well, but I have to ask you to do something you may find…uncomfortable."

"Okay, what is it?"

Darrius moved to his round dining room table, which only sat four people comfortably. He opened a dress box on the table and then turned to face Dena.

Curious, she moved away from the shelf and came to stand beside him. Tissue paper covered a beautiful white gossamer fabric fashioned into a Greek robe. Lifting it out of the box, she raised an eyebrow and studied the translucent garment. White satin covered the edges of the flowing floor-length gown. The satin design also covered the cuffs of the long bell-shaped sleeves. "This looks like a Greek wedding night negligée. Am I right?"

Darrius didn't know quite what to do with his hands. Still, he nodded. "I, uh, need several images to strike around the vase. Uh, you wouldn't have to be nude…not completely nude. You could wear your undergarments. I can just pretend that…." Darrius ran his right hand through his hair. "I'm making a mess of this. Believe me, I've worked with models before, but somehow this is different." When Dena laughed, Darrius frowned at her. "What?"

"If you wanted to photograph me wearing this, why didn't you just ask me?"

Darrius let out a pent-up breath. "Dena, would you wear this gown while I pose you and take pictures?'

She shrugged. "Sure. Where can I change?"

He pointed toward his bedroom and closed his eyes while shaking his head.

"By the way, it's good that you lit the fireplace. I'm not wearing a bra, only a thong. I forgot to do my laundry." She slipped into his room and closed the door on his stunned expression.

Ten minutes later, when Dena stepped out of his bedroom wearing the gown, Darrius thought he would swallow his tongue. She was a vision with the white gown against her brown skin. It fell to the floor and fanned out behind her like a train. When he chose this garment, he knew it would look fantastic on her, and she would look as sexy, yet demure as hell. He wasn't disappointed. She looked better than his imagination had conjured. "Uh, let me get my camera."

For the next twenty minutes, he took pictures of her from every angle, posing her leaning against a round column between his living room and dining room, and laying on a divan. Dena was long-limbed and model thin, but not inconsequential or boney. Her body was an enticing hourglass silhouette, as seen through the filmy fabric. Finally, he handed a bunch of yellow roses with white baby breaths and trailing green ivy to her. Then he captured her joy in smelling the fragrance. Still, Darrius felt that something was missing.

Going to her, he gestured to her hair. "Do you mind taking the braid a loose?"

"No, I don't mind."

As her fingers worked, Darrius took more shots, and then when her hair fell free, he asked her to bend forward. He luxuriated in causing it to fan out around her head and body like a shroud partially covering her face.

Dena didn't move as the camera repeatedly flashed.

Then, slowly, Darrius put the camera aside and approached Dena. Parting her hair from in front of her face, he closed his eyes and lightly traced the bone structure of her head with his fingertips. "You have European ancestry in your bloodline."

"Yes, I know. About ten percent English and North Western Europe and one percent each of Norway, Scotland, and Germanic Europe."

Darrius nodded as he continued to feel her jawline, chin, and nose. Finally, when he came to her mouth, he opened his eyes and looked into her upturned face. When she rose on her toes and pressed her mouth to his, he felt the thrill streak throughout his bodily systems from his head to his toes.

Dena removed the sash around Darrius's waist, and his jacket fell open to his bare chest. Her hands traveled up his firm, muscular body, and her fingertips pinched his flat nipples, causing him to tremble. Then, much as he had done to her, she closed her eyes and, starting with that thick pelt of wavy hair, she felt his bone structure with her fingertips. When Dena rubbed her thumb over his bottom lip, Darrius, holding her forearms, brought her in and slanted his mouth over hers. Then, sliding his hands down her rib cage, he opened the robe further to place his mouth on her neck and then her high grapefruit-sized breasts.

Dena could feel Darrius's heat at the apex of her thighs as her head fell back. Her hands stayed steady in Darrius's thick hair as he lowered, guiding his kisses across her abdomen to the parts of her body that needed his ministration. Kneeling before her, Darrius held on to her impossibly narrow waist and then her flared hips, bringing her thong down over her rounded bottom to her firm thighs. When he opened her and mouthed her hairless pubis, the move caused her to tremble, make a quick intake of breath, and end on a long moan of pleasure.

Darrius was so dazed and delighted with Dena's responsiveness and sounds of pleasure that he barely heard the buzzer. Standing and holding Dena at arm's length, it took a moment for him to steady himself to speak. He was so brick-hard and heavy in need of completion that he cursed liberally under his breath at the interruption. "That must be the food I ordered from your favorite bodega." Then, going to the door, he watched Dena as he pressed the buzzer and reached for his wallet. He opened his door when the bell sounded and was prepared to collect the food, tip the delivery person, and then return to pleasure Dena.

Yet, there stood Alana Fulton. It was too late to block out the view of Dena further.

"Well, hello, Doctor Montgomery."

"Hello, Ms. Fulton," Dena returned evenly.

Though Darrius had his arms up, blocking Alana's way inside, she ducked under and came in.

"Well, don't you look fetching. Actually, you looked interesting in western clothing. Are you two playing dress-up or dress-down? Darrius is wearing part of a Gi, and you're wearing what? A robe of some type?"

"Alana, why are you here?"

"I just got the word that today is your last day at Cambridge PD. Since you have blocked my calls and haven't returned my text messages, I thought I'd hurry over to share my good news with you before you left town. I'm pregnant, and you're going to be a daddy."

Chapter 29

Dena turned over facedown on the chaise lounge and sighed contentedly. This was the first full day of her vacation, and she was moving slower than a sloth. Earlier this morning, Drew roused her out of bed and forced her to take a dip with him in the huge lagoon. She had sighed over the beauty of the water features, the beach, and the Indian Ocean at dawn. Then, after breakfast on the lower terrace, she'd staked out a place to nest and lick her wounds. *So relaxed now*, she thought, when twenty-four hours earlier, she wasn't sure how to feel about not seeing Darrius Pappas again. Now, twenty-four hours later, the issue was solved when Alana announced his pending fatherhood.

Talk about an ice-cold bucket of water dousing the heat of passion between Darrius and her; it was a real doozy. Then, Dena remembered she couldn't dress and leave Darrius' condo fast enough. Clearly, he was angry about Alana's intrusion and questioned whether her pregnancy resulted from their intimate relationship or her long-term love affair with his married boss. At that point, the argument was getting intense, and Darrius' entreating for Dena to stay and not leave fell on deaf ears. Even the man, fascinated with her bike, lost his smile when she strode up.

However, by the time she parked in her condo's garage, Dena had shaken off the vision of her brief flirtation with Lieutenant Derrius Pappas. She did her laundry, packed her bag for the trip, helped Drew clean the refrigerator, set the condo to right, and set the alarm before turning out the lights. The Adventurer Executive Airline (AEA) ground transportation car service was on time and delivered them to the AEA private terminal at Logan International Airport fifteen minutes ahead of schedule.

After picking up Will, Linda, their boys, Gregory, Angelique, their children, and other family members in New York City, the family's 737 MAX 9 jet landed at Boston's Logan International Airport fifteen minutes after Drew and Dena's arrival. John and Jane were glad to see her, so she sat with them on the first seven-hour leg of the flight to Heathrow International Airport in London. There, with the dawn breaking and most of the children still asleep, they picked up Aunt Aretha, Russell Greene, and Bradley Smyth. The flight to Paris, France, for Grandaunt Mariah Benson took less than an hour.

A little over ten hours later, they landed in The Republic of Seychelles's capital city of Victoria. They were met at the airport by BlackHawk ground transportation, a division of BlackHawk Global, and delivered to the home of US Ambassador Jake Hawkins and his wife, Kelley Baylor. Jake and Kelley's palatial estate spanned forty acres of prime oceanfront land. Jake, a multibillionaire industrialist and owner of BlackHawk Global, arranged to have a new American Embassy constructed on the same grounds he purchased for his residence. In addition, he donated the use of the Embassy and its grounds to the US federal government cost-free for the duration of his tenure as ambassador.

Years earlier, the original embassy and its residence had been too easily infiltrated by terrorists while his family was visiting. So Jake ensured that his new residence and the embassy would have much more modern security protections. Slade Richardson's company provided state-of-the-art security systems through Nico Collins' satellite transponders, while Kenneth Alexander's CompuCorrect electronics and satellite services provided top-of-the-line equipment.

Sitting next to Dena, reading a report, Drew tipped down his Ray-Ban Aviator sunglasses and looked over at his pal, shaking his head. She had been so introspective since coming home from work the day before that he had been concerned. Unlike their usual after-work conversations, Dena didn't bubble over with enthusiasm for her students' successes. He needed his effervescent Dena the Dynamo back. "Are you alive?"

Dena moaned something unintelligible, but didn't otherwise move a muscle.

Jake Hawkins' beautiful young niece, Fiona Lizette Lowry, an architect and structural engineer, sat next to Drew. She leaned forward and looked across Drew toward Dena. "She may be a bit dehydrated or jetlagged. Unfortunately, both things happen to me each time I return to Seychelles from my home on Maryland's eastern shore."

Drew nodded. "Dena has also been working over her limit on a number of things. So I'm glad to see her relax. When was the last time you were in the states, Fiona?"

"Shortly after the New Year. My family and I were at Chuck and Vivian's New Year's Eve Ball, and I had a few more stops before coming back here. I was even in New York City for a short time." Fiona didn't mention that she left abruptly after her physician informed her that she was pregnant. She was well into her first trimester now and hadn't told her parents, six older brothers, or her uncle Jake and aunt Kelley. When she told Doctor Noah Mikasi, her baby's father, he didn't leave skid marks before he left Seychelles by dawn the next day, and she hadn't heard from him since then.

The circumstances that led to her pregnancy were purely a mishap. Before it happened, Fiona didn't even think Doctor Mikasi liked her as a person. She didn't know him from Adam's house cat and didn't care to know him at all. Yet, in the performance of their duties, she and Noah barely survived an earthquake on a remote island for seven days. Then, on their way back to Victoria, Noah had to land their seaplane on the water near an uninhabited island somewhere in the Indian Ocean to avoid a cyclone. They took cover in a cave to protect their aircraft for two days while the cyclone raged around them. Their nerves were stretched thin, and an overabundance of adrenalin got them started—the earthquake and then the weather emergencies. Of course, they may not have felt more than a physical need to release stress. Yet, given the timing, Fiona recognized that they were bound to have some type of proof-of-life episode. Neither of them expected their moments of madness to result in a pregnancy.

Drew set aside the report he was reading and picked up his refreshing drink of island fruit flavors. "I understand that you and Doctor Noah Mikasi are working on an extensive project for your uncle Jake."

Fiona nodded. "The project is called Operation: Uplift. The Republic of Seychelles comprises one hundred and twelve inhabited islands off the African Coast. Doctor Mikasi is a physician who has worked all over Africa and much of Asia, training others to perform basic medical services for indigent people. Most recently, he was with the NGO Doctors Without Borders. So my uncle asked him to head up a task force to evaluate the medical services here in the Seychelles islands and build clinics where necessary. He was also tasked with creating a cutting-edge hospital using the prototype that Uncle Jake's daughter, JaiHonnah, designed for him. Doctor Mikasi plans to staff the new facility with forward-thinking doctors, nurses, and other medical professionals from around the world.

"Uncle Jake also asked his son-in-law, Jefferson Logan, to head an education task force to evaluate the state of the academic systems in the islands."

Drew nodded. "I've heard of Doctor Jefferson Logan. He's a former ambassador, too, as I recall. Hey, wasn't he married to the Montrose heiress who died tragically in an auto accident?"

"That's correct. Her name was Felicia Montrose-Logan. She was riding Lady Godiva-style on the hood of one of her lover's Stutz Bearcat on the busy nighttime Washington, DC, streets in the popular Georgetown neighborhood when the accident happened. She was high on something or drunk, fell off the hood, and the man, also high, drove over her. Several other automobiles ran over her body. Jefferson, or Jeff, as we call him, was widowed and raised their three sons alone. He is married to Jake's first daughter, LaiLoni Skai, and they have five children, all girls now. They live in Summer County, South Carolina, where Jeff is the Dean of the flagship school, Summer County Academy.

"His role in Operation: Uplift is to make recommendations and implement school and library programs necessary to raise the literacy quotient through the unique program he manages at Summer County Academy.

"To assist the overall efforts, Uncle Jake purchased transponders on Nicholas Collins' satellite so that the medical and education programs would be interactive. Medical facilities on the islands will be linked with experts in the flagship hospital. The same will be true of the schools we build and link together. The schools will also have exchanges with Summer County Academy students and others like it in Washington, DC, Mitchell County, Maryland, and Chicago, Illinois.

"Uncle Jake asked me to take time out of my schedule to stay here and work with both programs. Each program needs facilities to accommodate the education and medical programs. So I've identified facilities on each island and had them retrofitted for the services they will provide."

"That's an incredible undertaking. I'm sweating through finding one piece of property in the Boston, Massachusetts, area to build a fitness center."

Fiona laughed. "My uncle doesn't do anything by halves. He convinced my six brothers to pledge a part of their time annually to come here to teach their construction skills and train workers to help complete the facilities I designed."

"This must be a very costly undertaking."

"Operation: Uplift expense is not an issue or a question to Jake Hawkins. He told us there is no such thing as a budget for this undertaking and we took him at his word. So we simply tell Uncle Jake's son, Adam, what we need or want, and it's his responsibility to get it for us, no questions asked.

"Everything we do for Operation: Uplift is under the BlackHawk Foundation umbrella, which you may know Adam heads. In another six months, we'll evaluate where we are and what we need to do going forward. This project is a prototype, a test area. If we are successful here, Uncle Jake intends to replicate this program in the poorest countries in Africa, starting with Burundi, Malawi, Niger, Mozambique, and The Central African Republic. Because of the multitude of legal systems associated with each country, Vivian Alexander Montgomery and her friend, Thomas Ashton Marshall, and his law firm, Marshall and Associates, agreed to spearhead that aspect of the project. He has offices in Washington, DC, and can work with the Ambassadors of each country who have an embassy in DC or representation with the United

Nations in New York City. Vivian's expertise before she became a judge was international contract law. Her niece, Whitney Ivy Alexander-Cavenaugh, is also on Mr. Marshalls' legal team and doing a great deal of the heavy lifting for the project."

"I thought so. Whitney Ivy and Dena are cousins. Dena and I saw her at KiLe Montgomery's celebration of life last month. She mentioned that she worked with Mr. Marshall."

Fiona nodded. "She's like her aunt Vivian, very diligent and resourceful."

"I haven't met Doctor Mikasi. I'll have to make time to talk with him while I'm here. We have medical personnel associated with the fitness center in New York City. We expect to have medical personnel at the new Massachusetts facility, too."

"Doctor Mikasi is away from the island now, and I'm not sure when he will return." *If ever*, she thought.

❦

At the Landstuhl, Germany, American military hospital, a private duty nurse stood beside Noah Mikasi's hospital bed and spoke into her cell phone. "I think he's coming around, Doctor Cavenaugh."

"Thank you for the heads up. I'll be there shortly."

Noah's breath caught as he began to climb to the surface of consciousness. He was on a ventilator, he knew, because he could hear the equipment breathing for him. He was a medical doctor, a surgeon, in fact, and although he wasn't fully conscious yet, he nevertheless recognized the sounds of the medical apparatus attached to his body and the monitor reporting his vital signs. At any moment, he knew he would be able to open his eyes and see his surroundings. Until then, he put his mind to work, tracing the episode that landed him in the hospital.

He had been called back to duty for an all-hands covert mission involving the…what? That was the part he couldn't remember. However, what was clearly evident in his mind was Fiona Lizette Lowry, the beautiful woman of color with an abundance of dark red hair, who announced that she was carrying his child.

They didn't know one another before and had only been working on Operation: Uplift for a matter of months. They barely spoke to each other, yet they were an effective and efficient two-person team when the earthquake occurred, and their lives were spared. Then, facing a cyclone at sea and taking shelter in a cave on a deserted island, they faced certain death a second time.

Now, here he was at death's door a third time in as many months. However, before he learned he would be a father, nothing much mattered to him except his skill as a physician. He didn't have biological parents or other relatives, of which he was aware. He'd been found in a restroom wrapped in a terrycloth towel and raised in an orphanage on the Canadian and American border. He and other orphans were educated and trained as warriors with unique skills. His skill set was medicine and mixing herbs and other vegetation for medicinal purposes. He added medical school and became a surgeon, along with his SEAL and Mossad training, to be a covert agent. From an early age, he had participated in hundreds of death-defying missions.

To the best of anyone's guess, he was still in his early thirties and assigned the code name: Stinger. Noah Mikasi was the name given to him at the orphanage. The name was American in origin, a native word that means Coyote, and he was fine with it. However, he never expected to procreate and bring another life into the world. That factor changed everything for him. Finally, he would have someone of his own he could love and care for, as no one, except the other orphans, had cared for him. He would not die and leave this new person to struggle through life with no identity to call his or her own.

As an architect and engineer, Fiona designed and built or retrofitted properties for use as educational and medical installations on over a hundred inhabited islands. However, Noah didn't think she was any better equipped to handle raising a child than he was. Like him, Fiona was an intellectual academician focused on precise calculations and design integrity. Or, at least, that was who she appeared to be to him. However, despite working closely together for months, he did not know her well. What Noah did know was every moment he was away from Fiona, he craved her like he needed his next breath. Noah had never truly made love to a woman until he and Fiona had their proof of life interlude in the cave during a typhoon.

Nevertheless, they would have to learn so much about one another in a relatively short time and synchronize parenting skills to ensure they didn't make a mess of their child's life. To do that, he had to return to Seychelles immediately. Unfortunately, he had left so abruptly that he didn't make time to explain that he had a mandatory covert mission to perform. Even now, he couldn't explain what he had to do or why he left her after her announcement. Noah didn't know what to expect when he returned, but he would deal with whatever when he was well enough to walk on his own two feet.

Covert Agent, code name: Satin, smiled. "Ah, there you are, Stinger. You've had us worried for a while." She placed her hand on his chest. "No, don't try to speak…okay, I can read your sign language." She laughed. "Well, that was rude. Yes, you've been out for nearly two weeks, but you needed time to heal, so you've been kept deeply sedated so that you wouldn't thrash around in your unconscious state. You'll be taken off the ventilator in a few moments. Here's the doctor now. Stay still and stop cursing the messenger."

Two hours later, Satin re-entered Noah's hospital room and frowned. The bed was empty. She went to the nurse's station and found his charge nurse keying data into a computer terminal. "Excuse me, but where is the patient in ICU?"

The nurse stood up and frowned while searching the area. Then, concerned, she went from room to room, searching for her patient. "I don't know. He was there sleeping an hour ago. He's in no condition to be out of bed so soon!"

Satin rolled her eyes and activated her specialized phone. "Delta, Stinger is gone."

"How did that happen?"

"I was briefing him on the missions that were underway. I think I made a mistake by telling him we have a credible threat in Seychelles. He got quiet after that, and I should have known something was up."

"He's got a head start, so we won't find him. He's too good at subterfuge and camouflage. He'll commandeer a plane and be in the air sometime today. Alert Avilla that he will likely show up at one of the islands there by this time tomorrow, if not sooner. Make sure that Doctor Montgomery knows he may have a patient coming his way. He's on the island vacationing with his family."

"Yes, sir. Satin Doll, out."

On Seychelles, Vivian strolled arm-in-arm along the lower terrace level with Jake Hawkins, chatting amiably. They had known each other since Vivian and Jake's daughter, JaiHonnah, were roommates at Spelman College and best buds since then. Jake taught Vivian how to play chess, which he claimed was the reason for his incredible success. He and his younger sister, Mavis, were orphaned when Jake was thirteen and she was eleven. They were sent to an orphanage near their home in the Louisiana bayou. When Mavis complained that she had been molested by one of the staff, Jake, big for his age, caught the man unawares and beat him with a bat to within an inch of his life. Then Jake and Mavis escaped to their former home in the bayou. Friends helped with food and what little money they had and sent the kids on their way, moving west to Texas.

On a back road, Ezra Neal, a teenage well-digger, picked up Jake and Mavis in his old, beat-up truck and drove them to the Texas oil fields. With Ezra's help, Jake got a job on one of the rigs. They put Mavis in school, Ezra claiming to be her uncle. Ezra, Jake, and Mavis stayed together for five years until Jake was injured on a well-rigging. When he was hospitalized, he woke to find a beautiful twenty-one-year-old Indigenous American nurse giving him a sponge bath. Eight months later, at eighteen, Jake married Skai Littlefeather in front of a Justice of the Peace. Nine months later, their son, Jacob Hawkins, was born.

The well-digging company paid the insurance claim, but when the carrier started asking questions about Jake's age, Ezra and Jake believed it was time to move on and head for the California oil fields. On their way after leaving San Antonio, they passed a deserted, old plantation. Because it was in a rural, sparsely populated area, conservators were selling the land for pennies on the dollar. Jake used his insurance money and bought it. A few years later, oil repositories were found on a remote section of his land. With an eighth-grade education, Jake built an empire using the strategies in chess Ezra taught him. Jake and Vivian started playing chess long distance and still challenged each other in chess, though many years have passed since she and JaiHonnah were in college.

Vivian was now a Supreme Court Jurist, and Jake was a US ambassador and diplomat.

Vivian looked at Drew and nodded to Dena. "How is she doing?"

"She's wiped out, but she'll be all right. I'll let her sleep a while longer, and then I'll coerce her into taking me horseback riding on the beach."

Vivian laughed. "You know her so well."

Jake frowned. "Is Dena all right?"

Vivian smiled and patted Jake's arm. "She's fine. Dena is my workaholic until she hits a wall, and then she hibernates for a few days or a week. Drew forces Dena to take breaks so that she doesn't face plant."

"She's so young to be so fixated."

"*Ha!*" Vivian scoffed good-naturedly. "My Dena doesn't know how to be anything else. She's addicted to learning and fervent about finding answers to impossible math paradigms." However, Vivian also knew more than she would say about her daughter. They had no secrets between them. Dena confided the detailed experience she had with Darrius Pappas and Alana Fulton.

"Ah, youth," Jake sighed, making everyone laugh.

Avilla Montenegro looked down the long, wide, polished conference table at Darrius. "Are you with us, Pappas?"

Darrius looked up from his note-taking and around at the other agents at the table. They were having a lunchtime meeting to discuss Jake Hawkins' estate and the strategic plans to protect and defend the guests on the grounds should it become necessary. However, given the issues under discussion, Darrius's focus drifted to encompass Dena Montgomery and her family's protection. Ordinarily, he would not have been brought on this particular mission. He was new to the team, and the Tiger Teams were the elite combat-ready members of Richardson Security. Each had military training and was ready to deploy at a moment's notice. They traveled in supersonic transports that reached speeds of MACH 2 or 3, the likes of which Darrius didn't know existed for civilian use.

The meeting was being held in the American Embassy in Seychelles. Overwatch, the sophisticated security system guarding the property, found what appeared to be a credible threat. An unmarked U-boat was stationary outside the five-mile perimeter of the shores of Seychelles. It had been there for more than a week. That wouldn't have caused concern except that the boat's occupants were using drones fashioned to resemble seagulls to fly over the on-shore embassy and residential property.

Fortunately, CompuCorrect's surveillance equipment was geared to detect any sound greater than a swarm of mosquitoes. The drones emitted sounds much greater than that and alerted Avilla's Rapid Deployment Tiger Team security contingent of potential trouble. First, they needed to identify the U-boat's origins and inhabitants. These boats were used to smuggle drugs into various countries bordering deep bodies of water. Yet, Avilla didn't believe that was its purpose for being off the coast. There were many islands in the Indian Ocean where drugs or other contraband could be off-loaded and not receive close scrutiny.

However, with Chuck and Vivian and their families vacationing on the island nation, it was a target-rich environment. Vivian, a US Supreme Court Jurist, was also one of the wealthiest women in the world. Her brother Kenneth headed one of the most significant tech firms and his wife, a US Senator. Another brother, Benjamin, a US Air Force General, was also an astronaut. Benjamin's wife, Stacy, was a US Navy Admiral. Gregory, Vivian's younger brother, was a former basketball icon and is now considered a Wall Street Wizard. He was married to the high-fashion model Angelique, who was also a famous restaurateur.

Vivian's parents, Bernard and Sylvia Benson Alexander, and her sister, Aretha, were all vacationing together with their families. Chuck's parents, Stephan and Harriet Jackson Montgomery, and the majority of his twelve siblings with their families, along with Harriet's five children and their families, were also escaping the cold for the two-week end-of-winter break. This family's close personal friends alone were among the Talented Tenth, very noteworthy people who sought to work for the common good. To have anything happen to them under Avilla's watch would spell disaster.

During his training sessions, it became clear to Darrius why Avilla was tasked to lead this aspect of Richardson's security operation. She was a warrior who had been a part of or led secret excursions into hostile countries and situations, but never failed to complete her mission. Furthermore, Darrius learned Avilla was not the only female with warrior creds. Someone only whispered about with the Code Name: Explorer One led the unique group of female warriors.

Darrius was beginning to believe that a super-secret entity was also somehow connected with Richardson Security. On the surface, the company was a subcontractor and provided covert specialized services to the United States federal government. However, it was becoming clear to Darrius through his studies that the company also provided clandestine services to the Central Intelligence Agency. In his reading material, Darrius learned that a Richardson subsidiary, International Investigative Services and Solutions, received nearly a billion-dollar contract from the State Department for security services to be provided worldwide. Like Erik Prince, a former US Navy SEAL who created Blackwater, Slade Richardson was also a distinguished member of the elite group. Richardson's groups provided law enforcement training, logistics, and close-quarter combat, stopping short of extreme rendition training in their security services. They were considered the best security management, full-service risk management consulting group globally. Darrius was learning a great deal of information from the reading material he was given, but there was so much more he was privy to in briefing sessions like this.

However, he was distracted because he hadn't had an opportunity to speak with Dena after she left his condo. Although he called and sent text messages, Dena had not responded. He understood her rationale for not wanting to speak with him, but still sought an opportunity to talk with her. Even if it were true that he and Alana were going to be parents, he would support his child, but he had no intention of marrying Alana. He recognized that he would have to remain in the Boston area, but he planned to stay with Richardson. He would have to work out a plan to co-parent with Alana, but that would be the extent of his relationship with her. He was not in love with her, but his feelings for Dena were becoming crystal clear. He wanted her as a permanent fixture in his life.

Chapter 30

Darrius sat quietly, reading a local newspaper in the lobby of Ambassador Hawkins's residence. Covertly, he watched the employees leave for the day and focused on one man, the majordomo of the residence. He was reasonably certain that the man was exhibiting symptoms of stress. Of course, managing the household of a multibillionaire with an estate the size of the Hawkins' property would have its challenges, but Darrius believed this man was under duress. Unfortunately, he had seen it too many times as a police officer purposely putting pressure on a witness or a perp. So he had taken it upon himself to test a theory.

When Avilla strode up and sat across from him, Darrius didn't look up from his newspaper, but spoke quietly to her. "Have you done a complete vetting on Douglas Charters?"

Avilla frowned. "The majordomo? No, I haven't, but I reviewed the profiles that Jake Hawkins' security people ran on all the employees Hawkins' people hired. Why?"

"I've been purposely following Charters and letting him see me watching him. He's very nervous about something."

"That's why you asked me to join you here?"

"It is, yes."

"Okay, I've been trained never to overlook someone's gut instincts. So what do you propose?"

"I've put a button tracker in his coat pocket. I'm following him on my phone. First, I want to give him a little time to get home and settle, and then I want to follow him. After that, we should have a covert meeting with him in his home and see if my instincts are right about him. Are you up for it?"

Avilla grinned and nodded. "I love a road trip."

Two hours later, Darrius and Avilla sat in the darkened kitchen of Mr. Charters' nicely designed home. The middle-aged man couldn't stem the tears as he related how he received a call indicating that his family, his wife, three children, and mother were being held hostage. Mr. Charters was being forced to provide a way for certain Japanese men to enter the Ambassador's residence, find the Japanese Emperor's grandnephews, take them, and leave without incident. The news had Avilla and Darrius eyeing one another and connecting this proposed abduction to the murder of KiLe. Someone wanted her out of the way so that they could take her children.

Later, as Darrius drove Avilla back to the Hawkins' residence, she turned to Darrius. "It doesn't take a Dun and Bradstreet lawyer to figure out who was behind KiLe's murder and why."

Darrius shook his head. "No, it doesn't. It's KiLe's paternal grandfather."

Avilla nodded. "I agree. We've had data on him since before KiLe and Brian married. Benny and Stacy Alexander came in contact with KiLe's parents when they were deployed as American attachés to the Ambassador in Japan. Their daughter, Whitney Ivy, and KiLe Hakamora were private elementary school chums up through the high school level. So we knew KiLe's mother was royalty, the Japanese Emperor's younger sister. Then KiLe and Whitney Ivy went to America together, and KiLe lived in Benny and Stacy Alexander's home in the Georgetown section of Washington, DC. KiLe and Whitney Ivy both attended Georgetown University. KiLe enrolled in undergrad, but Whitney Ivy was academically ahead of KiLe. While in Japan, Whitney Ivy did her undergraduate studies, and KiLe's mother was her academic advisor. So that when Whitney Ivy went to Georgetown, she was a legacy because of her aunt Vivian. She was accepted into the advanced studies law school program."

Darrius nodded. "Another gifted and brilliant member of the Alexander family."

Avilla nodded. "That's correct, but KiLe's father is a commoner, but a brilliant scientist. His father used Yakuza funds to bankroll his son's biofuel company. The company has been very successful, and the funds were repaid with interest; however, the grandfather pledged his first grandchild to the Yakuza as a part of the bargain. The only grandchild was KiLe. Still, she was promised at birth by her grandfather to wed a Yakuza man as a virgin.

"The Yakuza is a dangerous criminal entity. They wanted a hook into the Emperor and the royal family. That plan failed when KiLe rejected the men her grandfather selected, fell in love with Brian Montgomery, married him, and they had two sons. KiLe's sons are partially Japanese royalty. I believe that is why the Yakuza want to get their hands on the boys."

Darrius nodded. "Those boys are also Vivian Alexander Montgomery's grandchildren. She's a Supreme Court Jurist and one of the wealthiest women in the world. So imagine what kind of control the Yakuza would try to exert on her if they successfully abducted her grandsons."

Avilla shook her head. "All of Chuck and Vivian's children and grandchildren are at risk of being abducted. So they are cautious about people in their orbit."

"As I understand it, Whitney Ivy was abducted."

"Yes, but she was found quickly."

"Her quick recovery has something to do with the gold necklace she and others wear, didn't it?"

Avilla turned her head and looked at Darrius as they pulled to a stop at the gates of the Embassy. "That's beyond your pay grade and mine, Agent Pappas. For now, let me commend you on your protective instincts. While I've been focused on the U-boat out in the Indian Ocean, you were concentrating on an internal threat. Initially, when you seemed distracted, I thought you were fixated on Dena Montgomery." When he only looked directly into Avilla's eyes, she waved off further comments about what she witnessed between Dena and Darrius at the Alex-Mont Ranch. "Keep thinking outside the box, Pappas, and you'll do well at Richardson Investigation and Security.

"Let's get the rest of the team briefed. First, we must find Mr. Charters' family and simultaneously prepare for the assault on the residence."

It was nearing three in the morning when Noah Mikasi's taxi let him out in front of the American Embassy. The gate guards recognized him and permitted him to enter the property. Noah felt like roadkill, but he would not stop moving until he could talk with Fiona. He owed her an explanation for his behavior. Leaving the island immediately after she announced her pregnancy left a bad taste in his mouth. He could not imagine how his departure made her feel. Still, he needed to make it clear that despite his poor showing, he wanted his child, and he wanted Fiona Lizette Lowry more than his next breath.

Inside the residence, he walked as if in a trance through his bedroom suite, dropped his backpack, and proceeded out onto the terrace. He could hear a party underway in the ballroom. Fiona's suite of rooms was further down the terrace from his, and her lights were out, but if he didn't sit soon, he'd black out.

Since there didn't appear to be any after-action activity in the works, Noah presumed that either the threat had passed or it hadn't occurred yet. Still, it was too early to wake Fiona, but he'd remain alert and sit on one of the chaise lounges outside Fiona's suite until the awesome pain diminished and he got his breath back. Then, as soon as dawn broke over the ocean, he'd knock on Fiona's door and wake her up.

He had used up all the medication he appropriated from the hospital in Germany, but he had an ample supply here in Victoria. When finally seated with his feet up, Noah closed his eyes and purposefully slipped into a bat nap.

Fiona was feeling restless and turned fitfully in her bed. This behavior wasn't like her, but earlier in the evening, she felt twinges and fluttering in her abdomen that she believed must be her baby's first movements. That knowledge made her pregnancy real. There was a fetus that had the potential to become a human being growing inside of her. It was time to face the facts and tell her family what was happening. However, she dreaded having to explain how she became pregnant by a man she didn't know or like.

Although Fiona was having a great time, she had slipped away from the Alexander and Montgomery family party in the ballroom early. They were a great group of fun-loving people who knew how to enjoy themselves, singing and dancing up a storm, but reality intruded on her ability to go with the flow. Instead, she needed to focus on the demanding tasks ahead of her.

Earlier in the evening, after dinner but before the party, Fiona sat on the terrace and watched the tide ebb and flow. Mesmerized by the sight of the vast ocean, she allowed her mind to drift over her past with men. She had only been intimately involved with two men in her entire twenty-plus years of life. At least Aiden McKenna, her first lover, and she had known each other since birth. They became lovers in high school and together attended Carnegie Mellon University in Pittsburgh, Pennsylvania. Aiden went on to law school, and she trained as an architect and engineer. He became a US Congressman who was elected Maryland State Attorney General last November. Aiden expected they would marry and had asked her to marry him, but Fiona didn't want to be a politician's wife. Although she loved him dearly, Aiden had aspirations for higher public office, including the governorship and possibly the presidency.

Still, they remained lovers until she went on an impromptu three-month European and Asian tour with one of her clients, Maxwell Bishop Kennard, The Third, Trey, to his friends. That trip opened worlds Fiona had only read about in her textbooks and dreamed about while training as an architect and engineer. Fiona was designing and building a residence and studio where Trey could relax and create the incredible musical sounds he was known for worldwide. Her parents, siblings, and friends encouraged her to accept Trey's invitation to tour with him to learn about his need for a state-of-the-art sound facility. Along the way, their relationship became intimate, confirming that staying in rural Bay County, Maryland, and marrying Aiden would have been a mistake. Yet, although Fiona was fascinated with Trey's genius, warmth, and giving spirit, she didn't feel that succumbing to Trey's desire for her to move to New York City to live with him was the right path for her. Instead, she wanted to find her own niche for a satisfying life journey. So when her uncle asked her to join him in Africa to serve the common good for millions of people, Fiona didn't hesitate. It felt highly invigorating to use her skill in a way she had never envisioned. Working with talented people to create opportunities for generations to come made Fiona feel that she was finally doing something noble. She couldn't trade what she had now to be with either Trey or Aiden.

However, that was until she crossed paths with Doctor Noah Mikasi. What she was facing, she knew she would have to do alone. Fiona would never have expected it from him, but he had turned tail and run. His behavior was in complete opposition to what he said to her in the cave once their sanity had returned. He said at the time, *"If there are consequences, such as a pregnancy, without question, I want you and the child we may have made."* However, Fiona knew that her family loved her and would support her decisions. So she felt capable of setting a new path with the little person she was already beginning to love.

Standing from the bed, Fiona didn't turn on the lamp but went to the full-length mirror inside the closet door. Running her hand across her still concave abdomen, she again felt the flutter like butterfly wings and smiled. Taking her robe from the closet, Fiona wrapped it around her nude body, left her suite to stand on the terrace, and watched the ebb and flow of the Indian Ocean. It was a warm and beautiful night with a bright, full moon shining on the water. She didn't hear anything on the night air except the party still going strong in the ballroom.

Then suddenly, a hand clamped over her mouth, and an arm tightened around her waist, trapping her arms against her body. She would have struggled except for the whispered warning voiced in her ear. Instead, she did not protest when she was dragged back into her suite and told not to move or utter a sound.

Fiona did as she was told and watched as bodies passed by her door, silhouetted by the moonlight. Someone tried the lock, but the door did not open. Yet, she could make out Noah's shadow with his back to the wall beside the door. She never heard him lock the door, but apparently, he had mere split seconds before the silhouettes appeared. He was intently listening as he stood statue still. Fiona couldn't even hear him breathing.

Slowly, Noah moved away from the door and toward Fiona. There was a guard posted just outside her door, so he took her in his arms to whisper in her ear. Then, when Noah was sure that Fiona understood what was happening and the reason for his instructions, he guided her into her closet. Then, slowly he closed and locked the door with a latch on the inside. Turning on a penlight, he went to an interior wall and silently slid her hanging clothes aside enough to get his finger behind the shoe rack. Noah popped the back wall panel open, took Fiona's hand, and guided her into a narrow cavity between the walls. He reached up and popped the lock, securing the board back into place.

Then he braced his hands against his knees to ward off a wave of dizziness. He still had to get Fiona to safety and find the rest of the team he was sure were on red alert status. If he could see the silhouette of a submarine in the moonlit water moving closer to shore and hear the outboard motors of rubber lifeboats coming ashore, he was certain that Avilla Montenegro was not asleep at the switch. He just had to learn the game plan and do it silently.

Fiona's adrenaline was racing through her bodily systems. First, Noah had scared the crap out of her when he grabbed her on the terrace. Then his stern warning that they were being invaded by the Yakuza and to remain absolutely quiet had her fearing for the safety of her fetus if she didn't exactly do as he instructed. Now they were inside the wall cavity, and Fiona sensed something was wrong with Noah. When he held her to whisper in her ear, she could feel the excessive moisture on his face. His body was warm to the touch, and his shirt left a moist, sticky residue on her hands. Fiona wasn't at all sure what was going on now, but this silence was stretching her nerves.

Slowly, Fiona moved toward Noah, reaching a hand out in the dark to judge how close they were. When she connected with him, he clamped her hand, bringing her in closer and whispering to give him a minute. She nodded in understanding, but used the bottom of her robe to wipe at the moisture she felt on Noah's face. Finally, he nodded, stood from his bent position, took her hand, and slowly guided her along the narrow corridor. Suddenly, he collapsed and went down in the limited space.

Without uttering a sound, Fiona took Noah's penlight and surveyed his condition. Placing his head in her lap, she wiped away the moisture and noticed he was bleeding. Then, taking his phone, she sent a text message to her uncle, relaying where she was and Noah's condition. Immediately, a message came back to stay where they were. Help was on the way.

Darrius tried to keep an eye on Dena, but she was in the thick of the plans to protect the perimeter with her other siblings and cousins. First, however, they weren't sure where Fiona Lizette was. She had been at the party, but was the only one missing when they did a head count. Avilla was also looking at the monitors for someone whose code name was Stinger. Apparently, he was somewhere on the grounds but hadn't been located.

However, of the eleven Yakuzas who came ashore, five were deceased, four were in custody, but two were still missing. Huddled in the Embassy's SCIF, Dena listened, as did Simon attempting to pick up any sound that would alert them as to where the remaining two Yakuza were located. Finally, a message came through from Fiona, relaying where she and Doctor Mikasi were hiding and his condition. Holding up a finger, Dena vigorously nodded and keyed instructions for two cameras to focus on the door outside Fiona's room. One Yakuza criminal was keeping watch while the other one was apparently trying to pick the lock. Frustrated, their quiet discussion in Japanese concerned whether one of them had seen a woman standing on the terrace wearing a white robe. Little did they realize that while they were distracted attempting to get into the bedroom suite, a Tiger Team contingent was on its way to apprehend them, and their means of escape had been boarded and seized. Several US Navy submarines, a destroyer, and a frigate were all under US Navy Admiral Stacy Greene Alexander's command.

Epilogue

Benjamin Alexander, Benny to his family and friends, a five-star general in the US Air Force, a jet-fighter pilot, and an astronaut, smiled broadly at Dena, his niece, as she stood with tears streaming down her face. His sister, Vivian, and Chuck reached for their daughter, Dena, and she easily went into their arms.

Dena rubbed the tears from her cheeks with the back of her hands. "I can't believe it. Am I really going to fly?"

Her uncle Benny nodded. "Yes, you are, and I'm going to take you up myself."

Dena couldn't stem the flood that followed. "When did you know, Uncle Benny?"

He shrugged. "The word came down last week, but I delayed telling you in light of the invasion and the aftermath. We leave tonight for Houston, Texas. You've got four to six months of training to go through before we leave Mother Earth. I plan to work with you every step of the way."

Dena closed her eyes and shook her head. "You can't imagine how long I've dreamed of traveling in space."

Chuck laughed. "Oh, I think we have some idea. You still have a replica of the solar system hanging from the ceiling in your bedroom suite at the ranch."

Dena looked at the only mother she had ever known. "Mom."

Vivian's smile was beatific. "We are all so proud of you, daughter mine."

"You know when this hits the news, you and Dad will be inundated with news reporters and media hounds until I return."

Vivian nonchalantly shrugged. "Do I look intimidated to you?"

"Oh, Mom, you are absolutely the best of who and what I am. If you and Derrick hadn't taken me into your home and into your hearts, I don't know where I would be today." Then turning, she reached for Chuck's hand. "You've done so much for me and for all of us. There are no words I know that will adequately convey how much I love you both and how grateful I am to you for making a wonderful family for all of us."

Chuck shook his head. "Dena, each one of you has brought love and laughter into our lives. So you go shoot for the moon, baby, and you'll be among the stars in our universe."

Dena gave them one last squeeze and breathed them in before she went to share her good news with the rest of her family. Then she had to hurry and pack. Her destiny was waiting for her among the stars.

Darrius hurried to Dena's bedroom suite. He had a few hours to kill and wanted to see Dena to explain about Alana. This was the first opportunity he had to speak with her since they wrapped up the report of the invasion by the Yakuza. Shortly after the covert mission failed, KiLe's grandfather was found dead in his home. His wife could not be found. The Tokyo Metropolitan Police Department was not investigating, and the matter was closed at the direction of the Emperor of Japan. Avilla would continue to be watchful, but didn't believe there would be a problem for Brian and his boys going forward.

When Darrius tapped on the door, Drew answered and offered a curious smile. "Yes?"

"Oh, hello, Drew. I wanted to have a word with Dena."

"Uh, I don't think that's going to happen. Dena left hours ago."

"Left? You mean she's out touring the city?"

Drew shook his head. "No, she's left Seychelles. She's on her way to Houston, Texas. Her project has been given the green light. She'll be on one of the launches to SPACEHOME in about six months or so."

Darrius just stared.

After Doctor Chuck Montgomery completed his examination, Fiona sat beside Noah's hospital bed in her uncle and aunt's residence, reading a report about Operation: Uplift's progress. Despite Noah's departure months earlier, the project was on track. All the islands now had medical and educational facilities identified and were being outfitted quickly. There was a slowdown in the supply chain, but Fiona's cousin, Adam Hawkins, was doing whatever was necessary to deliver the needed goods, materials, and services.

Fiona's six brothers were scheduled to arrive next week with their parents. They would continue the training program at the Journeyman's College for construction specialties, like iron workers, carpenters, electricians, and plumbers. Her brothers would be there for six months training another contingent of qualified journeymen to work with the first graduates already on the islands building the facilities. Fiona was being flown from island to island to review the work underway. So far, she was pleased with what she saw.

Her architectural and engineering skills appeared to be needed for at least another year. That meant that her baby would likely be born here in the Republic of Seychelles unless she went home in time to deliver just before the holidays. Rubbing her abdomen, Fiona was concerned about her child's citizenship. She was an American citizen, but she believed Noah was Canadian. However, they were both people of color, and knowing how some politicians treated immigrants, Fiona didn't want any confusion because her child might be born in essentially an African nation.

She'd check with Attorney Marshall to ensure her thinking was correct on that score. So Fiona took out her phone, checked her calendar, and made a note to schedule one of her uncle's jets to deliver her to American soil before the date she was expected to deliver. Then she would have to remain in the states with her baby until she could get a passport for her child and safely return to the Republic to continue working on her tasks.

Fiona had to think beyond this initial project. If Operation: Uplift was victorious here in the Republic, her uncle planned to convince the

US State Department, other American ambassadors, and diplomats to implement the project in specific African nations, starting with the most financially challenged ones. Toward that end, Jake invited the American ambassadors and the leadership of certain African nations to a week-long conference at the start of Operation: Uplift. At the time, Uncle Jake and the leadership of the Republic broke ground on the Journeyman's College and the Medical Center simultaneously. Then, Uncle Jake invited the same group back every quarter to view the progress. In another month, the dignitaries would return to see the progress made in this first quarter of Operation: Uplift.

Fiona's attention was diverted from the report to a text message from her oldest brother. They were stairsteps, considering all seven of them were born a year apart. Nevertheless, her father intended to keep going until they had a girl. Fortunately, number seven was lucky to hear her mother tell it.

Her brother confirmed their plans to arrive on Sunday, but Fiona frowned. She expected her pal, Robinetta McKenna, to come to Seychelles for a visit. However, it seemed that Robinetta's entire family was coming along with her, including her younger brother, Aiden. As she continued to read the message, Aiden intended to ask her to marry him in front of his family and hers. He believed Seychelles would be a perfect location for a destination wedding and honeymoon.

Oh, hell, Fiona thought. *What a terrible conundrum this would be.* She had done everything in her power to dissuade Aiden from coming to Seychelles. Now he was upping the stakes by bringing his entire immediate family to convince her to become his wife? She loved the entire McKenna clan, including Aiden, but she wasn't *in love* with him. She wasn't *in love* with anyone, not Trey Kennard, and certainly not Noah Mikasi. Yet she was going to have a child with Noah. *What the hell am I going to do? Aiden's family and mine will be here in less than a week.*

Noah silently watched the myriad of expressions flow over Fiona Lizette's gamine face. This last bit of news on her phone had apparently struck fear in her heart because her beautiful eyes had gone wide, and her luscious mouth had rounded in apparent shock. Clearly, something had disturbed her seeming peace and tranquility.

He had secretly watched her day after day as she came in and sat at his bedside to give the regular nurses a break. It thrilled him that she was willing to sit with him after the monstrous manner in which he had treated her. However, there was only one way he could make amends for his bad behavior. Stretching out his right hand toward Fiona, he summoned his courage. "Marry me, Fiona Lizette Lowry."

For humming moments, Fiona just stared at Noah's hand and then his face. Then, she didn't know why she did it, but she put her hand in his and heard herself utter the single word of insanity. "Yes." Then quickly rising, Fiona started to leave the room.

Noah frowned. "Where are you going, Fiona?"

Without breaking stride, she flung over her shoulder. "To get Uncle Jake to perform the wedding ceremony and Aunt Kelley to be the witness. Don't go anywhere. I'll be right back."

Surprised, Noah frowned and then smiled while lacing his fingers behind his head. The monitor recorded his elevated heart rate. *Oh, no, I won't move a muscle until Fiona returns. After all, I am quite at my leisure with my thoughts of my wedding night with the woman who will be my wife for forever and a day.*

Six months later, Dena Montgomery closed her eyes and smiled her enthusiasm as the awesome engines ignited with an unbelievable roar. The trimmers were expected, but they were much more intense than they had been during the simulations she experienced in Houston's labs. Then Dena heard the Houston Control Center announce liftoff at 0800. From what she could see from her seat in the Space Shuttle, the Earth was falling away fast. They were riding piggyback on rockets with millions of pounds of thrust. Looking ahead, she could see through the wide windows of the cockpit the deep blue of space. Dena knew her role was to provide an environment out there in the weightless atmosphere in which astronauts could live in a permanently human-crewed space station known as SPACEHOME.

However, for the moment, Dena took advantage of every second of the experience of leaving Earth's atmosphere and the problems of daily life behind. Of course, she would miss her family, but they had come to Houston to wish her well. Dena carried a card they designed and all signed with special wishes for her success. It filled her up to see the pride shining in her parents' and grandparents' eyes. They and her siblings enthusiastically waved when she walked out of the building wearing her space flight suit to board the tram. Dena's heartbeat increased as she and the crew were delivered to the elevator to the shuttle. Yet, her confidence grew when her uncle Benny grinned at her, and they knuckle-bumped as the elevator rose. The other pilot, besides her uncle, was the drop-dead gorgeous Captain Shawn Baxter Rodgers. He, too, gave her a knuckle bump of encouragement along with the other twenty- three members of this SPACEHOME team. Shawn had been a joy to work with throughout her training sessions for the past six months. He was a daredevil jet fighter pilot like her uncle, and he had taken her up many times in his specially designed F-22 Raptor supersonic jet. He gave her the ride of her life each time and even let her hold the controls a few times. In addition to her uncle Benny and her sister, Eve, several of her siblings and relatives were flyers. As the first stage of rockets fell away and back to Earth, Dena promised herself that she would learn to fly when she returned.

SPACEHOME, the artificial planet, would be her primary residence for the foreseeable future. It would have to be designed and built to support a plethora of scientific research objectives, plus act as an engineering and support base for human journeys to the planets. It was a mind-invigorating mission, but Dena had no doubt she was up to the tasks ahead of her and the team she selected for this mission. She couldn't wait to get started.

The feasibility design study contracts for SPACEHOME were given to four aerospace contractors to present design proposals and provide materials for building the facilities. One of those companies was CompuCorrect's Aerospace Division, owned and operated by her uncle, Kenneth Alexander. His company was unanimously recommended by NASA based solely on CompuCorrect Aerospace's refined technical superiority. So Dena knew she would be working with the best of the best to accomplish her mission.

Dena also knew during this space program, she would be working with three primary agencies: the National Aeronautics and Space Administration for civil space; the Department of Defense (DoD) for military areas; and the intelligence community for specific space-based intelligence, surveillance, and reconnaissance assets. Dena learned during her six-month training program that these entities invested significant resources to advance technological approaches to meet specific program objectives. In addition, commercial interests emerged pursuing space solutions and expanded dramatically, especially with the significant investments made in recent years. Clearly, her uncle Kenneth's company had been at the forefront of technological advances for commercial uses.

To be among the crew for space exploration and multiple space stations and voyages to Mars or to deliver on the civilian space exploration mandate was thrilling. In addition, with other U.S. civil agencies, such as the National Oceanic and Atmospheric Administration and the U.S. Geological Survey, to deliver space assets supporting the weather and civil remote sensing mandates of those organizations was mind-bending.

The DoD military space program, Space Force, was the primary agent for delivering military space capability. Her uncle Benny, a five-star general, was an integral member of Space Force, the equivalent of the Air Force on Earth. Logistics, for the Global Positioning System, which is ubiquitous to users worldwide, were developed and maintained by the DoD. Yet, Dena would have to ensure in her design and implementation that missile warnings, defensive weather solutions, military satellite communications, and space domain awareness were a priority and received significant attention. That was another reason Air Force General Benjamin Alexander opted to take up this contingent of special agents. This trip was mission-critical because of the turmoil created by certain rogue countries and factions on Earth.

The intelligence community, through entities that include the National Reconnaissance Office, invested significant resources to deliver space solutions that advance the interest of the US in the national security domain. After all, Dena knew space-based surveillance and reconnaissance assets were the primary focus of these entities.

Yet, among the heady thoughts, Drew Hamilton's surprisingly warm, sumptuous kiss and the memory of Darrius Pappas's touch lingered as the last booster rocket fell away. The shuttle floated weightlessly until her uncle Benny and Shawn Rodgers took the controls and fired the thrusters which would bring the shuttle to SPACEHOME. So, Dena put aside thoughts of Drew and Darrius and let her excitement put her mind to work on the tasks at hand. She was now an astronaut.

Fiona Lizette awoke and watched the flatscreen image just as the booster rockets lifted the space shuttle off the deck at the Houston Space Flight Center. Her friend, Dena Montgomery, was aboard that shuttle and headed for an incredible task to build a series of homes for hundreds of people to expand the USA's reach into deep space. Fiona understood the challenges ahead of Dena. She had challenges, too, in completing the medical and educational facilities and co-located residential properties on over a hundred islands of the Republic of Seychelles here on Mother Earth.

Looking to her right, Noah Mikasi, her husband in name only, slept in a chair beside the twin bassinettes, which held their newborn son and daughter. Despite her best-laid plans, her little ones decided to come a week before her scheduled trip to the states. The babes were only hours old, and it had been a long night for Noah and her through the delivery hours. They were both incredibly tired. Because her uncle Jake, the American ambassador, and most American embassy personnel left for the holidays, Noah had to deliver their babes on his own. Still, Noah didn't bat an eye. Rather, he was steady as petrified wood in his delivery technique and keeping her comfortable and calm.

Fiona couldn't deny the unadulterated love she saw shining in Noah's eyes as each baby wrestled themselves from her womb. His joy reached inside her on an elemental level and drew her emotionally closer to Noah. Nine months earlier, they were strangers and co-workers who had a one-time proof-of-life episode that resulted in her unplanned pregnancy. During her pregnancy, they continued to work on their joint tasks but had not even become friends. Yet, they both shed copious tears through their laughter at the end of the delivery. So, due to her sudden motherhood, she would spend the holidays in Seychelles with Noah and her small family. As a result, the tasks Noah and she needed to complete before leaving for the holidays would have to be delayed for a while.

Fiona didn't expect to want to share her joy with this man she didn't know. Still, while she showered after the delivery of two healthy babies, Noah cleaned up and examined his son and daughter. He helped her get comfortable in a clean bed and then placed their babies in her arms. Noah sumptuously kissed her mouth and she was powerless not to respond to his tenderness. Then he slid into bed beside her and held her while the babies suckled her milk-ladened breasts. After they drank their fill, Noah burped one baby and she the other before he put them into the bassinets for their naps.

Now, as Fiona watched Noah sleep, she was conflicted about her relationship with him going forward. Noah had been there every step of the way during her pregnancy. He made healthy, but tasty meals for her and sparingly indulged her silly cravings for chocolate. He was an incredibly good cook who used spices and ingredients she'd never heard of or tasted. Noah showered with her to help wash her hair and areas of her body she couldn't reach and to ensure she didn't slip or fall. They swam together in the lagune and took long walks on the beach whenever she felt the need. Noah was at her beck and call every moment of the day and night.

As a medical doctor, Noah knew the pressure points that gave her the most discomfort. Giving her regular massages, he relieved any aches or pains from her head to her toes. His hands on her were magic and all too often aroused her with undeniable needs. Fiona vividly recalled how thoroughly Noah had made love with her that one time in a cave while a typhoon raged in the Indian Ocean surrounding them. Yet, she refused to allow herself the pleasure of his touch.

Fortunately, they could discuss their parenting philosophies and were of one mind where their son and daughter were concerned. Their parenting beliefs meshed and they had a solid foundation on which to start to build a co-parenting relationship. Noah made it clear that he would not define roles for either of them, but they would be equal partners in the care of their twins. However, they had yet to settle on a name for either child, so the birth certificates remained blank. They agreed that Mikasi would be the surname for each baby.

Fiona continued to let her eyes roam over Noah. He was an undeniably handsome man who appeared to be of indigenous North American continent origins. He was built like a Greek god with solid muscles on a six-five or six-six frame. He swiftly ran ten miles twice daily and made time to work out in the embassy gym. As a former US Navy SEAL, Noah kept himself in perfect shape as if he might be re-activated at a moment's notice.

However, beyond his attractive physical attributes, Doctor Noah Mikasi was highly intelligent, bordering on genius-level IQ. His tasks for Operation: Uplift were to design medical facilities, furnish the necessary equipment and supplies for each location, and staff the clinics. He was exacting to a finite level of proficiency. In addition to his role as a US Navy SEAL, Noah was an MIT and John Hopkins graduate. He had worked on the **Ship of Hope** and with the NGO, Doctors Without Borders. He was accustomed to international medical humanitarian work under dire circumstances. He had brought life-saving emergency medical aid to people affected by armed conflict, epidemics, pandemics, natural disasters, and healthcare exclusion. According to his bio, Noah had worked in countries in North Africa, South America, Asia Pacific, and the Middle East. That included villages not found on any map, refugee camps, hospitals and clinics, and projects serving the health needs of the vulnerable. He wasn't a glory seeker and generally kept a low profile for a man his height when around others. Still, he radiated an awesome power when simply standing still. For all he had done at an apparent early age, he had Fiona's respect.

Yet, when she announced that she was pregnant with his child, he abruptly left that day without a word of explanation. He was gone for months, and when he returned, he was injured but still managed to save her life. She appreciated his efforts, but she still didn't trust him. Yet, with insanity running rampant in her head, she agreed to become his wife for the sake of their babies.

Although she respected Noah, she didn't trust him or love him. Still, she was legally his wife, and he was the father of their babies. That meant they would have to find a way to co-exist and build a relationship from scratch. One thing was certain, she did not intend to live a monastic life, particularly since she craved Noah's skillful hands on her body.

Noah opened his eyes to see Fiona studying him. He could imagine what she was thinking. Now that their babies were a reality, how would they handle the future? They were married, and from Noah's perspective, he didn't intend their marriage to continue to be devoid of physical contact. He had wanted Fiona Lizzette Lowry literally from the first moment he saw her floating offshore too far out in the Indian Ocean. He denied his visceral reactions to her for months while they were paired together for Project: Uplift. However, after several life-threatening events, they had a proof-of-life episode that resulted in Fiona's pregnancy. Her announcement couldn't have come at a worse time as he had just been called into a covert mission with an organ so supersecret that it didn't have the benefit of an acronym. He couldn't tell anyone, and certainly not Fiona, that his duty to his covert missions would always be greater than his duty to his marriage vows and family and to the exclusion of everything and everyone else. Yet, he had to find a way to earn Fiona's trust, respect, and, ultimately, her love.

They continued to silently search each other's eyes.

Noah admired Fiona's beauty with the abundance of long, thick, dark red hair curling madly around her bare shoulders and between her plump breasts. He leaned forward, palmed his face rubbing briskly, and then tunneled his fingers through his thick, wavy hair before he rested his forearms on his knees and his balled fists under his chin. "I don't know what love is, Fiona, but you do. I saw it clearly when your parents and brothers came here expecting a wedding to take place between you and Aiden McKenna. They love him and his family, but they love you more.

They accepted and didn't question your decision to marry me instead of him. They respect, trust, and love you unconditionally. I don't know how to express that depth of devotion to you or to them. Yet, when I look at the two little golden nuggets we have made, I know that I would put my life on the line for them…and for you."

"That's the beginning of love, Noah. It's that all-encompassing feeling that nothing is more important than our babies. I would lay down my life for theirs any moment of the day and I only met them mere hours ago. You and I have worked together for nearly a year, but we don't *know* one another. We had impromptu sex once in a cave nine months ago, but we did not love one another. We did not even *know* each other that well. Of course, there is no guarantee that we will grow our marriage into a love affair, but I don't want our babies growing up thinking that we're just going through the motions of a loving family life."

Noah yawned, palmed his face, and nodded; his fatigue apparent. "Yes, I agree. We've been able to settle on basic tenants of parenting, and we have no disagreements there. However, I never had parents. I know who I've become, but I don't know *whose* I am so I can only tell you what my DNA reveals. I am of the Anishinaabeg, a group of culturally related Indigenous peoples present in the Great Lakes region of Canada and the United States. We include the Ojibwe, Saulteaux, Oji-Cree, Odawa, Potawatomi, Mississaugas, Nipissing and Algonquin peoples. The Anishinaabe speak *Anishinaabemowin*, or Anishinaabe languages that belong to the Algonquian language family. I can speak the languages of the Anishinaabeg and I want to teach our twins how to speak my languages.

"You see, I was found in a basket and wrapped in a towel apparently hours after I was born. I grew up in an orphanage on the Canadian and US boarder and didn't have what you had all of your life. Still, I want to know what it is to be *in love* with you. I want our babies to feel that you and I respect, trust, and love each other. You've had the experience, so you'll have to show me what you've learned. I promise to do whatever you want to make a loving relationship work between us…not just for our babies, but for you and me."

"I don't want a loveless marriage or a marriage in name only either. So, you'll have to open yourself to me, Noah. We can't have secrets and expect to build a solid foundation."

"I want to do that, and to a certain extent, I can share my life with you. Yet, I am a US Navy SEAL, and from time to time, I'm activated for missions that I will not be able to discuss with you…ever."

For ponderous moments, Fiona just stared into Noah's eyes. "I thought you were retired."

Noah slowly shook his head. "I am inactive for now. Once a SEAL, always a SEAL. The only distinction is whether I'm active or inactive."

"That's why you left when I told you I was pregnant, isn't it? That's why you returned injured. You were called back in for an active-duty mission."

Noah nodded. "Yes, but that is all I can say about it now or ever."

Fiona thoughtfully nodded. "I presume that I'll have to become accustomed to you leaving at a moment's notice."

"Yes. I can't predict when I might be called up, but as soon as the mission is over, regardless of where you are, I will come home to you."

Fiona knew there were many issues to consider and come to grips with concerning her relationship with Noah, but they were both too tired for a thorough conversation now. So instead, she simply nodded and moved over, allowing Noah to join her in bed. He stood, took off his clothes, and slipped under the covers to hold her. The kiss they shared was electrified, but tender.

Noah sighed contentedly. "The name Lowry is an Irish baby name. In Irish, the meaning of the name is: Crowned with laurel."

"Really? I didn't know that."

"It's true. I looked it up. Lizette is of American and Hebrew origin, and it means 'God is my oath.' It's also a variant of Elizabeth or Liz."

"I believe you're suggesting that we name our twins Lowery and Elizabeth Mikasi."

"Yes, I am."

Fiona closed her eyes and sighed. "Let's sleep on it."

"Done." Noah kissed Fiona's temple. His protective instincts engaged as he followed his wife into sleep.

About the Author

Ann Jeffries, the critically acclaimed author of the Family Reunion—Wisdom of the Ancestors Series, is a native of Washington, DC. As an only child, she enjoyed the benefits of a private school education at Allen in Asheville, North Carolina, and a public education at the University of Maryland. Ann began writing fiction for her own amusement.

Ms. Jeffries is the recipient of many awards for leadership and public service. A keynote speaker at colleges, universities, conferences, and conventions, she has extensively traveled the North American continent, Asia, and Europe. Among other endeavors, she is an entrepreneur, an avid supporter of public television, a genealogist, and a voracious reader.

Her pride and joy are her family members, particularly her Fabulous Four grands. She lives in Maryland and South Carolina.

Follow Ann on her website: www.annjeffries.net, Facebook @ Ann Jeffries, on Twitter @Ann Jeffries and her publishing house site: www.newviewliterature.com. Her novels are available in both e-book and paperback. Her autographed copies can be found on her website: annjeffries.net and also unautographed on Amazon.com and BarnesandNoble.com. All of Ms. Jeffries' novels are available in audiobook format through Audible, iBooks, and Amazon.